Head of State

Andrew Marr

Head of State

A Political Entertainment

THE OVERLOOK PRESS
New York, NY

This edition first published in hardcover in the United States in 2015 by
The Overlook Press, Peter Mayer Publishers, Inc.

141 Wooster Street
New York, NY 10012
www.overlookpress.com

For bulk and special sales, please contact sales@overlookny.com,
or write us at the address above.

Cataloging-in-Publication Data is available from the Library of Congress

Manufactured in the United States of America

ISBN 978-1-4683-1056-6

2 4 6 8 10 9 7 5 3 1

For Harry Cameron Marr

Author's Note

This book came about in an unusual way. I had long wanted to write a political satire that would help to lift the lid on how aspects of government and the media really worked in a way that's not possible in conventional journalism. Meanwhile Peter Chadlington, a member of the distinguished political Gummer family, had long had a notion for the plot of a novel centred on an explosive secret at the very heart of government. We were introduced through my agent, Ed Victor, and Peter described his idea to me. We subsequently met, and talked through the possibilities and tone of the book. I then wrote the novel, which was expertly edited first by Philippa Harrison, a legend in the trade, and then at Fourth Estate by Robert Lacey, another.

So I owe Lord Chadlington an enormous debt as the originator of the idea on which the whole plot of the novel revolves. He has also been kind in introducing me to certain political and financial figures who have helped ensure that the detail is as accurate as it's possible to be. However, it's fair to say that, left to himself, Peter would certainly have written a very different book. He may not approve of or agree with everything which has emerged; and he cannot be held in any way responsible for my private feuds, jokes and idiosyncrasies. Some of the characters and stories in the novel are derived directly from my thirty years as a political reporter, though of course almost everything here is fictional.

Andrew Marr
April 2014

Foreword

For the last fifty years, two of my abiding passions have been politics and the art of political persuasion. The basic idea behind this novel has been in my mind for much of that time. Andrew Marr has singlehandedly turned it into a political entertainment with verve and satire. Without him it would still just be swirling about in my head.

Some may read the following pages and declare the story too fanciful – 'It could never happen.' But we should remember that much of what we take today as 'normal' political behaviour would have been considered unthinkable fifty – or even twenty – years ago. Today, almost anything seems politically possible.

As Andrew has mentioned, the writing of this novel has been greatly helped by the advice of politicians and financiers, and also by access to several institutions – including Number 10 Downing Street – to ensure that the settings are as accurate as possible.

Peter Chadlington
April 2014

Contents

The people of Britain will vote on a definitive 'in or out' question on the country's membership of the European Union in a referendum to be held on Thursday, 21 September, the prime minister told the House of Commons yesterday.

'This will settle the question for a generation to come, and fix the course of this great nation for our children and our grandchildren,' he told the cheering backbenches of the 'grand coalition'.

The announcement follows many delays and disappointments for those campaigning for such a referendum, a matter which the PM said could not be delayed 'for more than a few months, for all our sakes'.

The prime minister, who was in Hanover last week to put the final touches to his agreement with the German chancellor for a looser, more market-friendly EU, assured the Commons that he would be campaigning unequivocally for a 'Yes' vote.

Leading the 'No' campaign from the opposition benches, Mrs Olivia Kite, who was until recently serving under the PM as home secretary, promised a 'no holds barred, passionate, honest and patriotic campaign' to persuade Britain finally to sever its ties with what she called the 'soft, corrupting dictatorship' of Brussels.

Polling for this newspaper suggests a close vote in three months' time, with the character and leadership abilities of the prime minister a major factor for swing voters.

National Courier, London, Thursday, 22 June 2017

I

Monday, 18 September

Referendum Day Minus Three

Cock of the Walk

A dirty wind gusted. There were just three days to go before the referendum that would settle Britain's destiny. The Golden Cockerel swung proudly from the balcony on the top floor of one of the City of London's most repellent buildings. Even among the swollen glass spikes, cheese graters and vegetables crowding the capital's horizon in 2017, this pastrami-and-lemon-coloured confection from the boom of the 1980s stood out — vile colours, ill-judged proportions, cheap materials. Architecture is one of the most certain measures of cultural and social decline. Inside the abomination, the Cockerel restaurant offered a cold-eyed English catering executive's idea of French peasant cooking. In recent years the 'Cock' had gained a certain notoriety, because its outside smoking terrace had become popular with City suicides.

A South Asian accountant, bullied at work, had thrown herself to her death after dinner. A City trader whose losses were about to be exposed had leapt the eight floors after a couple of Cock of the Walk martinis. The almost famous and thoroughly cuckolded president of the Society of Costermongers had made a witty speech to a gathering of his best friends, then vaulted over the guardrail into the traffic below, bouncing off the top of a passing bus before experiencing his last convulsions under the wheels of a kitchen-delivery lorry.

This Monday morning there lay, foetally curled in the grey half-light on the pavement below the Cockerel, the young constable's first corpse. She took in a dark-blue jacket of a Portuguese cut, a pair of German designer jeans pulled down around his ankles, scuffed but new-looking English brogues, arranged at unlikely angles; and finally a mop of dark, curling hair nestling in a half-dried archipelago of blood. This was a youngish, once-handsome man. There'd be a worried girl somewhere this morning. Or maybe a boy. As the wailing police cars screeched to a halt and disgorged more officers, who pushed aside the ghouls and surrounded the body with tape, and then a plastic tent, the constable stared up at the jutting metal balcony and the gaudy metal bird, squeaking nastily in the wind.

Odd, she thought.

Inside the tent, green-uniformed ambulancemen were bending over the body. But you only needed to glance at the twisted figure to know that there was nothing to be done. In the dark, the body could have been a rough sleeper, ignored for hours.

She walked over and rattled the door of the Golden Cockerel, which led to the lobby, which led to the lift. It was locked. Everything was locked. Too early. Even the cleaners wouldn't be in for an hour. So how had this happened? It was one thing for a drunken, despairing person to jump late at night, or even in the middle of a meal; but who would find their way into the Cockerel early on a Monday morning, and *then* jump? There were easier places – the bridges over the Thames, for one thing – all around.

It didn't make sense.

Three hours later, as the body was swaying slightly, tightly tied down on a gurney in a fast-moving van, a mobile phone began ringing in the dead man's pocket.

Ken Cooper, Upset

At the other end of the line was a heavily-built man sitting in the back of a chauffeured Mercedes which was stuck in traffic in central London. He was on his way to the offices of one of Britain's once-great newspapers, the *National Courier*.

Ken Cooper hated being in the back seat. He hated the taste in his mouth of a wolfed breakfast and the smell of warm leather. He hated the nauseous feeling caused by reading all those newspapers while the driver listened to some funny-moronic DJ doing a funny-moronic phone-in with his — Ken's — own readers. He hated the thought of the ill-tempered meeting with the marketing department weasels and circulation ferrets that would begin his office day.

How would it go?

'Kevin's done some more focus-group research, boss. There are too many older faces in the paper. We need good-looking young people. We need less politics. I've done some work, and you know our ideal story? Tasty rich kids being mugged for their Rolexes outside Annabel's. We need more muggings and more tasty rich kids.'

Reptiles. Water rats. But you could hardly blame them. All the papers were the same these days, run by scuttling, nervous children. Ken was coming to hate the trade he'd always loved.

He hated the clever rat-run route his driver had chosen, which had led straight into this hunched chaos, a clogged artery of barely moving German engineering. He hated the prospect of lunch with the proprietor's son, an Eton-educated stoat who affected purple tweeds and whose girlfriend was on the cover of half the colour supplements most weekends. He didn't mind the proprietor himself, a rough, cynical man who had made his money in property in the sixties. But he hated the son.

And he hated his Mercedes. He'd have been faster on a bike. He'd have been faster hopping on one foot, probably. Never in human history had so much engineering been expended to transport so few people such short distances so slowly. But try getting that in the paper.

Yet a car and driver was one of the last perks left for national newspaper editors, as their circulations shrivelled and their once-mighty legions of reporters were reduced to hysterical little platoons of underpaid dimwits. So he used the journey every morning to read his own paper, savagely underlining mistakes and striking through bad headlines, then scanning the opposition and drawing up lists of stories missed, or angles his guys had failed to see. Then he'd check Witter, jot down a few ideas for the morning news conference, and make some calls to cheer himself up.

At least in the office there was order and hierarchy and clear lines of command – Ken often reflected that had domestic life been as well-run as office life, the world generally would be a lot happier and better-ordered. At work, people knew their place, and could be rude or amusing to one another without offence being taken. Behind the front door of his house, the rules had been mysteriously different. His now ex-wife's flaming temper had matched his own, and on the few occasions when things had come to blows, she was faster with her fists too.

This morning his first call was to the news editor. Some good news, or at least real news. Yesterday afternoon a body had washed up on the embankment of the Thames, on a sliver of mud just below Battersea Park. The local nick, which was in the pay of his crime reporters, had tipped the *Courier* off. Christmas envelopes were the gifts that kept on giving.

As described by the police, the body was that of a heavily-built, naked white male in his late fifties or early sixties. The head and hands had been cut off. A Russian mafia killing? But the police had said that the only clue to the deceased's identity was a single Royal Navy tattoo. So whoever he was, he had been English.

The news editor had given the job to the paper's last proper investigative reporter, Lucien McBryde. But now Ken Cooper couldn't get the arrogant little sod to pick up his bloody phone.

McBryde, he reflected, had been behaving oddly in the last couple of days. He claimed to be closing in on a sensational political story. And certainly, these were sensational political times. The referendum was slicing the country down the middle. The British had always been a people slow to feel political enthusiasm – one of the great secrets of their national survival. But now, families were dividing over supper tables, and offices were riven by arguments about a subject bigger than football or waxing. Ken's car had already passed a dozen hoardings featuring the wrinkled, boxer's face of the prime minister – 'Your choice, your future. Vote Clever' – and as many, if not more, from the anti-Europe campaign, now led by the former home secretary Olivia Kite, who with her red hair, pale face and vivid crimson lips looked increasingly like Elizabeth I, or at least Cate Blanchett – 'Your country, your choice. Give your children the gift of freedom.'

But if Lucien McBryde had something to add to the earsplitting arguments over Britain's future, he hadn't shared it with the paper's political editor, or with Ken himself. He'd just said he was on to something that would 'change everything'. He had seemed even nervier and more excitable than usual, though that was probably down to the marching powder. He had also recently broken up with his girlfriend.

Whatever McBryde was up to, he wasn't answering his phone. Ken groaned, decided not to leave a voicemail message, and turned his phone to silent. Perhaps there wasn't really a story at all, and the whole thing was just an excuse. It wouldn't be the first time. Ken was glad that McBryde had been given the headless Battersea corpse. It would settle him down. Calm him. Give him something solid to get his teeth into.

But still, it was bloody rude of him not to answer his phone. It was past 9 o'clock. How dare the little badger not pick up?

Ken Cooper's World

The trainee was an experiment. The managing editor of the *National Courier* considered the trainee perhaps the crowning achievement of his career.

This morning, the trainee's job was to sit by the window that looked onto the street outside the *National Courier* and watch until he saw the silver Mercedes containing the editor. At that point he had to go – 'quickly, but not running' – to the managing editor's office and tell him. In the roughly one hundred seconds between the car being spotted and Ken Cooper shouldering his way through the revolving doors, the managing editor was able to summon the foreign editor, the business editor, the features editor and the sports editor. They would be waiting in the foyer with pointlessly ingratiating smiles as Cooper made his way to the lift.

'Just under the million. Eight per cent down on last year, and ten per cent since the spring promotion,' said the managing editor.

'Fuck off. We've cut the price in the Midlands, and we're still going down the toilet? The *Telegraph*'s only seven per cent down; *Guardian*, seven per cent down. Thought about hiring some journalists?'

The managing editor did not need to hire any journalists. But he did not tell Ken Cooper that.

The foreign editor was next in line. 'We've completely ignored the Malaysian typhoon, boss. Twenty thousand dead, and not even a line on the front.'

'Fuck off. That twenty thousand included a rich couple from Chelsea and their son who'd just started at Harrow. The *Daily Mail* had it. We didn't. Your fault. Not mine.'

Then the business editor: 'A cracking story from Sir Solomon Dundas, boss. They're going to split up that Scottish bank after all.'

'Fuck off. Dundas is a self-promoting wanker. His last tip was crap. I don't want another story with his sticky fingers on it in this newspaper, ever.'

The features editor was offering six of the best chocolate recipes, an article about why Bloody Marys were back in vogue, and an interview with Mia Farrow's son. Ken told him to fuck off and come back with something fucking interesting.

The sports editor, a lean, gnarled man with a bald head and rimless glasses, got him just before the lift doors opened. 'Boss?'

'Yes?' said Ken.

'Nothing really. . . Just – fuck off, boss.'

Ken laughed. He was beginning to feel better.

Exactly the same performance took place every morning. These days there was less tension than usual, because there was only one story in town. Everybody at the *National Courier* knew that the front page would be referendum, referendum, referendum. The cartoon would be referendum. The comment pages would contain referendum *yes* and referendum *no*. The editorial would be referendum *maybe*.

There were still twenty-five minutes before the morning editorial conference. Time enough for the foreign editor to tell his key staff to fuck off and bring him something interesting; for the business editor to tell his banking correspondent to fuck off and stop depending on the same old sources; for the features editor to tell everyone who worked for him that they were fucking useless; and for the sports editor to smoke three cigarettes. In this way, a great newspaper was coming together.

Nobody told the trainee to fuck off. Nobody even knew the trainee's name. He was a well-dressed young man in his early twenties, with beautifully cut hair, neat nails and a degree in journalism studies. He possessed, as all journalists must, a plausible manner, a little literary ability and a good deal of rat-like cunning. Despite these advantages, he was known only as 'oi'. When he protested about this to the managing editor, the managing editor quite truthfully explained that his name did not matter, since nobody would ever need to know it. Like him, most of the younger journalists at the *Courier* were work-experience trainees who lived at home with their parents in Ealing, Primrose Hill or Highgate. Because the paper was prestigious and jobs in journalism were almost impossible to find, none of them was actually being paid. Everybody benefited from this arrangement. Their parents could boast to their friends about their children's prestigious jobs. The paper got a steady supply of free labour. And the trainees quite enjoyed themselves. Occasionally the managing editor allowed himself to think of the many thousands of bright young people from poorer families who would never get the chance to work in journalism – but not for too long, because he knew that the current system made perfect economic sense.

One day as he was sitting at his desk, the managing editor had found himself wondering whether, as wealthy parents were clearly willing to subsidise their offspring, some of them might be prepared to go further, and actually pay the *Courier* to employ them. So the trainee's banker father was currently paying £30,000 in return for his son working at the paper. He regarded it as money well spent: if he paid £100,000 for a painting so he could boast about it at dinner parties, and many times that on dull holidays so he could boast about them, £30,000 was a small price to pay to allow him to boast about his dim but well-meaning son's journalistic career. Half of the money was going into the newspaper's coffers; the other half was going to the managing editor. The managing editor feared that one day Ken Cooper would discover what was going on; and that would be an unpleasant day. So the trainee could not stay forever. He was just an experiment. In the meantime, everybody called him 'oi'. The trainee, who dreamed of being a gossip columnist, was not put off, however. He had sticking power. He passionately believed that one day, somehow, someone would tell him too to fuck off.

How History is Made

At the moment that Ken Cooper stepped into the lift, Lord Trevor Briskett and his research assistant Ned Parminter were squashed together in a commuter train from Oxford. They were both scanning that morning's *Courier*. Lord Briskett read the paper from the middle outwards, starting with the editorial and the commentators, then checking the business and political news, before idly skimming the home pages, which were mostly filled with things he'd heard already on last night's news or the 7 a.m. bulletin on the *Today* programme. One celebrity was in favour of decluttering. Another was less sure. The girlfriend of somebody on a television show had drunk too much in a club. The age of newspapers, he reflected, was coming, whimpering, to an end.

Ned Parminter was brushing through the iPad edition of the paper with his forefinger, flicking the screen at great speed. The *Courier* at least still covered politics with some vigour, although the news pages seemed to be in favour of Britain leaving the EU, while the comment pages were aggressively the other way.

Neither of them paused to read the short report on the headless Battersea corpse. Corpses, particularly headless ones, were clearly something to do with the criminal underworld, and were therefore politically unimportant. Briskett and Parminter were following a bigger story than that. 'Vote clever.' 'Vote for freedom.' A nation torn in two.

Dressed in his trademark coarse green tweeds, with his halo of frizzy white hair and heavy horn-rimmed spectacles, part A.J.P. Taylor, part Bamber Gascoigne, Trevor Briskett was famous enough from his TV performances to attract second glances from his fellow commuters. On the streets of Oxford – that crowded, clucking duckpond of vanity and ruffled feathers – he was stopped-in-the-street famous.

And rightly so. For Briskett was the finest political historian of the late twentieth and early twenty-first centuries. His early biographies – Blair, Thatcher, Johnson – were still in print, while the memoirs of scores of almost-forgotten politicians had long since vanished to charity shops and recycling dumps after selling only a few score copies. Briskett's account of the modern constitution had been compared to the works of that Victorian master-journalist Walter Bagehot. His history of British intelligence during the Cold War had been praised by all the right people. Emeritus professor at Wadham, winner of numerous literary prizes, elevated five years ago to the Lords as a crossbencher after chairing a royal commission on security lapses at the Ministry of Defence, Briskett was regularly tipped to be the next member of the Order of Merit.

Yet somehow these decorative embellishments, which might have weighed him down and made him soft, slow and comfortable, had had little apparent effect on Trevor Briskett. At seventy he was as sharp, as boyishly enthusiastic, as wicked a gossip with as rasping a laugh, as he had been at thirty. The exact nature of the pornography discovered on the minister's lost laptop. The attempt to blackmail a senior minister over his wife's cocaine habit. Just who Olivia Kite was taking to her bed these days. . . If you really wanted to know, you went to Briskett, and he would tap his nose, lean towards you, give a wolfish smile and a 'dear boy', and spill all the beans.

Thus, it had generally been admired as a rather brave decision when the prime minister announced that he had appointed Briskett as the official historian of the great European referendum. The PM, himself an amateur political historian, had argued that such was the momentous nature of the choice now before the British people that they were owed – the nation was owed – a proper, in-depth account by a proper writer. Briskett, he had promised, would be given unparalleled access to the members of his inner team for the duration of the campaign. He would be welcomed at Downing Street, he would be given copies of the emails, the strategy documents – everything. And after it was all over, people might actually read his book.

No sooner had the PM announced this than Olivia Kite, on behalf of the get-outers, issued a press release declaring that she too admired Lord Briskett, whom she regarded as an authoritative and independent voice, and that she would give him the same level of access to her team.

The political commentators said that the PM's decision to give contemporary history what Briskett had called 'the ultimate ringside seat' was evidence of his great confidence about the outcome of the referendum. His evident conviction that he would win, and that victory would be the ultimate vindication of his premiership, was itself damaging to his opponents. Olivia Kite had had little option but to make Briskett as welcome in Prince Rupert's tent as in Cromwell's.

Basking in this hot limelight, Briskett moved lightly. He wanted to do all the work himself, so far as he could. He had brought in only his protégé Ned Parminter, a shy but brilliant PhD student who, Briskett thought, might one day be a significant contemporary historian himself.

Parminter, with his wiry black beard and intense dark eyes,

looked like an Orthodox priest in civilian clothes. Although he shared Briskett's urbane sense of humour, his romantic English patriotism had a fanatical streak.

Together, the two of them made up a balanced ticket: Briskett's delight in Westminster gamesmanship inclined him towards the larger-than-life, principled yet unscrupulous figure of the prime minister. Parminter, a specialist in the seventeenth-century development of Parliament, was a natural Olivia Kite supporter. They had, of course, never discussed their allegiances on this matter between themselves.

Now the two of them were on their way to meet the prime minister himself. As the train wriggled through West London towards Paddington, Briskett leaned forward in his seat.

'You're seeing that. . . girl, Ned, after our rendezvous?'

Parminter scratched his beard under his chin, a sign of anxiety, before slowly replying. 'She's invaluable. She's across everything in the Kite campaign. She reads all the emails, all Kite's texts, on her official BlackBerry and her personal one. She's copying us into every piece of traffic.'

'And does the ever-lovely Mrs Kite know this?'

'Apparently. I think she must. Jen's nothing if not loyal, so I guess Kite's fine with it.'

'*Good* girl. Good for you, too.'

'There is one other thing. It's a bit odd. She also seems to know rather a lot about what's happening on the other side. Far more than she ought to. Hidden channels in Number 10, perhaps.'

Briskett rubbed his hands with pleasure.

'Really? Sleeping with the enemy, is she? Delicious. At a moment like this, what is happening in each HQ is our primary concern. Let us wallow, Ned, in the panics, the little feuds, the unwarranted pessimism and the foolish overconfidence. But in a sense, what matters most is what is harder to discover. I mean, what is happening *between* the camps. It's there that the deepest secrets lie. And what is this fascinating creature's full name, Ned?'

'Jennifer Lewis. But she prefers Jen. I've known her since uni.'

Briskett exhaled an irritated hiss.

'You mean you've known her since you were up at Oxford, Ned. I really cannot understand this squirming self-abasement about "uni". It would be a different matter if it were Keele, but I assume — given her youth and prominence — that she was at Oxford too. Or, poor girl, Cambridge?'

'Somerville.'

'Hmm. PPE?'

'PPE.'

'Well. . .'

The two men lapsed into silence until the train was almost at Paddington.

Under a Rebel Flag

But Jennifer Lewis was not going to make her appoint-ment with Ned Parminter that afternoon. Some fascinating new polling results had come in overnight which called for a few late changes to the campaign, so she was more than sixty miles to the east of London, crunching numbers in the gorgeous surroundings of Danskin House. Olivia Kite, meanwhile, dressed only in a short, almost see-through kimono, walked between the rows of campaign volunteers checking the messages on her mobile phone. Nobody even thought about taking a picture. They were a tight, loyal team.

After breakfast Olivia changed the kimono for a vibrantly-coloured Issey Miyake suit; she made a point of dressing up for every day at work in her own home as if she were being presented to the king at Buckingham Palace. He had, after all, called her half a dozen times in the course of the campaign. Some of their conversations had run on late into the night.

Danskin House was the beating heart of the nationalist move-ment. It was rebel camp headquarters, as much a symbol of defiance of Westminster as Oxford had been when King Charles I had raised his standard there almost four centuries previously. Yet it was an odd place for British patriotism to take its stand. The house was vaguely Renaissance in shape, and was hung with Dutch tiles. Its roofs and turrets glittered pale blue and orange. It boasted an Italian garden, complete with eighteenth-century reproduction Roman statuary, and a Greek temple overlooking a lake. Inside, a long hallway was decorated with suits of German armour and some quite good paintings, not least by the Dutchman Pieter de Hooch and the Spanish papist Murillo. What had once been an insanitary Tudor patchwork had been extensively rebuilt in Northern European style after the Glorious Revolution – the glazed tiles, the statues, the limewashed inside walls.

The house's current master, Olivia Kite's husband Reeder, was half American and half Egyptian. Yet, because it happened to nestle alongside a tiny Essex river, Danskin had long since become an emblem of Englishness, featuring in Jane Austen television documentaries and *Christ Almighty*, a recent Hollywood adaptation of Evelyn Waugh's biography of Ronald Knox.

On this particular morning, a dim boy leaned on his rake in the grounds and watched a procession of cars crunch along the gravel drive, then disgorge their passengers between the pillars and into the main entrance of the house. He spat on the ground. He may have been a fool, but he was not so stupid that he didn't know what was going on.

In the formal garden to the rear of the house, Reeder Kite strolled past the chipped and forlorn Venus and the amputee Adonis and arched his back against the late-summer heat. Already-blown roses oozed a sensuous, sickly scent, intensifying when it met the livelier stench of a trellis of sweet peas around the sundial. Butterflies and bees drifted over borders of rich, moist soil, thickly strewn with astrantia, allium and aquilegia, mildly invaded by vetch and willow-herb. Fertility was everywhere.

Reeder scratched his inner thigh, probed himself, and wondered how soon after lunch he could escape back to London, where his mistress would be idling in her mews flat. He admired his new Nike trainers, his still-strong legs, then tensed his gut – there were still a few muscles there – thrust his arms out in front of him and squatted down. At that moment Olivia happened to glance through the window, and saw her near-naked husband performing his strength and balance training. He looked, she thought, like a walrus attempting ballet.

There was a curious mismatch between the temperatures inside and outside the house. Within its walls, Danskin felt as cold as death. Over the past few months the woman in the mews house in London had destroyed whatever human warmth had once been found there. The effect of Reeder's adultery had spread like an icy mist, floating down corridors and lurking under beds. Olivia no longer ransacked his email inbox or stabbed her way through his mobile phones, but had instead redirected her fury into a last spasm of energy in the referendum campaign. Each morning the family exchanged chilly platitudes over the breakfast table. Protracted silences and accusatory glances had replaced the former veneer of civility.

As if to echo the dismantling of the family, the main downstairs rooms had been cleared of pictures, books and domestic clutter. Boxes of old photographs, football boots, scented candles, CDs and unloved Christmas presents had been crammed into cupboards and forgotten. The ghostly outlines of Turkish rugs lingered on the bare wooden floors. Where once there had been elegant reproduction antique chairs and polished occasional tables, there were now rows of hurriedly-assembled flatpack desks and plastic chairs. Cables coiled in every direction from computers and printers set up throughout what had been the dining room, the sitting room and the second kitchen. Piles of cardboard boxes filled with files and labelled with thick ink marker teetered in the corners.

Maps of parliamentary constituencies, graffitied with numbers and names, had been pinned onto the walls, and flatscreen televisions were in every room, permanently broadcasting the BBC and Sky news channels. During working hours the rooms were full of smartly dressed young people crouching over their desks with serious expressions, their heads pressed to phones, their necks eternally cricked even as their fingers danced on keyboards. Outside, the background noise was hum and whoosh, living rural England; inside, it was tap and mutter.

At first Olivia Kite's decision to move the headquarters of the No to Europe, Democracy First campaign away from Westminster and into the expensive country house where her marriage was ending had seemed inexplicable. In fact it was a stroke of genius, distancing the campaign from the political establishment in London, and fusing together its couple of hundred dedicated staff out in the sticks. Their sequestered camaraderie meant that their movement had come to feel like a popular insurgency – and so, in a way, it was. Greece had exploded, Spain was dividing, France was on the march; and now it was Britain's turn. Far away from elderly, cynical Whitehall, this was a Spitfire summer. For the men and women serving under Olivia Kite, Danskin House was Fighter Command.

The house was not in fact quite as remote as it might have seemed. Just beyond the forest of oak and Scots pine that surrounded its formal gardens and strip of parkland was a busy coastal town, with a good road link to the M11, along which an endless stream of lorries trundled, bringing cars from Germany and containers full of almost everything else from China. Its railway station required only one change from Liverpool Street, and the local taxi drivers had become accustomed to cabinet ministers and minority party leaders, never mind television journalists and other hangers-on, arriving off the morning and evening trains with a self-important air and asking for 'Mrs Kite's place'.

Despite the container ships that arrived in the port every few hours, the European Union was deeply unpopular in this northern corner of Essex. Union flags flew from pubs and public buildings, and Mrs Kite, partly because her husband's reckless infidelity was a rich source of local gossip, was hugely popular here.

As for Olivia herself, she had recovered her domestic territory and stamped it with her own political identity; her skulking, pirouetting husband was beginning to feel like a stranger in his own home. Lionel, their eldest son, who was going through an REM phase, referred to his father simply as the Oaf. 'Living Well is the Best Revenge' echoed along the upstairs hallway as Olivia stared at her husband's froggy face flushing in the garden and thought, 'No, it bloody isn't. Stamping on his face with stiletto heels, before burning all his dreams in front of his staring eyes, ripping his fingernails off one by one and humiliating him in the newspapers. . . that would be the best revenge. But if that's not an option, I suppose living well is an acceptable second choice.'

Olivia was the Cavalier commander. But she had no intention of losing her head. She had more of Oliver Cromwell about her than any languid Stuart. Jennifer Lewis, by contrast, definitely had the looks of a Cavalier lady: a long, serpentine body, delicate, pale features and hair for whose colour there was no adequate description – corngold and copper, silver birch with licks of flame. With her green eyes and large, capable hands, however, she was a fighter too, and an eager footsoldier in Olivia Kite's parliamentary insurgency. Olivia treated her almost as a daughter, and relied very heavily on the younger woman's uncanny grasp of numbers and down-to-earth political sense.

Through the frantic weeks of the referendum campaign Jen was at her boss's side most of the time, expressionless, taking calls and giving orders. But today her provocative eyes seemed lost in thought. She couldn't get her mind off her last meeting with her former lover, the newspaper reporter Lucien McBryde. A man with a considerable talent for self-destruction, he now seemed to be falling apart at a spectacular rate. Texts she had received over the weekend told her he had been leaving her messages, even now, through their very private system.

2

Saturday, 16 September

Referendum Day Minus Five

Fathers and Sons

Two nights previously, Lucien McBryde had been walking slowly up St James's Street, deep in thought. (Not deep enough: this was his last weekend alive, although he wasn't aware of that fact. Had he known, he would more consciously have drunk in the salmon-coloured light on the sides of the buildings, the indistinct urban scent of late summer, the kestrel hovering over St James's Palace.)

Samuel Johnson held that to live a good life meant acting morally as if you were about to die, while conducting your daily business as if you were going to live for another fifty years. Lucien McBryde failed on both counts.

Morally, his main failings were idleness and irresponsibility mitigated by charm, an addiction to a stimulating powder, and another to stimulating, strong women. In his defence, he would point out that while many men regarded them simply as complicated and expensive instruments for their own pleasure, he was a genuine admirer of women – their smells and tastes, the way they walked and the way they talked – and that they tended to sense this. 'I am essentially a male lesbian,' he would declare.

In his professional life, McBryde acted as if he had an endless, charmed life, with unlimited possibilities for second chances and eleventh-hour renegotiations. His tax returns, bills, investments, pension and passwords were in an entirely chaotic state. For the best part of a decade Lucien McBryde had lived blissfully from day to day. But his supply of rising suns and golden sunsets was about to run out.

Tonight, McBryde had a nagging toothache. Eventually his tongue located it. Pain sought pain. Probing the back of his palate, he thought back to the events of two months before, when his father had died and his own life had begun to spin out of control.

Old Robson McBryde, Lucien's widowed father, had been a hard man to love. In Lucien's case, this was perhaps partly because they were closer to two generations apart in age than one. But it was mainly because his father was an impossible man to live up to. With a face like an American bald eagle, hacked and fissured by many decades of concentration and humour, Robson McBryde was a legend in Fleet Street and beyond – the wartime hero who pursued a career as a foreign correspondent in the Middle East, reporting on the first Gaza camps for the *Guardian* with a ferocity which led (thanks to a quiet word from a major advertiser to the paper's impeccably liberal editor of the day) to his summary dismissal on the unspoken charge of anti-Semitism.

Robson migrated to other newspapers as a pitiless moralist in the foreign affairs field, churning out endless lucid and fact-packed columns on the immorality of British foreign policy across the Middle East and beyond. As early as the Suez debates of 1956 he was cited in the House of Commons as an authority, and regarded as the then prime minister's personal nemesis in the press.

Lucien had grown up in the menacing shadow of his father's moral certainties. It had been a boyhood of newspapers flattened out on the breakfast table and fingers stabbed down angrily in emphasis, of after-school harangues and sad shakings of the head over his lack of interest in current affairs and, more generally, his academic performance. Old Robson, a liberal and Fabian of the old school, would never have raised his hand against a child, yet in his perpetual disappointment, punctuated by occasional door-slamming tantrums, the old man proved a brutally destructive humanitarian, a *Guardian*-reading human-hater. His son, lying on the floor with his chess set or watching television, had dreamed of being taken in and adopted by the parents of his best friend Jonathan. They were kindly people, of no known opinions.

The father had never regarded the son as his intellectual equal. Lucien's attempts to impress him, whether through his school essays or in conversation, tended to result only in hard-eyed silences or sarcastic rejoinders. ('Ha! Islington's home-grown Mencken has, I think, mistaken Ernie for Nye'; or, 'Young Woodward, I presume? Iran and Persia are *the same fucking place.*') It is surprisingly easy to destroy a young man's sense of himself.

When Lucien finally got a job after university as a gossip reporter for a midmarket newspaper, he did not even try to persuade his father that this was a respectable way of earning a living. The old man nourished his disappointment for years, missing no opportunity of praising his son's award-winning contemporaries, and asking awkward questions about the sources of his minor scoops.

Early on in his career, Robson had given a leg-up to Ken Cooper, now the editor of the *National Courier*, and they had remained drinking friends ever since, having lunch together every few months. Once they had been three, but the intense, wiry-haired young politician who had been such brilliant company, and who had kept them gasping and spluttering with laughter for years, had drifted away, too busy and too ambitious for alcoholic afternoons. Having kept his head down during the Blair, Brown and Cameron years, neither journalist was surprised when he rose, comparatively late in life, to become party leader and then prime minister.

With Ken and Robson left by themselves, their lunches became almost silent affairs, but somehow they survived Ken's continued success in the glittery, shallow, modern newspaper world. From opposite ends of the political spectrum, the two friends had agreed an armistice in which the only fit subject of conversation was the catastrophic decline of the country. Their habitual game was to try to identify fresh signs of this, and to probe their origins.

After twenty minutes of gloomy silence, Ken would say, 'Inappropriate.'

With any luck, Robson would show sufficient interest for Ken to continue.

'Our forefathers talked about human *evil*. You and I . . . well, we'd say that something – I don't know, child abuse, or trying to strangle your wife in public – was *wicked*. These days, it's just fucking *inappropriate*. That's the worst fucking word they've got.' (*They* was code for everyone under fifty.)

Robson would continue to slurp his soup, and Ken to smash his salad to pieces. Eventually one of them would say, 'Butchers.'

And so it would go on. Sometimes a gambit wouldn't work. 'Velcro. Bloody Velcro,' Robson might say, but Ken would only look up blankly and shrug. Another thirty minutes or so of friendly, despairing silence was then guaranteed.

On only one subject would Robson frown and show displeasure.

'That boy of yours isn't completely stupid, you know,' Ken might say. 'Brought in a decent little story last week. . .'

Lucien had been hired by the *Courier*'s deputy editor, but Robson refused to believe it wasn't patronage, and never forgave Ken for his supposed weakness.

But Ken was right: Lucien McBryde really wasn't completely stupid. And so he had fluttered, broken-winged, from perch to perch, eventually making enough money at the *Courier* to be able to enjoy himself, and to dress well, while never hanging on to it long enough to own property, or any of the other appurtenances of serious, grown-up life.

Lucien was not on the run from his father. That level of exertion would have appalled him. He was, rather, on a gentle jog from adult responsibility, and as he continued up St James's Street he flattered himself that, in that respect at least, he had been doing rather well. But then he had tripped over Jen Lewis, and had fallen, hurtling head-down, parachute-free, in love.

Mothers and Daughters

On the face of it – and hers was an ivory, oval face, offset by a sensual, challenging mouth – Jennifer Lewis's background could hardly have been more different. She had been brought up by a strict aunt in an old Devon rectory, and had attended the Royal Girls' Academy outside Exeter. There she had appeared gloriously normal. But Jennifer's cross, the painful burden chafing her slim shoulders, had always been her mother. Myfanwy Davies-Jones, a Welsh poetess and novelist with a cloud of yellow hair and a scarlet reputation, had arrived in the King's Road in July 1963, not quite straight from her pit-village school, and had thrown herself headfirst into West London society during the most exhilarating and self-indulgent years those dirty terraced streets and dusty parks had enjoyed since the Second World War.

She attracted the rich and the dangerous – men such as Lord Croaker, the asset-stripper and zoo-owner; and the right-wing journalist and politician Sir Rufus Panzer. Way back, Panzer had been a communist, even volunteering as a machine-gunner in a red corps during the Spanish Civil War. In his sixties he had been a lean and extreme supporter of the rising Tory right, though he was later rejected by Margaret Thatcher: 'Brilliant man, but a little too much gleam in the eye.'

After half a dozen relationships with such wild characters, diluted by the occasional *artiste*, Myfanwy's first novel was acclaimed as the satirical *roman à clef* swinging London had been waiting for. Sidetracked from her new celebrity by a doe-eyed performance poet from Liverpool, she gave birth to a son, quickly palmed off to a couple who for some reason wished to adopt him. She would have preferred an abortion, she frankly admitted to her friends, but had been too disorganised, lazy, and perhaps frightened, to go through with it.

The hospital long remembered Myfanwy Lewis – for this episode she had chosen to revert temporarily to her real name, rather than the one by which she was known to her public. Its nurses had never before had to deal with a strong aroma of marijuana smoke in the maternity wing, let alone a constant stream of arguing and back-slapping visitors in leather jackets and kaftans who stayed late into the night playing Joan Baez songs. Myfanwy had treated the birth pains and what they brought forth as a baffling surprise, unpleasant enough at the time, but soon afterwards useful material for one of her most successful books.

Then, many years later, when Myfanwy was on the very brink of the menopause, she had swanned back to the hospital, still striking, still attended by adoring young men, hugely pregnant and hugely irritated at this second unexpected turn of events. Thus arrived the small and cross Zuleika Maria-Guadeloupe Attracta Gonne Lewis.

In later years, the unwanted Jen – as she preferred to be called – had never thrown her mother's evident lack of interest, or even maternal instinct, back at her. It would have been as futile as complaining to a bird about its song. As a baby, as a toddler, and as a striking, solemn-faced young girl, she had been passed from friend to relative to acquaintance. 'Who's on Jenny Wren duty tonight?' literary editors would ask publishers' secretaries. Jen remembered only a haze of kindly, feckless faces, wooden floors and Turkish carpets in colourfully furnished flats and houses across

West London. From time to time Mother would appear briefly, brandish her like a prize at a party or barbecue, then disappear again, after flinging her a bouquet of incomprehensibly flowery language and a warm, nauseatingly perfumed farewell embrace. Jen still recalled the moist, sickly, lipsticked mouth and the wet, lolling tongue, imbued with tobacco and wine, with a shudder.

In many other families, both Jen and her mother would have got over all this, and thrived. Jen would have turned her early years into a funny late-night story for the benefit of boyfriends, and become increasingly admiring of her mother's genuine, exotic literary gift, and even her famous face, like that of a fine-boned elf in a wig, which had popped up so often, sketched or photographed, on the covers of extinct magazines and *Sunday Times* colour supplements. Myfanwy, meanwhile, would have come to appreciate her daughter's precocious intelligence and her looks, which echoed her own, and woven her childish triumphs, pearls of wisdom and delightful mistakes into brittle newspaper columns. Eventually, the two would have become friends.

It never happened like that. Jennifer was, at least, spared those newspaper columns. She had the wrong temperament to understand her mother. Temperament is fate, and Jen was temperamentally literal rather than literary, almost male in her self-absorbed preference for order and systems. She hated sloppiness, and the slopping around of personal secrets. And when she eventually read her mother's novels — *Seven Sermons for Secular Sinners*, or *Leprosy and the Ladies' Room* — she found them emotionally incontinent, plotless and frankly embarrassing. Myfanwy's love affairs, described with an earthy, sensuous detail that in those days was very rare from a woman, had made her rich. First editions of her early books now changed hands for thousands of pounds, while the paperbacks could be found, squeezed between Jackie Collins and Margaret Drabble, on bookshelves across North London. To her daughter, this literary celebrity was incomprehensible.

Jen's life only began to make sense to herself when, aged eleven, she was dispatched from London to go and live with her mother's sister, a stern, quietly religious woman married to a dentist in Devon. Hundreds of miles away from the nearest literary party, she enjoyed the clipped lawn and the piano lessons in a large, oak-timbered room that smelled of old fires and damp Victorian sofas. She loved her school, the biology and chemistry lessons in particular, and made a group of friends, quiet, serious girls like herself. She collected stamps, butterflies and even football cards. For days – even weeks – at a time she felt herself happy.

Oxford was another fresh start, a place of wonders. A natural scientist, in both senses, Jenny found herself being pulled towards politics during the short-lived Johnson administration. Repelled by the beery and yobbish advances of young men who proclaimed themselves socialists, or even revolutionaries – and not simply because her political heroine Margaret Thatcher had herself been a scientist – she joined the Conservative Party. Jen believed in reason and efficiency. She didn't much care about the European Union one way or the other – that would come later. Her politics did not make her universally popular. But, confronted by the self-righteous arguments of the college lefties, she prided herself on never losing her temper, and on hitting back with carefully memorised figures and quotations. She was quickly spotted.

In her second year Jen switched from 'nat sci' to PPE, and became an active Tory student, elbowing aside moist-palmed, stammering young men as she rose through the ranks of the Union, until in her final year she was elected its president. Nothing could have mortified her mother more. In college she was known universally as 'June', which she had assumed was the result of a mishearing, until one evening in the student bar she overheard a girl explaining to her friend, 'No, not Jen. *June* – cold and bright.' When her mother, a regular in the letters pages of the *Observer* and a prominent campaigner for the arts, came to speak at the Union, Jen did not attend. By then she had led the winning side in many Union debates herself.

So it came about that after university the girl who had assumed that she would spend her adult life as a laboratory assistant or a research scientist went instead to work at Conservative Central Office. In that boys' world she was recognised as brilliant but difficult. She had spent a happy year working for the man – now much heavier and with silver through his wiry hair – who would become prime minister. But a disastrous love affair with a young, married MP who managed to keep his seat despite his exposure in the press, ended in her leaving that job both sadder and wiser.

It was then that she was snapped up by Olivia Kite, who recognised her brilliance and made her the number-cruncher and analyst-in-chief for the increasingly powerful Eurosceptic group inside the parliamentary party. Slim, pale, and with her mother's shining hair, Jennifer Lewis continued to be much admired – though mostly from a distance.

Sex and Marriage

Who could ever have predicted that cold, bright June Lewis and Lucien McBryde, the tousled, coke-snorting lobby hack who had once been thrown off the prime minister's battle bus, having been caught in the toilet, red-eyed, with crusty nostrils, would experience such an instant and intense mutual attraction? He was dishevelled, she meticulously shevelled. He disreputable, she shinily reputable. He a dark and ragged squiggle of a man, she as beautifully balanced as a complex quadratic equation. That both of them felt the same inside, both having been ruined by a selfish and indifferent parent, was something few people could have guessed. To a friend, Jen had explained: 'He was the last person on earth I was ever likely to fall for. That's why it happened.'

The sex, when they eventually got round to it, was intense and revelatory. (The shift from the time when people 'had' each other to when they 'did' each other had been the subject of a conversation between Ken Cooper and Robson McBryde.) In bed Jen experienced the only area of his life in which Lucien was not selfish. Two bodies became one. Away from bed, their friends said admiringly and jealously, each became more engaging and lovable.

Perhaps the happiest day that either Jen or Lucien would know in their lives centred around a lunch in a chaotic and cheerful Italian restaurant by Victoria station. No wedding, but a wine-and-pasta-fuelled meeting of two writing tribes, it was hosted in their honour by Robson McBryde. Racy literature and fervid political journalism acknowledged each other, and made dignified bows. Jen's mother performed many of her most successful anecdotes, and was grudgingly admired by the wary elderly journalist, while their two children, both secure and both feeling that they knew who they were at last, looked on.

'Luce, let's never ever have a *wedding* anniversary,' Jen had said as they teetered back up the street towards their respective offices. 'Let's celebrate this date as our special day, and come back here for years and years.'

Lucien had said nothing in reply. For once, he couldn't speak. He was still trying to come to terms with this strange new feeling – not drunkenness, not 'a rush', but something calmer and more delicately coloured: perhaps it was happiness.

But nothing happy ever lasts. Just two months after the pair of them had been bound together, unable to keep their hands off each other, driven to nuzzle in public places and to stifle their conversations with kisses, London began one of her amazing changes of costume. For a few weeks her temperature rose to that of Paris, and even Rome. Magnesium glares splashed across her glass towers. Down in her shaded alleys and half-lit canyons, her citizens shucked off their grey woollens and padded jackets. Torsos, suspiciously tanned or thickly hairy, were openly displayed. Unhappy cats found themselves sharing urban gardens with pot-planters and barbecue-lighters. Damp pavements, now dried, hosted families of chairs and little tables, and brightly-coloured young people sat outside pubs and restaurants. The smells of charcoaling meat and fragrant tobacco filled the air. Dogs gambolled deliriously in the public parks. Annually, the people of London became inmates released from prison into a brighter world of possibilities. And amid all this chirruping and fluttering, Lucien and Jennifer had a terrible, terminal row. Like most of the worst rows, it seemed to blow up out of nothing at all. Yet it ripped their oneness apart forever.

Lucien had casually mentioned that an ex-girlfriend had asked him to supper. For no particular reason, he had never told Jen about this girl before. Jen froze, then snapped at him. Lucien went cold, and sneered at her. In an instant Jen found herself looking at him differently. Who was he, this stranger? Her face zipped shut, her melting eyes turned to ice, and when Lucien finally brought himself to look at her properly after a long silence, he found he barely recognised her either.

In the bitter public argument that followed, both spat out plosives and fricatives like shrapnel. Each, suddenly feeling sick inside, had been in subconscious training for this combat of ugly words, this tournament of misery, for weeks. Never conversationalists, they now discovered in one another a genius for invective. After twenty minutes they were standing silent and stiff-legged, like mannequins, at the Trafalgar Square end of Whitehall, before turning and hobbling off in opposite directions. By the time evening fell Jennifer had taken her things out of Lucien's Notting Hill basement flat, and gathered a group of sympathetic friends to empty wine bottles and shred his already tattered reputation. His addictive personality had been too much for Jen. It had been slowly pushing the walls of her ordered life apart. Now she tugged them firmly back together again.

Lucien had been damaged the more severely. In the days that followed he realised that the first person who had ever made him feel like a fully functioning adult human being had walked away. He tried to comfort himself with the memories of earlier lovers and the promise of new erotic freedom, but felt nothing stirring at all, except irrepressible self-disgust. He thought about throwing himself off Hammersmith Bridge. But he was not a jumper.

Perhaps the break-up was inevitable, was even for the best. Had

Lucien and Jennifer stayed together and had children, they would have passed their self-destructive traits down to the next generation. The French say that the children of lovers are orphans.

A few days later, Lucien's father was in his local when he noticed that he was pouring his pint of bitter directly down the trouser leg of the man sitting to his left.

'Oof. Groourrgh,' protested the man. 'Hoi, hoi.' Nor did he say this in a friendly way. Robson tried to right his glass, but there was no strength in his wrist, and the rest of the liquid gurgled onto the man's crotch. He said 'Hoi,' again, sounding as though he meant it. Robson tried to explain and apologise, but no sound came from his mouth. Then he suddenly slid backwards off his bar stool, and landed face-up on the floor.

He was still feeling an overwhelming sense of irritation when the two ambulancemen arrived. One said to the other, 'Shall we blue this one?' The other replied, 'God yes, we'd better blue *him*.' Robson rather liked the sound of that – it made him feel important – but the stroke killed him even as the flashing and wailing ambulance pulled away from the pub.

The funeral had taken place at a crematorium in North London, attended by a ragged platoon of newspaper editors, including a stunned and bewildered-looking Ken Cooper, as well as famous foreign correspondents and columnists from the less popular papers. The rain cascaded down on the backs and hats of some two hundred people who could not be fitted into the chapel. Lucien was not there. He spent the day in his flat, emptying a bottle of his father's favourite malt whisky, and sobbing.

He survived the weeks following his father's death by drowning himself in the large, wet eyes of a series of sympathetic girls, and managed to keep working by snuffling fashionable stimulants. But his timekeeping, as Cooper noticed morosely, became ever more erratic.

Library Game

That Saturday, idly admiring the forthright, no-nonsense
names of the old shopkeepers on the street – Lobb for boots, Lock
for hats, winking, scarlet Berry Bros & Rudd for booze, Hockney
for tobacco – Lucien McBryde turned right just before the *Economist*
building, and wavered his way towards the north-west corner of St
James's Square, and a narrow building with tall windows that was
the nearest thing he had to a spiritual home. This was the London
Library, a private-subscription affair founded by whiskered and
idealistic Victorians, lifelong membership of which had been a gift
from his father during a brief phase when he'd showed some promise
as a writer. Its collection was unsurpassed by that of any other
private institution. Its dark reading room, smelling of old books
and old men, was as calming a place as could be found in this square
half-mile of clubland.

But that was not why Lucien McBryde used the building. Well-
versed in the dangers of email, texting and mobile phones, he had
made the library, in effect, his private communications hub. By this
time on a Saturday it would normally have closed its doors. But
tonight the annual party was in full swing, and McBryde lurched
his way inside. For once he was not looking for another drink, free
or otherwise. He was here, as usual, to send a message.

When pursuing a woman, or dealing with a particularly private
source of information, McBryde avoided all the modern commu-

nications systems, which were vulnerable to being spied on by everyone from spotty youths in the pay of rival newspapers to, so the *Guardian* said, GCHQ, the Americans and probably the Chinese as well. He passed his most sensitive messages on by simply texting its recipient the title and author of a particular book, and leaving an old-fashioned handwritten note inside the London Library's copy of it. All the girl, or civil servant, or junior minister, had to do then was to go to the narrow, metal-grilled stacks, pull out the book and retrieve the message. They would then repeat the process, texting him the location of his own 'book-note'. So far, all parties had found this method entirely secure.

Others cottoned on, of course, and the waiting list for membership of the London Library had jumped remarkably. The venerable stacks began to reek of passion and secret liaisons. Many of those apparent bibliophiles fingering a history of the early French kings with an affectedly vague expression, or rubbing their palms along an anatomical sketchbook, were in reality trying to hunt down a passionate letter from a married man or woman, or a proposition for an indecent or politically sensitive rendezvous.

The crucial thing about the London Library postal service was that the messages had to be left in books which were in no danger of being taken out by the wrong person – some wandering visitor who was unaware of the system. They had to be secreted in books about thoroughly dull topics, books no one in their right mind would ever want to open. McBryde had experimented with obscure Swedish philologists, unknown Victorian novelists, and dense tomes of twentieth-century structural Marxism, but had finally settled on the works of the journalist and sometime historian Dominic Sandbrook. Sandbrook had been the unwitting Pandar for McBryde's life-changing love affair; at last, flickers of energy had pulsed between his pages.

Tonight Lucien was on his way to deliver a message to Jennifer, but one that had little to do with romance, although just writing her name had given his heart a sickening lurch. He swiped his membership card and entered the library, then went upstairs to the History of England section, where he took down the latest of Sandbrook's tomes, an eight-hundred-page history of Britain from 1982 to 1983. Into it, he slipped his note.

He felt clammy and weak as he made his way back out into St James's Square, shouldering past the party guests – Sir Tom Stoppard was deep in conversation with Andrew Wilson. Once he was outside he checked his phone, which was full of increasingly terse messages from the office. He scrolled through them. Then deleted them. There was absolutely no point in being a reporter if you had to attend meetings or communicate with your bosses.

McBryde was planning a long – a very long – night. Even so, he remained just slightly more journalist than dipsomaniac. The tip he was passing on to Jennifer had come from Alois Haydn, the notorious Svengali of Number 10. Haydn knew everyone in London. He *was* London. His deepest secret was McBryde's last romantic gift to Jen. Passing it on to her was a stroke of genius. . . Or so McBryde thought. But ever since their meeting a question had been nagging away at him. Why had that famously manipulative little man sought *him* out? He owed him no favours. *Haydn?*

A good journalist does not simply receive what is given; he always asks *why* he was given it. Loitering in a nearby pub over a whisky and soda, McBryde concentrated hard as he began to look his gift horse closely in the mouth. Alois Haydn only ever looked out for Alois Haydn. Everyone knew that. But the story he'd told him was one that put Haydn himself in a bad light – or would, one day. So if it wasn't about power, what else could it be about? Was it money?

For all the wrong reasons – involving Soho clubs and drug dealers

— Lucien had made some quite good connections in the murkier fringes of the City. He texted Charmian Locke, a school friend from many years ago who he had heard was currently working at one of the larger merchant banks, and arranged a clandestine meeting for the following evening. Both would probably be pretty pissed by then, Lucien thought, but he prided himself on being able to hold his drink. He would remember everything that was said.

3

Monday, 18 September

Referendum Day Minus Three

Who is Alois Haydn?

The cool of the Monday morning had lifted. A cloudless sky, and eye-scorching brightness, reflected from top-floor windows across the capital. A body had been deposited in the mortuary reserved for suspicious deaths. The pavement had already been cleaned, the police tape removed, and commuters were now passing heedlessly over the spot at which a young journalist had died. A mile or so to the west, almost equally invisible, a perfectly groomed little man was gliding purposefully along Piccadilly, his tiny feet barely touching the pavement.

It was once said of Josef Stalin, no less, that during his rise to power he was like a grey blur, always in the background, never quite in focus. Alois Haydn had the same talent. Somehow, one never looked at him closely. No matter how hard you tried, you could never remember his face, even after a difficult meeting. If he ever threw a shadow, it was a thin, vaporous one. This morning he was on his way to an important meeting with the executive members of a somewhat mysterious company, Professional Logistical Services, or 'PLS'.

Alois Haydn's name had been on the lists of the Most Influential Britons for more than a decade. All the political parties paid him court. His summer parties in Oxfordshire attracted ministers, celebrities and intellectuals alike. By the lake and in the marquee, prize-winning novelists and rising politicians mingled: the Lucasian professor could be found deep in conversation with the Eton-educated star of a hit American TV series; Prince Andrew and the crop-haired, boyish editor of the *Guardian* might be seen sitting at the same table. To receive one's invitation, a month ahead of the event, had become part of Britain's unofficial honours system, on a par with appearing on *Desert Island Discs*, being lampooned on the cover of *Private Eye* or speaking at Davos. Ordinary snappers clustered at the gate to capture the arrivals; a royal-connected fashion photographer took informal pictures inside the grounds.

Yet the host, Alois Haydn, was rarely photographed. Gatsby-like, he was little more than a linen suit glimpsed in the background shadows. And this year, to widespread disappointment, the party had been cancelled. Haydn had moved his home from the Cotswolds, rural heartland of the English establishment, to the Essex coast, on the edge of the island, where he was building a new house. The symbolism was much commented on.

Having bought Rocks Point, an elegant Victorian seaside mansion perched on a spit of sandy soil, Haydn had caused local uproar by demolishing the whole building, from its brick turrets and fancy battlements to its sprawling stables and wrought-iron greenhouses. In its place there had arisen a bleak outcrop of cubes, pyramids and mushrooms, as if a shoddily constructed alien spacecraft had crash landed on the site. Intriguingly, it was just a few miles from Olivia Kite's Danskin House.

There was a lot of snooping. Mini-drones, tiny helicopters equipped with cameras and microphones, had just begun to be used by the mainstream media. Wildfowling in the marshes had long been a local tradition, so Haydn invited friends from London, county types and shadowy Eastern Europeans alike, for the shooting. Again and again they brought down the drones. Website owners were outraged. Lawyers rubbed their hands.

He could afford that: Haydn Communications had smashed through the old world of gentlemanly corporate public relations back in the 1980s, not long after Nigel Lawson had smashed up the cosy old world of the City: one of Alois's big breaks had come from the privatisation of British Gas. His early years were lost in mystery, but he appeared to be a member of a famous family. His much older sister Camille Haydn had won the Turner Prize with her installation on the history of female sexuality, and his much younger brother Liddell Haydn was the eponymous creator of the successful TV production company. Haydn himself was of almost Middle Eastern appearance, and some said he had been plucked from a children's home – there were no pictures of him from his early childhood. But he never spoke of such things, either to friends or in public.

Haydn's bride, the daughter of the radical Tory peer and land-owner Lord Mortlake, had brought him modest inherited wealth and an entrée to the highest levels of the Conservative Party. The wealth and the contacts lingered on after the dissolution of the marriage when Alois came out. He was now in a civil partnership with the Indian short-story writer Ajit Gupta. It was often stated by those who claimed to know that Haydn was 'more New Labour than anything', and he had certainly prospered under Tony Blair. He had given Tony, Cherie and the children the use of his holiday villa in Umbria, and had been pictured playing tennis with Tony at Chequers. Peter Mandelson was said to have him on speed dial.

Alois Haydn was, it seems, a hard man to pin down, and a hard man to describe. On this particular morning, walking past the Ritz in the late-summer sunlight, he was on his way to meet a roomful of people who prided themselves on being good observers – some of them professionally so. What might they have noted down?

They would have reported that Haydn was a man of something

below middle height, and of average weight, and of middling years. His hair was hazel, and slightly curled. His face was olive-shaped and avocado-coloured, with dark, sunken eyes like two soft dates. He could almost have been Indian. His suit was Ozwald Boateng, and his shoes were Italian brogues. He wore a light-grey silk tie over a cream shirt, and his nails appeared to have been varnished. His views? Unfathomable. His educational background? Unknown. His psychological drive? *Hush*. He carried a small leather bag neatly in both hands, and he walked so lightly it was almost as if he were being blown gently along by the wind.

The Dither Fund

Alois Haydn carried his wealth lightly too. He called the substantial reserves of money he had amassed his 'dither fund' — inheritance and earnings he had been thinking about investing in property, shares or holiday treats, but had never got round to using. Because it was just sitting in the bank, slowly losing value, he also called it his 'ice money': drip by drip, it slowly shrank in value and leaked away. When, just before the previous Christmas, he had finally stopped dithering, the dither fund stood at £4,745,201.20. He wired most of it to a new account in the Gulf, cashing out the remaining half a million in £50 notes. This took a lot of paperwork, tedious discussions with bank staff and nervous packaging, but he eventually had the sum wrapped in waterproof paper and jammed into a rucksack.

Alois may have had an obscure background, but he had a very clear mind. Britain, he believed, was finished. Thirty years of spending ever more money on ever pleasanter lifestyles, while working ever less hard and ever less efficiently, had done the once-great nation irreversible damage. Tory and Labour alike: locust years. It wasn't politics. It was decadence.

As Alois saw it, there were now two possible courses of events. Either the socialists would get back, and in the prevailing mood of public outrage the demands for higher taxes would drive the rich and the foreigners out, fleeing London like flocks of migrating birds affected by a sudden chilling in the weather. Or, despite the best efforts of the current prime minister, the radical and nationalist right would take over, doing enormous short-term damage to everything, including employment. Either way, property prices would crash, and those who remained in Britain would have nowhere safe to put their money. Alois didn't trust government assurances about the security of the banks. He knew a little history.

He had screwed up his courage to talk about his worries with the prime minister. It wasn't easy. The PM had a way of looking at you, his forehead creased and his thick, shaggy eyebrows casting dark shadows over his eyes, his mouth twisted in a wordless disdain that had you beaten in argument before he said a word. When it finally came, his voice – all gravel and pebbles and fast-running water between them – reminded Alois of his recent personal triumph in Germany, and the possibility of a negotiated solution acceptable to all sides. The very thing he was putting to the country in a referendum.

'Why, Alois, do you suppose I am ruining – *ruining* – my health, and shredding what's left of my popularity, if not to steer the poor old British people deftly between the two disasters you so eloquently describe? Grab the tiller. Port and starboard: the economically illiterate socialist Scylla and the saloon-bar nationalist Charybdis. My job is to jam wax into the ears of the people and get us past the Sirens, through the white horses and out into the open sea. And I will, if it's the last thing I do. Believe me, Alois. Stick with us, and leave your money where it is.'

Alois had always admired the prime minister just this side of idolatry. It was his only weakness, and he rather liked himself for it. But after this conversation, and despite the prime minister's almost hypnotic stare, he walked away unconvinced. Two days later he liquidated the entire dither fund and bought tickets for himself and Ajit to Dubai.

Various interesting people from the Islamic Republic of Iran and the Pakistani security service had found Dubai more discreet than Switzerland and as secure as Singapore – as well as much nearer than either. The banks there would open an account for a large amount of currency passed across the counter with the minimum of questioning or paperwork. The architecture, the heat and the vulgarity of the shopping were minor inconveniences compared with the helpfulness of the financial institutions.

Ajit, dejected by the appalling British weather, had jumped at the idea of a brief break in Dubai, and was touched when Alois packed for him. It almost made up for his steerage-class ticket – Alois, as always, travelled first class. But when Ajit discovered, while delving in his rucksack for his washbag at Dubai International Airport, that he had just unwittingly carried a vast sum of sterling through customs, while Alois had brought only a few T-shirts and a credit card, the couple had their first big row.

'But you got away with it,' Alois had defended himself.

'That's not the point. You deceived me. You did it coldly, and you put me in danger. You behaved like a shit.'

'For God's sake, Ajit. Nobody travelling in steerage with a rucksack is going to be checked for currency. You get past the dope-sniffer dogs and you're home free. It would have been much more risky if I'd had it in *my* luggage. And if I'd told you about it you'd have been pathetic – all camp and sweaty and scared – and you'd certainly have been caught.'

'Don't call me pathetic. And don't you dare call me camp. I'm not "camp". I'm not "gay". I'm not "queer". I'm just an old-fashioned, straightforward bugger. And I'm damned proud to be a bugger. All I ask, Alois. . .'

Their voices had been raised enough to attract the attention of the businessmen and white-robed taxi drivers standing around the arrivals hall. The country was full of proud buggers, but they didn't often talk about it in loud voices in public places.

The argument fizzled out, but it left Ajit in a terrible mood, and spoiled the holiday for both of them. Alois had taken the money off to the bank recommended to him by his wealth manager at Raworth & Reid in London and opened a new and untraceable account, the ultimate insurance, which even in Dubai took an entire morning. Ajit was left to sun himself by the hotel pool, which proved to be greasy with tanning lotion and full of writhing, screaming Arab teenagers throwing footballs and splashing each other. And the sun was far too hot. He decided that he hated Dubai, and retreated indoors to the fitness suite to work off his bad temper on some kettle bells and the treadmill.

A wiry, tousle-headed man, dressed only in a pair of shorts, was grunting away on the rowing machine. Both of them did a hard forty minutes in the gym before starting to talk under the refreshingly cold showers. The rower introduced himself as Charmian Locke, a 'sort of banker' from London, and added nastily, 'You musht be the only Indian staying in a fuck-off place like thish.'

The speech impediment – made all the more noticeable by his huge teeth, like gleaming white tombstones – bothered Ajit. It seemed to come and go. Could it be an affectation? Nevertheless, he explained that his partner had come to invest some money here, and said that Dubai struck him as a bit of a hole.

'It'sh not so bad. The trouble ish, it isn't Arab and it isn't Western,' said Charmian. 'It *ish* a hole, I shpose – the hole between the two.' He and Ajit talked about why so much money was being made in this surreal, gritty little country. Ajit, as a writer, both respected money and was frightened by it. But Charmian's evident greed and cleverness were catching, and Ajit began to find his new acquaintance's conversation as interesting as his teeth were alarming.

However, by the time he and Haydn, both of whom were still disgruntled with one another, returned to the airport a few days later, he had forgotten Charmian. But then they bumped into each other in the queue. Ajit introduced him to Alois as the brilliant money man he'd met in the hotel gym. Naturally, Charmian was travelling at the front of the plane, and he and Alois talked non-stop all the way to London. One of the great things about first-class air travel is that it puts all the crooks together.

Charmian Locke had worked for one of the biggest investment banks in the world before his blog about life in the City after the financial crash was tracked to his trading computer and he was fired for breaking the firm's confidentiality clauses. The truth was, he had been bored. His deserved reputation as one of the shrewdest brains on the trading floor meant that he was soon contacted by a friend of his father's, Sir Solomon Dundas, a flamboyant former private banker now with a company called PLS, with a proposal concerning his future employment. The money wasn't great, but the job was.

'He's a damn clever fellow. New generation. Perfectly respectable – just don't let him smile at you,' was the judgement of Solomon. And so it was that Alois Haydn came to have yet another link with Professional Logistical Services.

Professional Logistical Services

At his insistence, the group of eminent public Britons had convened to meet Alois Haydn in a private club off Shepherd's Market. He'd ordered them over there, and now he'd ordered them over here. The man was a maniac for secrecy. There was an air of irritation in the room, as they had all left urgent work. They were unaccustomed to being summoned, and unaccustomed to waiting.

This club was a remnant of a London that — so far as outsiders imagined — had long disappeared. It was the London in which gentlemen never wore brown shoes except with corduroy trousers and tweed jackets; the London whose tobacconists mixed cigarette blends just as sir preferred, and where Purdeys were bought in pairs for young sons; the London of unmarked doors, of Albany chambers (not 'flats', still less 'apartments'), where the tea was forever Darjeeling and the gins only came pink. It was a London, frankly, that was mostly now for sale to wealthy foreign nostalgists. But there were still a few pockets of the old ways.

A circle of padded leather chairs had been arranged in front of an ornate marble fireplace. One of those present was actually smoking — tobacco. A discreet handwritten sign on the door told club members that the Red Library had been reserved until lunchtime by 'PLS'. The full name of the company whose executives had gathered in the small, stuffy room in Mayfair had been deliberately chosen because it was the dullest and most meaningless available.

The average age of the people assembled in the room was well into the seventies, and one weatherbeaten and famous face must have been ninety if he was a day. Yet the gathering unmistakably exuded power as well as experience. An informed observer – Ken Cooper, say – would have recognised everyone there.

Admiral Lord Jock Dalgety, former chief of the Defence Staff, was rubbing his long red nose and muttering something to General Sir Mike Patten, who had led the British forces in Iraq and who still failed to look convincingly like a businessman. Dame Cecily Morgan, former director of MI5, was sitting utterly still and silent, her hands neatly folded in her lap. She had been recruited by General Patten after a late-night club dinner when they had found themselves the last two guests remaining at the table for ten.

'What, really, do you have to look forward to, Cecily?' he had asked her as they nursed their brandies.

'Well, Mike, I guess five or six more years of independence in my flat, learning to cope with just a little more pain each year, and then the usual expensive, overheated, piss-scented home. Suffocating, those places. I've got a few nieces and nephews, but no children. That's what the service does to you. I'm luckier than most: there's enough money left for decent wine and a film-channel subscription until I finally kick the bucket.' Even as a young woman, Cecily had been known for her blunt speaking.

The old general nodded vigorously. 'For me, what I really dread is the old girl going first. Left to myself it'll be too much whisky every evening and then a fall in the bathroom one night when I'm stumbling around on my way for a piss. Can't even enjoy the theatre any more. Weak bladder. The old girl does a decent omelette, and keeps an eye on me, but she's not well. They train you for the battlefield and what might happen there, but where's the situation report for those last ten years?'

Patten then began to describe a more interesting possible final chapter to Dame Cecily, earning decent money and travelling, even at her advanced age, to some interesting parts of the world where she might actually meet some rivals from the old days whom she had never dreamed of seeing face to face. The powers that be wouldn't be happy, but what could they do? God already Called her God. She hadn't been hard to convince, particularly when she learned that the mysterious company contained many people she had known for most of her working life. Lord McDonald, the fire-eating chairman of United Meats, and Baroness Tessie Fremantle, the Miss Marple-featured former permanent secretary at the Treasury, would be among her colleagues. As would Dickie Greene, the hairy-eared, scarlet-jerseyed former director of the Secret Intelligence Service and chairman of the Joint Intelligence Committee.

Every one of those now assembled in the room had done things in their past that they would prefer didn't become public – cooked figures, spread deceptions, strangled careers, and in Dame Cecily's case looked the other way while enemies of Britain were tortured, even killed. All of them were lined and creased by years of responsibility and hard choices. None of them had many years left. They were all 'comfortable' in the narrow financial sense, but they had all been uncomfortable, itchy and uneasy in the constricted world of retirement. One last adventure mattered much more to each of them than any paycheque that might be involved.

Despite the high average age of its senior board and their general air of languor, PLS was a comparatively recent organisation. It had been founded in 1988 by some former members of the intelligence services, senior military officers and a few financial eagles to bring 'advanced research techniques' to British companies that found themselves in some sort of trouble. In the letters of association and early discussions about contracts, nothing remotely illegal was ever mentioned. 'No guns, no bugs, no break-ins. Except as a last resort' was PLS's unofficial motto, and the company prided itself on maintaining a façade of utter respectability.

Much of its work was simply about reaching the right people, and putting the right people in touch with each other. You wanted to build a power station in Turkey? PLS would find the minister whose approval was essential. You had failed to win a major contract in Russia? PLS would find out why, and would even be prepared to sell you the most confidential details of the winning bid. If a major bank was in trouble with the FSA over allegations of money-laundering in South America or the Caribbean, PLS could find out exactly who had opened certain accounts, who had been paid to do so, and quietly negotiate with the appropriate law-enforcement agencies in the US to smooth things over.

Ex-ambassadors would pick up the phone to call State Department officials they used to play golf with, or former SIS officers would drop in on old contacts in Florida or Mexico City. If there were difficulties over some necessary but discreet payments being made to a Saudi prince in connection with a contract for a turboprop training aircraft upon which many hundreds of jobs in Walsall depended, Professional Logistical Services soon came to expect a call. Everything would be explained in due course: the no-doubt-necessary but not-discreet-enough payments had been 'misunderstood' – the prince, who was a humanitarian as well as a patriot and a businessman, intended to use the money to improve the working conditions of Bangladeshis in the Kingdom. The money was not baksheesh, but aid. And so the world turned, and the client book grew thicker. PLS opened doors most people didn't even know existed. It was virtually unknown in the wider world. But its success rate was very high.

The company's offices were in a cul de sac by Green Park, a hundred yards north of Clarence House, sandwiched between a boutique hotel and the headquarters of a hedge fund. Analysts, number-crunchers and secretarial staff worked long hours in the small, cream stucco building's quiet, wood-panelled rooms.

In the hot, smoky room in Shepherd's Market, Dame Cecily turned to Admiral Dalgety.

'*Really*, Jock. Where *is* the little cunt?'

The Romance of Fleet Street

Every senior member of Professional Logistical Services had a file devoted to them in the offices of the *National Courier*. There were blurred old photographs, articles about long-forgotten defence-spending rows and minor departmental scandals, queen's birthday honours lists from the old days, and obituaries waiting to go. But there was nothing that connected the names to each other, and not a single reference, even from the business pages, to PLS. And this, by the standards of the day, was a decent enough news-paper, still just about hanging on.

All newspaper offices are much the same – the filthy beige walls, the desolate expanse of cluttered desks behind which wise old sacks of human indolence order the young and stupid about. Ken Cooper was the editor here, the commander of his own poop deck, not because he was the oldest, or the cleverest, or the most frightening – though he was fairly old, and very sharp, and borderline scary – but because he was more *alive* than anybody else in the office. His heart pumped richer blood. His lungs sucked in more of the sparse, air-conditioned oxygen. He laughed louder. His rages were more extreme. Even between the desks, even in the narrow corridor leading to the lifts, he didn't walk so much as romp. He bounced and roared and flung his arms about when everybody else was catatonic with exhaustion; and so he raised up the cynical and made them care, he roused the bored and made them curious. He was the model of a newspaper editor, and his Anglo-Saxon was famously fluent.

'Quintfuckingessence of fuck, in twelve-fucking-point bold fucking Bodoni. Fuck in eleven fucking dimensions.'

'Well, fair point, boss.'

'Fuck this fucking paper and all who fucking sail in her. We're all fucking drowning. Fuck you. Fuck me. In fact, fuck me sideways with an Atex machine and a lot of fucking enthusiasm. And fuck my fucking wife while you're at it.'

'Didn't know you'd remarried, boss.'

'I haven't. Fuck off. . . you. . . you. . .'

'Fuck?'

'Fu. . . fu. . . fu. . .'

But by now a small smile was creeping across Ken Cooper's face. He started to laugh. Eddie Fitt, the news editor, was laughing too. The pair had known each other since they had both started out as down-table subs on the *Newcastle Chronicle*. Fitt had made it to London first, and found himself hired by the great Harry Evans, before hopping over to little Donald Trelford's *Observer*. By then he was 'out' in the great gay city, and having fun for the first time in his cramped, nervous life. Cooper had come down a year later, stayed on Fitt's sofa, had his eyes opened about various people in the public eye, and worked his way through the Murdoch papers before the flit to Wapping, staying on after they'd made the move, surviving the siege and surviving Charlie Wilson, the Glaswegian editor he partly modelled himself on, who had called him 'Fingers'. ('Why Fingers, by the way, Mr Wilson?' 'Because that's all you're fucking hanging on by, sonny.')

In time he'd tired of life in Andrew Neil's considerable and growing shadow, and had migrated to the *Mail*. There it was said that the fabled Paul Dacre called him a cunt 'more affectionately than he had ever called anyone a cunt before'. He'd had enough bad relationships and gabby colleagues, and a salty enough tongue, to be a regular in *Private Eye*'s 'Street of Shame' column, but his experiment in marriage had turned him darker. It left him with a slouching, angry son and explosive weekly confrontations with his former spouse, who was then working for the rival *Correspondent*. When he got the call to go to the *Courier*, he'd rung Eddie Fitt, whom he'd long since outpaced, and asked him to come aboard ('Poisoned fucking chalice, Eddie. Just your cup of tea').

'But Jesus, Eddie,' continued Cooper, who had calmed down a bit by now. 'What the fuck? Where the fuck is fucking McBryde?'

'Dunno, boss. It's very odd. He's a bloody good reporter, but a bloody messed-up guy. I've left dozens of messages, voice and text. I've told him the headless corpse is our splash whatever happens, whatever he gets. I've thrown my bread. But from across the great black pond of Soho dissipation there comes back no response, no echo at all.'

'OK. Well. . . he'll show eventually. Meanwhile, here's this to be getting on with.' Cooper slung across the heavily marked and annotated wad of newspapers he'd been working on during his car ride to the office. 'Tell McBryde to call me as soon as he turns up. And ask Carole, would you, to cancel my lunch with Lord fucking Fauntleroy. No reason. Oh yes, and get Scadding to come to my office pronto.'

Lucy Scadding, the political editor, arrived with her deputy in seconds. She'd been loitering outside Cooper's door for nearly an hour, her mobile clamped to her head, nodding and grunting mono-syllables. Lucy wasn't a fence-sitter – she strove to keep words like 'may', 'might', 'is said to be' and 'rumoured' out of her copy. She knew the golden rule: any headline with a question mark at the end of it deserves the answer 'Nah, not really.' She also knew all too well that over the next few days she would either establish herself among the wiser heads in the Westminster lobby, as one of those who had called the referendum right. . . or she'd fail. No pressure, then. She'd become a bit of a favourite of the prime minister, mainly because she read the political biographies, and could quote them back at him. (Most political reporters have virtually no understanding of or interest in politics; serious politicians adore the few who do.)

'Hello, Ken. How long have we got? Things are getting interesting over at Number 10.'

'No more than twenty minutes, Lucy. The country may be about to commit political fucking suicide, but I'm running a newspaper on life support, and I've got to go and grovel to some fucking marketing meerkats before conference. So keep it clear and keep it snappy.'

Lucy Scadding sat down, though her editor was standing at his desk, and flipped open her iPad, dabbing a finger on it until she found what she was looking for.

'Well, first off, general sit-rep. Everyone still expects a "Yes" to Europe, although there are signs that the gap's narrowing. Ipsos Mori, YouGov, Populus – different methodologies, but all pretty much in the same place. The City boys say gilts are holding up well, and the top Footsies are all bobbing on a rising tide. We're expecting the PM to do a final regional tour, and a big presser either today or tomorrow. We think he'll choose the Birmingham area, because it's very tight there. I've been talking to the usual suspects at Number 10 this morning, and the mood there's pretty chipper. Some of the inner circle seem a bit frantic, though. Something's up, I know it is. I just can't put my finger on it.

'On the other side, Olivia Kite's people are insisting it's still all to play for. They say they're going to be unveiling a few renegade

Tories and some very senior Labour people later today. Again, I'm expecting them to do it in Birmingham. But I'm not convinced it will be enough. I think it's time for a big, bold prediction on the front page – we're staying in.'

'Whoa, girl. Steady. Let's not cross the fucking finishing line before the nags are out of the fucking boxes,' said Cooper. 'It's playing out more or less as we predicted. The PM out on the stump, and Olivia just a little too far behind. But you're right, it does look like game over. So what happens afterwards? We'll have a reshuffle almost immediately, eh, Lucy? He can't keep the rebels in the cabinet after what they've been saying over the past few weeks. Get ahead of the fucking game, girl. I want a down-page piece giving me the new cabinet.'

'I'm not so sure there'll be a reshuffle. After his deal with the Germans, and assuming he pulls this off, he'll go down as the most successful PM since Thatcher. He'll be a hero for a few weeks at least, and he'll be able to pick any international job he wants in due course – but he'll still be party leader, and he can't expect to win a general election with the party in splinters. He'll want the maximum party unity he can salvage out of this smash-up. He'll try to settle the succession – he won't be able to, but he'll try – and bind the wounds. So I think he'll be very cautious in victory. He's got a tight little cabal of good people around him, but I expect he'll resign, probably by the end of the year.'

'Well, fucking fine for him. Fucking good for us too. We'll have called it right anyway.'

Cooper meant, of course, that he himself had called it right. The proprietor's increasingly obstreperous son was a convinced 'patriot' and 'No European tyranny' man. The proprietor had agonised for weeks about the line the paper had chosen to take, and the pressure had been unpleasant. Cooper had regarded himself as a friend of the prime minister's ever since his early days in Parliament. They ate the odd meal together even now. So he had gone with his man, and with the PM's utter conviction that the referendum had to be won – and would be won. His veteran political columnist, a frog-eyed intellectual, took the opposite line, as did half the newsroom, mainly the younger ones.

Once, Cooper would simply have sacked the columnist and intimidated the others. He had always made a point of the *Courier*'s tradition of dissent, holding out against the Cameron government's new press censorship law for two long years. There had even been talk of jail. But with the owner not knowing what to think, and his son on the warpath, sales weak, and fucking bloggers and other assorted digital wankers making so much of the running, Ken Cooper's old certainties had long gone. He also believed in creative tension between his journalists, and had just about held the editorial line. Lucy Scadding had become an important ally. Perhaps, he reflected briefly, that was why she'd taken a seat on his office sofa so comfortably. But the frog-eyed columnist was now standing at the door, and he pitched in.

'The thing is, Mr Cooper, it's not quite adding up. All respect to Lucy, I agree that something's up at Number 10. I think it's the latest polling figures that are making them uneasy. All that cash that's been slung into the "Yes" campaign seems to have moved things very little – if at all. There are signs that it's getting too close for anyone to assume anything. We haven't even got a clue how many people are going to come out and actually vote. So I really don't see why everyone seems so confident.'

Lucy Scadding stopped playing with her mobile phone, and started to talk Ken Cooper's language. 'It's really down to the PM. They – we – still believe in the bugger. He's a shit, and he's fucked up so many times – but he's *our* shit, and he's got that smile that makes people want to smile back. And he's never lost an important fight. Not one. He's leaving it a bit to the last minute, though. I can't think why he didn't do the Andy Marr show yesterday. Barney Jones was beside himself. I'm guessing he's got something special up his sleeve.'

'Most likely. Will he write us that fucking piece, do you think?'

Lucy tapped her mobile again. 'Yes, yes. I got a reply back about half an hour ago. He says it'll be mostly by "the team", but that he'll personalise it for an old friend like you.'

Good, thought Cooper. There are some places where I still count. Leaving Lucy Scadding and frog-eyes behind him, he bounced out into the newsroom – which, as always, struck him as sadly quiet compared to the old days. Half the people there were poor, benighted 'media studies' graduates working for nothing. What a fucking con, thought Cooper. All those student loans piled up to keep obsolete hacks-turned-professors in work, on the hollow promise that the deluded kids would get gainful work. Well, there was no gainful fucking work left. Maybe when they finally fired him he'd tour the universities with a placard: 'Media Studies? Starve in Fucking Style.' They'd probably arrest him. That would be a fucking story.

At the newsdesk Eddie Fitt was on the phone. He saw Cooper and shook his head. Still no McBryde.

'Fuck, fuck and fuckety fuck,' muttered Cooper. They had been a pretty unimaginative lot, he admitted to himself, those Anglo-Saxons.

Conversation Piece

Two figures lay in adjoining frosty cubicles, awaiting the folding steel tables on small rubber wheels. One was the headless and handless body of the sixty-ish man recovered from the Thames, now cleaned of mud and slime. The other was the broken but otherwise intact body of the twenty-eight-year-old newspaper reporter Lucien McBryde, by now also naked. That the latter had been given the task of investigating the former was something nobody present could know.

The mortuary was a long, low building with a high brick wall and an electric steel gate, lacking any sign or distinguishing number. Not far from the fashionable Chelsea Harbour, and opposite a bland international hotel, it was the designated holding place for central London's sufferers of violent death. Here had come the torn victims of the 7/7 bombings, the possibly murdered, the certainly murdered, the suicides, and the children who had killed and then been killed in the gang wars of Brixton and Hammersmith.

Locals knew about the place, and noticed the unmarked vans and ambulances that regularly passed through its gates; but to most Londoners it was a blank, a built-up vacancy in an anonymous triangle of lost real estate. Google Maps gave it no description; on Streetview there was only a blurred strip of brick wall and a metal gate. It was, however prime development land, and developers had had their eyes on the site for years. As one local estate agent put it, 'Leaving a bit of juicy riverfront like that to cadavers rather than living punters is pure insanity. It isn't English.'

On the other side of the wall, once a call had opened the gate, there was generous space for parking and then a small office – velour chairs, a dusty rubber plant, two ancient computers, a calendar with pictures of fat naked women – staffed by an unshaven, exhausted-looking man and a tired secretary. Behind it, corridors with photographs of English seaside towns led to heavy doors and thick plastic curtains. Beyond these, the atmosphere under the strip lights was both chilly and stuffy, with the vinegar smell of formaldehyde not quite hiding something sweeter. Porters moved the bodies from cold storage to the cement-floored rooms where the autopsies took place, and then sluiced down the fluids after the coroners, the police and the pathologists had done their jobs and left.

What kind of people sought such work? Not bad people, necessarily. Rather, those who combined a yearning for quiet financial security with flickers of a gothic sensibility. Graveyard humour didn't stop with Shakespeare. Famous corpses sometimes found themselves decorated with lipstick or stick-on noses before the mortuary closed for the night. At Christmas, a certain amount of inappropriate tinsel was not unknown. There had been one near-scandal, when relatives from the Indian subcontinent turned up unexpectedly to find a steel tycoon dressed in women's stockings. Lucien McBryde's slender and remarkably long penis had been the source of much comment today; but he had not been tampered with.

Had the Thames body and the investigative journalist been able to, they would surely have turned and gaped at one another, surprised by their clammy propinquity – wondering who would show up next, disturbed by the thought of what the white-trousered menials might leave as a goodnight gift. But as one of them had a broken neck and the other was missing his head, they could exchange no such look.

Constitutional Monarchy

The chief whip, Ronnie Ashe, was experiencing something he hadn't felt since he had been a small boy at his first preparatory school. He felt inadequate. This was not surprising. He had been summoned to Buckingham Palace by the new king's private secretary half an hour earlier, to explain why the king's first minister was apparently too busy to attend his regular audience with His Majesty – moved to Monday mornings at the beginning of the new reign. And the king was not amused.

Ronnie had decided to walk across St James's Park in order to prepare himself – it would be almost as quick as clambering into the official Jaguar and being driven, he'd thought – but he had underestimated the time it would take, and arrived late. His Majesty was not amused about that either.

Ronnie was taken by an equerry through the courtyard and up a surprisingly small staircase to the king's private study. There a portrait of the late queen dominated the wall behind the desk, while the rest of the room was filled with the king's own watercolours of Scotland, India and Windsor. A pair of green-silk-covered armchairs had been set out in preparation for the meeting, a couple of yards apart. Ronnie bowed, beamed, but remained standing until the king waved an irritated hand towards one of them. Had the prime minister been there, a footman would have been waiting with a glass of his favourite Talisker malt whisky. For Ronnie, there was not even the offer of a cup of tea.

Yet Ronnie Ashe and His Majesty were acquainted. Early in his parliamentary career, Ashe, who'd made some real money by almost doubling the size of his father's agricultural-equipment business, had been approached to become a trustee of one of the then prince's pet charities. Ronnie was enough of a man of the world to understand that 'trustee' was a short way of saying 'Pay up, or find people who can.' He did a bit of both, was invited to a couple of what he told his wife were 'snob lunches', and eventually they both spent a weekend at the prince's country house. With his engineering background, Ronnie often had some useful tips to pass on for royal speeches, and he'd spent a few days over a few months explaining how Parliament really worked to the young princes. A regular at Cheltenham, Lingfield, Epsom and Ascot, as well as a genial, attentive listener, he was the kind of man the Windsors found easy to have in attendance.

But, like many who had found themselves in this position, Ronnie Ashe had once made the mistake of 'presuming' – of being just a little too friendly – and had immediately experienced the famous Windsor chill. He had felt knocked off-balance, like a schoolboy caught doing something obscurely shameful, and surprisingly upset.

The prime minister, who was twenty years his senior, had put him right. 'The secret of monarchy? Fast exits, Ronnie. Out goes the hand. On comes the smile. You feel like a million dollars. Then you suddenly realise they've skedaddled, moved down the line. Or you're having a conversation and HM goes, "Really? How fascinating? Now why has nobody ever told me that?" You make the mistake of jabbering away some more, and then you notice a glaze behind the eyes. A fog has descended. I've seen it a million times – ambassadors and actors, cabinet ministers and editors, suddenly going "How did *that* happen? Where did they go?" It's how it has to be, old man. No idling. No getting too close. And of course it's worse for those who are a little closer. So if you want to keep being invited, if you want to sit on those boards, maybe get a Victorian Order one of these days, you have to play the game, and understand their rules. Don't *presume*. Don't dream of being a friend. Remember, always and forever: quick exits.'

Ronnie Ashe had remembered, and learned, and so in time he had been asked back. He'd had an eat-and-sleep at Windsor. He'd accompanied the king to see children's clubs, and he'd managed to get a royal opening for the new business college in his constituency. He'd made jokes and heard kingly laughter and laughed at kingly jokes – which actually weren't bad, though they often made you feel sorry for the man.

Today, though, was rather short on kingly humour. The brick-red Windsor face was trembling with anger. The back was ramrod straight.

'What the bloody hell is going on, Ronnie? What the bloody hell is he *thinking*?'

'Your Majesty, I'm so sorry. I know it looks bad. . .'

'Bad? It looks bloody rude. It looks rude to his monarch, and it looks as if he's forgotten his position. As if he was some bloody continental president.'

'Your Majesty, the prime minister meant no disrespect. He's tried to reach you by phone. It's just that in these last few days before the country votes he's completely. . .'

'Oh, "snowed under", I'm sure. Too busy to explain to the sovereign head of state of the United Kingdom of Great Britain and Northern Ireland whether or not its destiny is to remain a member of the European Union of nations or – what's the phrase – "reclaim our sovereignty for a new age of greatness", hmm? I'm sure he's got memoranda and briefing papers and polling results to look through. It's just that he seems to have lost his sense of bloody perspective. Perspective is what these audiences are all about, Ronnie, you know.'

'Sir, if I may, the prime minister is very anxious. . .'

'*She* wouldn't make that mistake, you know, Ronnie. I am above politics. I have no views on any of this. But Mrs Kite has been most attentive. *She* wouldn't leave her monarch kicking his heels.'

'Sir, the prime minister has sent me to apologise to you personally, and to ask you to forgive him this once – this once – during what have been the most difficult and testing few days of his political life, at a time when he feels – the prime minister feels very strongly – that the fate of the nation rests in his hands. He tells me that he has had many conversations with you, sir, which have led him to believe and to trust that you understand one another on this subject *completely*, and he further says that he is hugely strengthened by the wisdom and judgement you have imparted to him over the past year, and upon which he is relying even now. . .'

As the chief whip continued speaking he detected a slight relaxing of the kingly shoulders. The monarch's face had moved from storm-cloud purple, through damson, to traffic-light red, and was now merely a hot pink. If not yet mollified, he was at least no longer livid. The tempest was passing. Ronnie Ashe pressed on.

'Sire – sir – the PM feels that in what has also been the biggest test of your reign so far you have completely confounded your critics, who said that you would be unable to remain above the fray. And that notwithstanding your – wholly justified, and indeed unanswerable – criticisms of the EU and its impact on your country, you have seen the wider picture, and indeed imparted to your government a sense of perspective which individual politicians have entirely failed. . . ah, failed. . .'

The king nodded. He allowed himself a wry smile. 'But it's not a very. . . *kind*. . . way to treat a batty old monarch, who may *perhaps* know a thing or two, is it? Simply not to turn up? You might mention that.'

Ashe thought the time was now right to press him. 'Sir, if you would be your truly generous self and speak to him on the telephone, I know the PM would be both moved and grateful. He does need you, sire – sir – at this time more than ever.'

Again the king nodded. He leaned over, picked up the old white telephone and pressed a single button. 'The prime minister, please.'

He looked across at Ashe, as if he'd forgotten already that the chief whip was in the room.

'You can go now.'

In the Little Brick Terrace

The call from Buckingham Palace was put straight through by 'Switch', as the Downing Street switchboard was always known. The prime minister had a special place in his heart for Switch. Britain, he liked to reflect, had become a nation in which many things that had once been taken for granted had all but disappeared. A cheap, efficient postal service; prudent, morally unimpeachable bankers; unbureaucratic and reliable police who didn't leak stories to the newspapers; vicars who spoke elegant, direct English in churches, and people who gathered in those churches to learn to be kinder and generally better; patriotic, bloody-minded trade union leaders. . . where had they all gone? But among the quiet institutions that still thrummed along, unchanged, utterly reliable, Switch was a little gem.

The women of Switch could find anyone, anywhere, any time. A part-time and notoriously alcoholic consul in Jakarta; a delinquent backbencher hiding from the government whips on Skye; a shadow minister with a suspicious and awkward question down for the following day – Switch had them all at the end of a line in minutes. No one knew quite how they did it. 'You're the spirit of Bletchley Park and Agatha Christie rolled into one,' the PM had toasted them during the staff Christmas party.

The phone rang in the PM's inner sanctum, now out of bounds to all but a chosen few, and a mottled, beefy hand reached out to pick it up. 'The king is on the line for the prime minister,' said Switch.

'Your Majesty. This is very kind,' growled the familiar prime ministerial voice.

The PM was on magisterial form, apologetic about having missed the weekly audience but persuasive about the closeness of the vote, the huge importance of keeping his agreement with Berlin about the future of the EU, and the imminent danger of a run on the banks if the polls kept shifting against Britain staying in. After just a few minutes the king was so caught up in the political drama that his protests about protocol sounded petty even to him. He didn't dare to raise the subject of his late-night conversations with Mrs Kite. 'Abashed' was a novel feeling for the monarch, but abashed was how he felt.

Meanwhile, Lord Briskett and Ned Parminter were sitting in the tiny waiting room to the left of the Downing Street hallway. In the fireplace, where there should have been a grate there was instead an ancient iron safe. Bored visitors sometimes opened it to have a look inside; they found only a few broken pieces of outmoded office equipment.

After being ushered through the security gates, Briskett and Parminter had had their mobile phones politely removed and placed in a wooden cabinet whose numbered chambers were perfectly sized to hold BlackBerrys and iPhones. Now Parminter was showing Briskett the latest printed-out emails from inside the 'No' campaign.

'You see,' he said, 'it's really no longer quite as clear-cut as everyone's been saying. We can discount most of the press and their surveys. They're loading the questions and suppressing the full data. They all have their spin. On both sides it's become too serious for fair reporting. Behind the scenes the polling companies are going bananas. But the real deal is the data that's coming straight to Kite – and to the PM too, I'll bet. The figures for Manchester and Sheffield will be interesting, for instance.'

Briskett rubbed his forehead. 'It really *is* close. I'm sure Olivia Kite has a big surprise or two in store for the final days – I see we're no longer being sent anything that passes between her and the big-business boys. I wonder if one or two of them are going to come out for independence. That's what she needs. Last-minute reassurance from the big money. But I don't know. Perhaps the "No" camp is beginning to panic after all. I'll be fascinated to see how the PM interprets his own polls.'

Ned shuffled his papers. 'Do you think there's any chance of getting an objective view from him? I mean, he really loathes Kite and the rest of them.'

'Oh no, Ned, you're quite wrong,' said Briskett. 'Quite wrong. I've known him for years. He's got lots of special qualities – charm, energy, self-belief, physical strength, likeability, even a little of the old charisma still. Take him into a room full of strangers and he seems to know their names instinctively. I've seen him ask after spouses and children of whose existence I could have sworn he hadn't a clue. And tell him just once about an illness, or a son in trouble, and – years later, even – he'll remember and ask.

'Oh, he's a remarkable man. But do you know his greatest quality as a politician? It's his objectivity. He can take any situation he's in, turn it round, step out of it as it were, and look at it from the outside. He can think like the opposition, like people who hate everything about him, and understand exactly what they're thinking. He's completely unsentimental. He knows his own weaknesses, and their strengths – but in his guts, not just abstractly. He *feels* a problem from every side. So if there's one person in this whole blessed kingdom who really knows what's going on, he's sitting down there along the corridor. Waiting for us.'

After a long pause Parminter asked, 'But *is* he? Waiting for us I mean. We've been here for thirty minutes now.'

Briskett stood up and re-knotted his bright yellow tie in the reflection from a glass-fronted painting by Spencer Gore, a Number 10 favourite.

'Nonsense. Thirty minutes is nothing. History's being made all around us. You can smell it, Ned.' And he sniffed and grinned.

The door opened, and there, with a broad smile of welcome, mirroring Briskett's, stood a tall, handsome woman, hands on her hips, in a red jacket and a skirt few fifty-somethings would have attempted to carry off.

'Hello, darling,' she said in a gravelly, mischievous smoker's voice. 'How is the most fabulous historian in the entire world? Looking as wicked as ever, Trevor. And who is this gorgeous young man?'

'This, my dear Amanda, is my research assistant Ned Parminter, who – come to think of it – you yourself must have cleared to come with me today. Ned, may I introduce the prime minister's gatekeeper, private secretary, Girl Friday and long-time chum, Amanda Andrews.'

Parminter reached out a hand. 'You are a very intriguing and, if I may say so, elusive woman,' he said. 'I'm delighted to meet you at last.'

'The pleasure is all mine, boys,' said Amanda. 'And I have some excellent news for you. I have just been cleared, by the PM himself, to show you the minutes of this morning's referendum steering group, which is about as up-to-the-minute as it gets when it comes to the thinking on our side. I've also been authorised to take you through the PM's personal email inbox. Some interesting messages,

I think you'll find, though obviously I'll have to sit with you while you go through them. I've ordered sandwiches and coffee.'

Briskett looked almost taken aback, though he just managed to maintain his usual air of imperturbability. 'Dear Amanda! That is of course a great treat and an unexpected little extra *bon-bon*. But I do wonder, when are we going to be able to sit down with the great man himself? We have been promised our *tête-à-tête*, and this whole project does rather depend on getting his thoughts from him, fresh, as it were, as the situation develops.'

'Yes, Trevor, I do understand. We've promised that, and we will deliver him. The only thing is that, unfortunately, something rather delicate and unexpected has come up. We did set aside an hour for you, as I said, but the PM thinks it would be better if you could reschedule for later in the week. He promises he'll be able to give you more time, and that he'll be even franker – "dangerously frank" was his phrase, I think.' Amanda beamed, her eyes crinkling with pleasure.

Briskett could feel himself failing, retreating. 'Yet there's nothing quite like a proper face-to-face conversation. . .'

'We've come all the way from Oxford just for this,' added Parminter.

'Darling,' said Amanda, 'you yourself have *not* made the rather short journey from Oxford just to see us. A little bird tells me that you will also be meeting a certain Jennifer Lewis, the very shrewd and formidable young lady who advises our not-quite-best-friend Mrs Kite.'

Parminter goggled.

'How do I know that? Well, my dear, I have a whole flock of little birds tweeting and twittering their way round the place, with their little phones and their little pictures and their endless, loveable curiosity. And do we mind that you and Miss Lewis – who seems, by the way, quite smitten – have been in cahoots? We do not mind. Not at all. That's your job. To keep in with both sides, as agreed. And what an enjoyable job, Mr Parminter, yours seems to be.'

By now both men were pretty much beaten, resigned to the fact that there would be no meeting with the PM. Amanda led them out of the waiting room and past the portrait of Lord Walpole, the bewigged old sinner who was Britain's first prime minister. She licked her lips in front of him before delivering the *coup de grâce*.

'Since you are both looking so doleful and disappointed, I have one final treat. And this time I'm not passing on a message from the great man. This time I'm acting on my own initiative. He might be cross. Goodness, he might even *spank me*.'

Briskett could barely speak.

'Nevertheless, I have decided, in the interests of fair play and full disclosure, sweeties, that I will tell you exactly what the PM is up to at this very moment, and just why a certain person had to take precedence over my favourite historian and his floppy-haired researcher who's half in love with the enemy. He's on the phone right now – and has been for some time, and will be for some time – to the king.

'Kingy is rather flustered. Kingy knows very well which side his organic home-baked wholemeal bread is freshly buttered on. Despite his occasionally strange views, Kingy understands that if the UK were to leave the European Union many fine companies would quit his realm, and many peasants would lose their jobs and their pensions, and thus become quite seriously revolting. Once you begin a revolution – and believe this, boys, cutting fifty years of ties with continental Europe is a revolutionary step – history teaches us that you can't tell where it will end. Kings know their history, even if they don't know much else. So Kingy is with us, in his head at least.'

The trio had passed down the corridor that was used as a place in which to hang good British paintings from the previous century – Briskett noted a Spencer, another Gore and a Nicholson; they were changed every year, around September – and were advancing in the direction of the Cabinet Room, the door of which was locked as usual. They turned right towards the prime minister's private office, but Amanda briskly led them past it and up the famous staircase with its photo gallery of prime ministerial heads to the white drawing room, with its fine gilding, restored under Margaret Thatcher, and the excellent Turner over the fireplace. They were in the grandest of Downing Street's state rooms, in which foreign dignitaries were greeted with drinks and prime ministers gave television interviews. The views over Horse Guards Parade and St James's Park were magnificent.

But Lord Briskett was far from dazzled. Being brought here was, for him, no compliment. He was all too aware that the real work went on one floor below them, in the Cabinet Room and the PM's office and the private secretaries' rooms. Down there was a buzzing hive of activity, all tiny staircases and crowded, noisy, hot rooms. This drawing room was calm, comfortable and quiet – but it was all for show. Briskett's irritation was, however, slightly blunted by his curiosity about the king's attitude to the referendum, which sounded just the kind of insider story that would make his book talked about.

Once they were all seated, Amanda continued. 'Kingy's heart, though, is a rather different organ. As we all know, it has led him into the odd spot of bother in the distant past. Well, it now beats rather fervidly for Old Britannia, roast beef, and the romance of independence from foreign Johnnies. Kite's a clever bitch, and she's taken him to the top of the mountain and shown him a golden vista of rolling organic pastures, no nuclear power or wind farms, the Household Cavalry restored to its former glory, more money for the jolly old navy, and above all an end to those pestilential health-and-safety rules which Kingy believes are holding back the common people. And Kingy – to be frank – is wobbly.'

Long before Lord Briskett had finally stopped writing with his gold-nibbed antique Parker and Ned Parminter had turned off his recorder, both men knew they had a real story.

Amanda then brought in a transcript of the PM's recent email traffic, which was more interesting for its tone and its jokes than for any real new information it revealed, and after that the two of them went through the minutes of that morning's meetings downstairs. All good stuff, even if it didn't quite make up for their disappointment at failing to meet the prime minister himself.

As they were leaving, passing along the small corridor that led to the PM's office, they bumped into the foreign secretary and the chief whip, engaged in an urgent whispered conversation. Briskett knew them both, but they seemed disconcerted to see him. Perhaps the possible defection of His Majesty was putting the wind up the inner circle.

The two men separated after they left Downing Street. Parminter, whose mind was mainly on Jennifer Lewis, tried to call her for her take on the Buckingham Palace story, but only got her voicemail. As he walked across St James's Park towards his lunch, Lord Briskett called an old friend in Buckingham Palace. To his relief and mild surprise, this man, a member of the king's research department, pretty much confirmed what Amanda had told him: it was not impossible that, unconstitutional though it would undoubtedly be, the monarch might intervene in this crucial referendum at the last moment and make plain his worries about Britain's continued membership of the EU.

All this made Lord Briskett very happy. A multicoloured thrashing of birdlife exploded across the pond – Oriental ducks, swans, acid-green parakeets and pigeons. A splash of sunlight, leaching through the fast-moving clouds, landed on the scarlet tunics and silver breastplates of the Life Guards over in the direction of Whitehall. Suddenly the world seemed brighter and more unpredictable. This was what *living* felt like. Briskett experienced a surge of excitement, and paused briefly to stare back at Downing Street. He could just see the windows behind which the prime minister must be sitting. Then he turned around and marched past the ducks, dicentras and daisies and Horse Guards Parade. He crossed the Mall, took the long flight of stone stairs two at a time and made his way towards the white-stuccoed Palladian building that housed his club.

A Club Lunch

As it was a Monday, thought Briskett, there would be a decent piece of beef on the trolley. And he might find his old friend Ken Cooper of the *Courier* in the bar, along with that merry old bat from MI5 who had found some lucrative cushy berth selling secrets to the private sector. They would both be worth talking to. And he had something to tell them that would make their eyes pop. What fun history in the making was, actually being inside it for once, not just on the outside looking in. He rubbed his hands briskly and blew through them, not because they were cold but because he felt the need to mark his mood in some physical way.

The Universities and Constitutional Club had a basement swimming pool, which with its old-fashioned wooden changing cubicles lured health-conscious broadcasters and civil servants, while the cosy bar, decorated with hundreds of political cartoons and yellowing front pages, provided the best-value wines in London. Club members left their coats and bags in a black-and-white-tiled lobby, using hooks and open shelving – that anything might be nicked was unthinkable. In the dining room there were special round tables set aside for the ultra-regulars like the crusty old novelist and the ITV executive who always dined together. Another was reserved solely for permanent and under-secretaries. At the centre of the room was a long, narrow table for the waifs and strays who arrived unexpectedly without company.

As Briskett strode in he inhaled the strong and appetising aroma of roasted meat. Ken Cooper was indeed at the bar, nursing a small glass of champagne. Nobody in fucking journalism drank any more, Cooper was musing grumpily at that moment. Certainly not at lunchtime. Even as fucking editor he felt he had to retreat to a private club. When was it that all the fizz had gone? Probably when the fucking Americans had started taking over the City of London and brought their mineral-water culture here, along with their fucking perfect smiles and their gym-built bodies. In this country, Cooper had always said, water was for turning your coat collar against and dropping a fishing line into, not for fucking drinking. He went back to brooding about the missing Lucien McBryde and, like everybody else, idly rehearsing in his mind the likelihood of the country voting to leave the EU in a few days' time.

Cooper brightened as Briskett waved to him across the crowded bar, and came over to join him.

'Pink one?'

'Oh, I think something fizzy for me if you don't mind, Ken. I have some news for your shell-like which I suspect will make your day, and necessitate a change of tomorrow's front page.'

Cooper ordered two more glasses of champagne, and the two men headed to a small table by one of the long windows overlooking St James's Park. Observing them from a sofa on the far side of the room were Dame Cecily Morgan and Admiral Jock Dalgety, who had been discussing PLS's irritating and demanding new client, Alois Haydn. The elderly spy – who bore a distinct physical resemblance to Margaret Rutherford – had lost none of her instinct: although she and the admiral were deeply engaged in their conversation, she could still read the body language between Lord Briskett and Ken Cooper. Did they know something? The historian was not normally an excitable fellow, and even from this distance she could tell that something was up.

She turned back to the admiral. 'As I say, Jock, they can't keep it up, even with our help, for much longer. In fact, it looks to me as if that absurd busybody Lord Briskett has cottoned on to something already, and is spreading the word to the yellow press even now. Will you excuse me for just a moment?'

Making her slightly unsteady way to the table by the window, Dame Cecily waved her hospital-issue walking stick in Ken Cooper's face.

'I always said we shouldn't let you vermin into this place. What slush are you hoovering up from modern history's answer to Jeremy Clarkson? Don't lie to me, Ken. I can tell from your piggy little face that something's going on.'

'It's the king, Cecily dear,' Briskett replied, nettled by the Clarkson jibe but taking care not to let her see that. 'The most wonderful hoo-ha is about to break out. The poor old king is panicking, and the prime minister has a fight on his hands that could well destroy either him or his monarch. We haven't been here since Pitt the Younger and mad King George.' He sighed. 'I only wish that Ken here understood quite how big this is.'

He was right to be miffed. Cooper was gazing vaguely into the middle distance, having been a complete disappointment as the receptacle for the sensational political news. His day had just been ruined by a vibration in his pocket. Nobody at the *Courier* was allowed to call him at lunchtime – it was a rule that everyone in the office understood. But Lucy Scadding had texted him.

The brief and cheerful chirrup of his telephone had been received in the dining room with the kind of reaction you might have expected from an earth-shaking fart. Angry heads swivelled. Irritable women tutted. A waiter allowed his jaw to flop open as if he were a trout approaching a fluttering insect. Ken, oblivious, had idly checked Lucy's message just as Briskett was getting going. Nothing the historian had said after that had registered. The text read: 'There's bad news about Lucien, boss. Really bad. We're onto it, and we'll know more when you get back.'

Cooper found himself breathing heavily. The club seemed dim, sub-aqueous, its denizens oddly distorted. Briskett was still talking, but Cooper ignored him, his thumb moving rapidly as a humming-bird over his phone. 'When? Where? How? Are you sure?'

A few seconds later that insistent, optimistic electronic noise caused another shudder around the room.

'Body found this morning. Could have jumped, but the cops don't think so. Very mysterious timing. Lucy.'

Cooper suddenly felt physically sick. So McBryde was dead, not just off on the piss somewhere. His first thought was that he might well have killed himself. He'd fallen apart after the ending of his relationship with that woman from Olivia Kite's campaign. Besides, who could possibly want to kill Lucien McBryde? He was a clever enough fellow, but really only a conduit for other people's dirty water – the sewer, not the sewage, as someone had once put it. In the sentimental fashion of old Fleet Street, Cooper had always taken a vaguely paternal interest in the son of his old friend.

Looking pale, he turned back to Dame Cecily and Lord Briskett.

'I'm sorry, but I have to get straight back to the office. There's been a terrible tragedy. Rather close to home, I'm afraid. Please excuse me.'

With that he left, shouldering his way through the now thronged and noisy dining room.

Briskett, who just a few minutes ago had been feeling rather like a disgruntled, tweedy bird which has laid an egg to no applause, was mildly regruntled by the old spy's suggestion that he have lunch with her and Jock Dalgety. Dame Cecily's real object was, of course, to find out just how much he knew, or at least suspected, about what was going on in Downing Street.

Knowing nothing of this, Briskett felt himself transported to a suburb of heaven. Throughout the meal he could feel his mind moving like a beautiful piece of machinery. A chapter was written in his imagination; it would emerge through his fingers the following weekend, fully formed, not a colon out of place. He mashed the last of his Stilton onto a cracker, and was masticating it with intense pleasure as he leaned over and said to Dame Cecily, 'Here's what I don't get, old thing. What's the PM up to, hiding away on the last weekend before the big day? It isn't like him to lurk. He didn't even do Marr yesterday. No one I know has seen him for days.'

'You're quite wrong, Trevor. You know *me*, and I was with him only last night. The truth is, half the movers and shakers from the financial world, and the ambassadors of every significant country, are desperate to know what he plans to do if, by chance, the referendum result goes the other way. There's a whole universe of parallel planning going on, and he has to be part of that even as he's leading the "Yes" campaign. The man is just insanely busy. I've seen people work hard, but I've never seen anything like this. Anyway, you've just told us yourself that he's spoken to the king this morning, besides doing that radio phone-in with Dermot Murnaghan. And you're going to see him in person tomorrow. So I really don't understand your point.'

Briskett swirled the last half-inch of house claret around his glass. Dame Cecily and Admiral Jock Dalgety were staring at him with identical chilly expressions. He stared back.

'You've *seen* him, you say? He wasn't at the Palace himself, and I have a strong suspicion that I'll be put off again if I try to meet him tomorrow. I'm only asking. What's going on? Is he ill or something?'

The admiral leaned aggressively towards him. 'You of all people, Lord Briskett, should be aware that unlike the Americans, we have no right to pry into the medical condition of our leaders. All we can ask of them is that they perform their bloody job. I can see no sign whatsoever that the prime minister is failing to perform his many bloody jobs. The House, of course, is not sitting during this referendum campaign. So his duties are to rally the forces of the pro-European cause, and persuade the public of its rightness, while at the same time calming down the panickers and the knicker-wetters from the business world. Poor bastard. It would kill a lesser man. But so far as I can tell the PM has been performing remarkably effectively.' Dalgety, rolling a small piece of bread into a perfect sphere, switched into pompous Whitehall-speak. 'Speaking for myself, I could only deprecate any attempt to spread despondency at this point.'

Briskett flushed and leaned back in his seat. 'Writing contemporary history, Admiral, is not simply a matter of reading letters, or indeed opinion polls. If I have some modest reputation, it is because of this.' He tapped his nose. 'I have an instinct, a feel for the game, and I can smell when something's not right. The pair of you are as plugged in as anyone could be. The fact that you don't like what I'm saying makes me more suspicious, not less. Dammit, it's beginning to feel as if we don't have a prime minister at all.'

Dame Cecily was a formidable woman, and she did not quail. 'Trevor Briskett, we may not be close friends, but we are what I would call cordial acquaintances. I respect your body of work, and I enjoy – most of the time – your company. So please understand that I do not relish telling you what I must: you are making an utter fool of yourself. I don't know whether it's the lunchtime wine or whether you're just bored with the real world, but if this conversation became widely known – if Mr Cooper were still here, and reported it in his newspaper – you would be the laughing stock of London. And London, candidly, would be quite right. You would have the same kind of reputation poor Hugh Trevor-Roper had after he authenticated the Hitler diaries.'

On that unhappy, insulting note, the meal ended.

As he was leaving the building Briskett paused on the steps and tried to call Ned Parminter, but got no reply. He stared out towards Whitehall, with the hoop of the London Eye visible past the three white towers of the Ministry of Defence. Trevor Briskett had come to believe in his nose as a Christian believes in his Redeemer, and he was not inclined to be bullied by Dame Cecily Morgan or Admiral (Retired) Jock Dalgety. He could smell the acrid stink wafting across from Number 10. Something was definitely up. And he was going to find out what it was.

4

Friday, 15 September

Three Days Earlier:
Referendum Day Minus Six

A Queer Turn of Events

The prime minister had served his queen and country during the Falklands War, and had then left the Royal Navy to enter politics. He had remained on the backbenches for only a year, and in office he had decided and decided and decided, argued and persuaded, winning many notable victories in the face of formidable opposition.

He had brought back an industrial policy which, driven by experienced business people and local leaders, was just beginning to bear fruit. He had revived a proper technical education, so that a generation of young British men – and even a few women – would have the skills they needed to do something useful. By radically devolving welfare he had cut costs yet produced a fairer and more popular system. Any one of these achievements would have made him a significant leader; taken together they were extraordinary, and he knew it.

Away from Parliament he had loved women and abandoned them, and loved and lost his own children even as his public reputation swelled. But now he felt weary. It was late on Friday afternoon, but that hardly explained it. The PM – by now even he thought of himself as 'the PM' – was a tough old bird. In his veins flowed not ordinary blood, but vim – vintage, sparkling vim with a splash of *premier cru* gusto.

Like any good politician he was best-known to the public for a handful of trivial public sayings and his occasional failures, while his real achievements remained largely hidden. His flashy wit and easy repartee, which had been evident ever since he was a young sub-lieutenant, made Prime Minister's Questions considerably more entertaining than they had been under Brown or Cameron. His swift brutality in dispatching incompetent ministers and appointing lesser-known names kept the bloggers and the news sites on their toes. His louche private behaviour, which the *Guardian* editor had told him privately came dangerously close to sexual harassment, had so far caused him no problems with the electorate.

His wife had chosen neither to suffer in silence nor to bring him down, but to opt instead for an elegant, unhumiliated exit, and to live an almost entirely separate life. During the annual party conference she appeared, expensively coutured, by his side. For the rest of the year she lived in an apartment overlooking Regent's Park. Various prominent businessmen escorted her to parties. If this pained the PM he gave no sign of it.

What, in essence, had been his real achievement in office? It was certainly profound, but it was hard to define. It had been to consider the deeper historical shifts; to nudge his country, with subtle changes of emphasis, away from the rocks. He rarely fought on the brightly-lit daily battleground of U-turns or passing scandals, but hung like a shrewd, vigilant old buzzard, high overhead. In a sense, he felt, his only real job was to *take responsibility*. And the only thing that really mattered, in his view, was how the country stood in the world, and how it would make its way in the future.

He gazed around the cramped but comfortable office – the easy chairs and sofas on which so many historic conversations had taken place; the framed political cartoons and newspaper front pages; the meaningless bric-a-brac exchanged at G8 and European summits. He was no simple-minded enthusiast for the European project; it was clear to him that the Union was incompatible with democracy. For the public, parliamentary democracy required a bursting bubble or a hubbub of loudly raised voices, plenty of good salty abuse and a cast of familiar, easily caricatured faces. How else could normal, busy people give their attention to something so abstruse and slow-moving?

Oh yes, the undignified compromise that was parliamentary politics – the only political system left standing in the modern world that had any merit, and that had been invented in the busy half-mile around him – needed violent speeches and grotesque exaggerations, those bloody newspapers and those stupid television comedians. One language, one democracy, one country. You simply couldn't do it in twenty-odd tongues, sprawling across proud old national cultures which still knew little about each other – and more to the point, didn't want to know. The internet, Brussels propaganda, pan-European TV channels and the sophisticated commentaries in the expensive newspapers; in forty years of trying they had hardly changed things at all. So to pretend that British democracy could survive and thrive inside this new superstate was a lie.

Yet this prime minister saw further and thought more deeply. Unlike Heath, unlike even Thatcher, he had never deceived himself. He'd known instinctively for most of his adult life that the countries of Europe, including his own, were bust, in rapid historical decline: 'For two generations,' he had declared in the House, 'we have consumed too much, like spoilt teenagers on a spree.' Now he gazed mordantly at a framed cover from *The Economist*, a cartoon showing a tiny, frightened European gazing up at a pair of American and Chinese titans. It was true enough. From the once bold and ruthless Spanish to the once ingenious and hard-working Hollanders, the European peoples were now frankly decadent, adrift in a time when better-organised powers were preparing to replace them, and the swarming millions of the Arab and African worlds were elbowing their way in. A Europe that fragmented now would soon become a mere vacuum, a playground for American technology, Chinese money and Russian political ambition.

And Britain? Britain would again find itself desperately trying to negotiate the balance of power between Berlin and Paris, from a position of no significance. It would be impossible. A Wellington today would have had to serve his time wearing a blue UN beret, guarding food supplies in Ethiopia. Europe was nothing but a huddle of timid and half-naked polities, crouching together for warmth. But even that, the PM felt, was better than the alternative.

There was a knock on the door. Sam Mulligan, who worked on his diary in the private office downstairs, poked his friendly, scarlet face around it, his blond eyebrows raised. The PM smiled, but shook his head and waved a weary hand. He needed thinking time, and the staff here understood that.

Slow collapse, then, and a long, grim struggle to prevent it. None of this could ever be said in public. Not a word. Decades of slow economic rebuilding, learning to work harder again, squeezing both the greedy rich and the feckless poor, meant that politics would be no fun, in his judgement, until about 2050. Grind and slog, slog and grind. All serious politicians knew the truth – the finance ministers and chancellors, the presidents and foreign secretaries – but none dared to express it openly in front of the hostile eyes of the ignorant masses. '*Pas devant les enfants,*' the French president had sneered at their last meeting.

And so, sitting in his private office behind the Cabinet Room, gazing out at the sprays of blown pink roses tumbling over the brick wall that separated the Number 10 garden from Horse Guards Parade, the PM reflected that his job was simply to carry the burden of decline as elegantly and calmly as he could for a few more years before handing over to the next poor sod, hoping that he too had good strong arms and a dash of common sense.

But just now, as the band of the Grenadier Guards tuned up for yet another rehearsal, he found the tiredness was irresistible. Just now, an unfamiliar pain pushed its hands up towards his shirt collar. Just now, he leaned his head with its famous mane of hair gently down on his desk. An unexpected turn of events. Tired. Sore. Pleasantly unalarmed. He idly wondered what Olivia Kite would make of this; and he closed his eyes, and he died.

'He Can't Do This'

Olivia Kite was far away in Essex, but Number 10 was swarming. Only half a dozen or so of the 150 people who worked there full-time had the right to enter the prime minister's office after a quick knock, and Sam Mulligan had passed it on that 'The old man's in one of his dwams.' The first person to ignore this gentle warning was Amanda Andrews. Surprised to find the PM asleep across his desk, she shook him gently by the shoulder.

But he was not asleep, as some kind of instinct told her almost immediately. She pushed her fingers inside his shirt collar to feel for a pulse. Amanda did not scream; she was of the old school. She cried a little though, and her cheeks were still wet when Jason Latimer, the foreign secretary, walked in for a meeting that had been in the diary since the previous week. Many people assumed that Jason was the PM's favoured heir apparent, although Amanda knew better. Even so, as he stood over the prime minister's desk he shook his head with every appearance of genuine anger.

'He can't do this. Not now. He can't go and bloody die on us. Not now, just when we need him most. Amanda, I absolutely *forbid* it.'

Latimer cracked his long fingers, arched his back for relief and plunged his hands through his long golden hair, which he then shook as if it were wet. A natural actor, he strode to the long window then turned around so that he was silhouetted above the slumped prime minister, like an angel of judgement.

'This man was my friend. I will succeed him as prime minister, as you know very well. There is no place here for sentimentality or false emotion. I feel what I feel *here*' – he smote his breast with apparent emotion – 'but this is a moment for thinking' – a long bony finger stabbed the high, ridged forehead over which his golden locks fell – 'and a moment's thought tells us. . . What does it tell us, Amanda?'

'You tell me, foreign secretary,' Amanda replied drily. 'You're the politician.'

Buttoning his jacket for effect, Latimer flung a hand towards the window.

'Yes. I am. And my political instincts tell me that out there, where the millions are waiting, we simply cannot afford to lose our leader. I believe the party is ready for me, and that the country will be too. But this is the height of the battle, the furious flurry. Lose our king, and our forces will lose their heart. The people are with us – just – because they love this man. We have all followed him through so much. He has friends in Berlin, in Paris, in London. He has shouldered the burden' – by now Latimer was enjoying the sound of his own voice rather more than Amanda was – 'and if they out there know that the leader has fallen, I fear that the cause will fall too. Mrs Kite will plunge down on us like a. . . like a. . .'

'A kite?' Amanda offered.

'Quite so.'

At that moment a new voice was heard. It was low, resonant and Scottish.

'Or perhaps an Assyrian?'

Amanda and Latimer turned to see a tall man standing in the doorway that connected the PM's office to the stuffy little room that housed his inner staff. That afternoon it was almost empty, apart from the usual dozen computers and the private secretary in charge of speechwriting, who could be seen peering into a hole in the wood-panelled wall. In a nice nostalgic touch, all the paperwork from the floor below, the real, highly secure hub of Number 10's operations, arrived by dumb waiter, a device installed in Edwardian times, presumably to deliver tongue sandwiches or veal cutlets, but now used for messages deemed too sensitive to appear on the Downing Street intranet.

The man who had joined them began to recite:

'The Assyrian came down like the wolf on the fold,
And his cohorts were gleaming in purple and gold;
And the sheen of their spears was like stars on the sea. . .

'The old man loved his Byron.'

The speaker was Nelson Fraser, the PM's communications secretary, well known to the general public because he habitually affected traditional Scottish dress. Now he stood fondling his sporran and surveying the scene.

'The foreign secretary in the prime minister's inner sanctum, apparently playing to the upper tier at the Royal Opera House. Miss Andrews with a smear of mascara on her cheeks. Our great leader – well, prone. I am inclined to think the unthinkable. I always worried that he'd never make it through to retirement. Poor, lovely man. Isn't it rather early, Latimer, to be calculating the political odds? But I suppose the old man would have expected nothing less. He might even have approved. And as it happens, I entirely concur with you on one subject. He *can't* do this now. Take our leader out of the equation just a few days before the referendum and Olivia Kite will win the bloody thing. And once it's done, it's done. We'll be out of the EU once and for all, now and forever. Which would be a bloody disaster. No, he can't go and die on us. Dereliction of duty. For once, foreign secretary, I have to agree with you.'

Amanda dabbed her face, from which the colour had drained. 'Are you seriously suggesting that we can keep the news of the prime minister's death from the entire British public for long enough to get us through the referendum? That's six days away. You know what this building's like — 150 paranoid gossips squeezed together in a small ship in the middle of a hurricane. How could we possibly hide something like this?'

Fraser and Latimer both knew she was right. Number 10 Downing Street is a small, cramped village with lifts and back stairs, tiny offices slotted next to one another and a large permanent staff constantly bringing news from Moscow and clean towels, the latest polling information and coffee and sandwiches, telephone calls from Washington and freshly polished shoes for the prime minister. It's a village in which everyone knows everyone else, everyone is jealous of each other, and there is only one truly valuable currency: proximity to the PM. Trying to hide his death would be harder than trying to hide the death of the Pope inside the Vatican.

But Amanda had only just got started. 'And what happens then? What happens to those of us who kept the secret when we have to confess that we lied to the British public, and Parliament, and the king himself? Because this is going to come out. It's just a question of when. There are the speeches, the interviews, the public occasions, all the times when the PM has to be seen and heard. They'll string us up, one at a time, darling boys, from the lamp posts outside the Commons. I can feel the hemp around my darling neck. I can feel my long legs kicking.'

Jason Latimer, who had been standing over the prime minister, now moved away and sat down in his former leader's favourite armchair, from which the PM had plotted strategy, sipping black coffee laced with whisky, with his closest ministers and advisers.

'Amanda, think. Calm down. All we have to do is move the PM's unfortunate death on by a few days, so we can announce it after the vote. It could be like Nelson at Trafalgar: death at the moment of victory, the commander on deck at the heart of the battle. Not a dry eye in the house. We just need to buy some time. It can't be impossible. What we need above all is a cover story. I know it's difficult, but Amanda, let me ask you: how many people know for sure where he actually is at any given time? Hardly anyone has unrestricted access to this office or to his apartment upstairs, and he has his private lift.'

Amanda was far away, wondering what it actually felt like to be hanged. She'd heard that men. . . But she was a resilient woman. Her mind picked up on what the foreign secretary was saying.

'In one sense, Jason, we're lucky. The darling referendum means we can virtually ignore Parliament. Almost everyone's away. Most of the cabinet are out campaigning for one side or the other, and Whitehall's pretty much at a standstill; the PM has no meetings scheduled with the Treasury or anyone else for the next few days. But I come back to my first point, which is that this place is the real danger. There are at least twenty people, from the diary secretary to the PM's private detective to the key private secretaries, who could knock on that door at any time. The chief whip. Stately, plump, Sam Mulligan. Margaret with the tea. And so on. One of us could sit in the corridor outside and deflect them all for an hour or two, but not for much longer than that. You know how this place is, Nelson, better than anyone. Somebody's bound to talk to the press or to some pet blogger. If we're to have any chance at all we're going to have to shut down the ordinary Downing Street routine somehow, with a cast-iron cover story. But how we do that is beyond me. . .'

'Me too,' confessed Jason Latimer.

Nelson Fraser ran his fingers thoughtfully along the hem of his kilt, an Ancient Hunting Tadger, one of the rarest tartans of all, with its moss greens, faded pinks and tea-stain stripes. His sporran had been a present from Vladimir Putin after a Moscow summit; it was made of genuine mammoth fur. On a close day it stank slightly of brimstone and treacle.

'It's beyond me too,' he said finally. 'Frankly, I think it would be beyond anyone. You'd need Beelzebub himself to pull this off. So that's the fellow we need.'

'Now I've heard everything,' grunted the foreign secretary from his armchair. 'Ever since Alastair Campbell, people have assumed that being skilled in the dark arts was an essential part of your job. But even I never guessed you had a hotline to Hades.'

'Not quite. Not actually to Old Nick himself, but the next best thing. Who did the PM always turn to when there was something really difficult, something really dodgy, that needed doing?'

The Gamble

Amanda was staring at the crinkled, acrid bag of mammoth hair. Its smell was really quite something. 'You're not suggesting we tell Alois Haydn about this?'

'Who the hell else could pull it off?'

When the prime minister had been alive, it was said that if he was alone in a room there was more political understanding and intelligence there than anywhere else in Western Europe. Now he was gone, but the three people left in his office had a lot of nous between them. Amanda Andrews had been his Girl Friday since way back in the bleak years of opposition. In her time she had arm-twisted, cajoled and entranced hundreds of MPs and thousands of lobbyists. Jason Latimer had held most of the great offices of state, as well as once being Britain's Commissioner in Europe. In his youth he had worked for the Democratic party machine in Washington. Nelson Fraser understood the British media backwards, upside down and in its every changeable mood.

Even so, the three of them silently assented that this task was beyond them. The job of hiding the prime minister's death convincingly enough, for long enough, was so dangerous, so fraught with risk, that they needed Alois Haydn.

It was Amanda who made the call.

'We need you, Ally boy. I'm afraid the PM has had some kind of seizure.'

'Tsk tsk. But I'm not a doctor, Amanda. Is it serious?'

'Well . . .–ish. He is, in point of fact, dead. That's why we need you. Can't happen, you see, can it? Not from a political point of view.'

There was silence at the other end of the line. Amanda could sense that Haydn was weighing up this new situation, calculating just what it meant politically and personally. Finally he said, 'Nooo, no it can't, Amanda. Not at all, certainly not now. *Dead* dead?'

'Dead dead. So put your thinking cap on.'

'Reaching for it now. I'll be with you in half an hour.'

The truth is that once we begin to ask ourselves how a thing can be done, we are already on the slope to doing it. How many madcap escapades, unlikely plots and criminal conspiracies have started with the theoretical question, 'If I was going to, where would I start?' Take a handful of experienced political operators, set them a challenge, and the mechanism has already started to tick. By the time Haydn arrived Fraser was sitting outside the PM's door, keeping intruders at bay with a flimsy story about an urgent call to Washington.

Whatever people said about Alois Haydn – and they said a lot – nobody denied that he was a very fast thinker. He walked in, brushed the dead prime minister's hair briefly with the back of his hand, then turned around.

'This can only succeed if we do two things. We have to maintain the illusion that the PM is still alive, by which I mean that he must fulfil his engagements, and be heard and seen. Simultaneously, we have to find a way of preventing anyone from getting into this room or into his flat for the next five days. I've given this some thought already, and I can tell you that we're going to need some serious, organised and professional assistance. Have any of you heard of PLS – or Professional Logistical Services, to give them their full name? None of you? I'm disappointed, but not very surprised. Anyway, those are the people we need.'

Fraser objected: 'We can't possibly widen the circle at this point. Certainly not to people we don't know.'

Haydn gave a thin smile. 'First, as you will discover, you do know a lot of them. Second, it's already too late to try to keep this to ourselves. Sometimes longer walls are stronger walls, and as you'll find, we couldn't be dealing with a more discreet organisation. I've made a call already. Once I've explained the situation to them in person we're going to need to bring them here, in house, but I promise you that nobody will even notice.'

If you leave the private secretaries' antechamber to the PM's office in Number 10 Downing Street and turn left, the first thing you come to is a rabbit warren of tiny offices, where the private secretaries do their real work. Then comes a corridor which leads, through a security door rather like an airlock on a submarine, to the larger bureaucracy of the Cabinet Office. Number 10 people can choose to pass through the Cabinet Office and to go anywhere in Whitehall from there, including – via a secret tunnel – to the Ministry of Defence. It is much harder for Cabinet Office staff to go the other way, as the electronic pass system is cleverly configured for mostly one-way traffic. There are other interesting places in that part of Number 10 too, from the police secure room where the CCTV cameras are monitored to a small cupboard containing the flags that are brought out and displayed when foreign dignitaries visit. But the most important room is the kitchen, where tea, coffee, biscuits and sandwiches are prepared. It was there that the foreign secretary now went, returning to the PM's office bearing a tray.

The four people in the room had suddenly felt exhausted and famished. They sipped and munched in solemn silence. The full implications of what they were attempting were beginning to sink in. They planned to deceive the British people at the very time that they were taking a vitally important decision which would affect the future of the nation, and possibly that of the entire European continent. They were doing this, they all understood, because they had loved the former prime minister, and because they thought that a victory for Olivia Kite, and Britain's exit from the European Union, would be a national catastrophe. But that didn't alter the fact that what they were doing was treason. If they were found out they would be remembered for decades, perhaps for centuries, as villains. Yet each of them had private reasons for choosing to go ahead with the plan.

Jason Latimer wanted to be the next prime minister. If Olivia Kite won the referendum it would almost certainly be she who inherited the crown, and any hopes he had of Number 10 would be dashed. But if the deception worked and the PM 'died' at the moment of victory, Jason would be well placed to succeed him. That the PM had always cordially despised him no longer mattered.

Amanda Andrews, despite her provocative manner, was perhaps the most political person in the room. She had adored the PM, and was an ardent, Tuscany-soaked Europhile. But more important than any of that, she had a seething, almost uncontrollable hatred of Olivia Kite. In the days when Kite had had access to Number 10 the two women had experienced an instantaneous mutual antagonism. Amanda despised Olivia's face, make-up, clothing, smell, shoes and accent. Olivia felt, if anything, slightly more strongly about Amanda. From the family kitchen to the boardroom such irrational antagonisms hedge us all, helping to shape our fate whether we succumb to them or try vainly to resist.

As for Nelson Fraser, he saw his moment in history arriving. Whether he emerged from it as a hero or a villain, it would provide the raw material for one of the greatest books on politics ever written. Also, being trapped in this building for several days of intense crisis management might well present him with a long-awaited opportunity of becoming considerably more intimate with Amanda Andrews.

And Alois Haydn. . . was Alois Haydn. He could no more turn down a conspiracy than the late Alan Clark MP could turn down a 'filly'.

By the time the sandwiches had gone and the coffee pots had been emptied, Fraser had slipped out of the office and returned with a thin stack of small, typed pieces of card – the PM's daily engagements, extracted from the electronic diary and normally carried in his top pocket. The process of preparing them was like reducing a good sauce. The raw material for the day arrived electronically: all the requests, routine meetings, hoped-for private engagements – everything from a birthday that must not be forgotten to the time set aside to prepare for a visit from the Portuguese prime minister. These were typed into the electronic diary in the secure private office one floor below. It was the private secretaries who, deciding that a newspaper editor must be disappointed, and juggling the conflicting demands of Parliament and the PM's constituency chairman, assembled a daily briefing document. This, together with the red box that went up to the PM's private apartment last thing each night, gave him everything he needed to get through the following day. From it were drawn the small pieces of card, the *aides-memoire* that Nelson Fraser was now flicking through.

'Nothing in Parliament of course, thank Christ. There's the Sunday-morning telly, but there's a question mark against that already, so we can get out of that. That's it for the weekend. Then there's the audience with the king on Monday morning. And lots of campaigning – we've promised that he'll visit Edgbaston and Wolverhampton in the early part of next week, and we have to fit the Bluewater shopping centre in somehow too. That's what we have to deal with immediately. Could have been worse, I guess.'

Fraser was about to slip the cards into his sporran when he caught Amanda's glare, and quickly placed them on the desk.

'No souvenirs, Nelson.'

'No souvenirs, Amanda.'

Jason Latimer was leafing through the PM's daily briefing folder as if to the manner born. He pointed out that Buckingham Palace could hardly just be ignored. At the very least an emissary would have to be sent to see the king. He suggested that the only go-between who might work was the chief whip, Ronnie Ashe. 'I know it must seem that we're widening the circle all the time, but there simply aren't enough of us in this plot yet to make it work. And after all, Ronnie was the PM's closest friend, and he does know the king, as well as being a wise old bird. Besides which, attempting any deep skulduggery at Westminster without the chief whip would be as futile as trying to run a revolution without the secret police. All in favour?'

There was a low murmur of assent.

'Right, then. What about this radio interview? The country is clearly going to have to hear the PM's voice. My view is that we call in the best impersonator around – and that's still Rory Bremner – swear him to secrecy, promise him the Order of Merit or whatever, and give him a really good crib sheet. We'll sit beside him and he can do it from here. Actually, do you think we could get him to talk to the king on the phone?' A low whistle from Amanda; expressions of disbelief, amusement and excitement from elsewhere.

Now Haydn broke in. As he was talking, Latimer observed that his legs were so short that his feet dangled from the PM's sofa and swung six inches off the ground. 'The old queen had a saying: I must be *seen* to be *believed*. These days, with twenty-four-hour news channels and YouTube, things are a lot trickier. Even so, there are tricks, and I know the people who can play them. But it's going to take time. So. . . the Sunday-morning telly would have been Sky's turn, wouldn't it? Amanda, get on to Dermot Murnaghan and tell him this: the PM no longer regards these long set-piece interviews as an effective means of getting his message over to swing voters. Instead, he wants to do an on-line radio phone-in on Monday morning, with Dermot chairing it.

'The Sky bosses won't be happy about it – although since Sky radio supplies the commercial news stations, they should be. But I think we can get away with it, particularly if we float the idea in tomorrow's papers: direct democracy, unmediated, the PM brave enough to take on unscripted questions, that kind of nonsense. We should stage a photo-op right here in this office, with the prime minister working hard on his papers.'

Amanda butted in: 'That might be a little tricky, darling, since all we have to work with is an ex-prime minister.'

All four of them paused and turned to look at the heavily-built figure sprawled over his desk. Haydn began to talk about propping him up somehow, and what could be achieved with a bit of clever lighting, but Amanda hadn't finished yet.

'And that brings me to the next thing. There are still five days to go before the vote. It's some years since I last watched *Prime Suspect*, but what do you think happens to a human cadaver left in a warm room for that length of time? Sorry to be distasteful and all that, but what we're planning to do is going to cause enough of a stink without a real stink to make it even worse.'

Alois Haydn bounced to his feet. 'Agreed. We need a plan. And we need it tonight. Meanwhile, Amanda, you're on door duty. Nelson, you handle the phone. Jason, you need to be seen coming in and out of this office on urgent business. Tell the private secs there's a big storm brewing from Berlin, or whatever you like. As for me, I need to get to PLS right now.' With that he slipped out through the door, leaving behind a very faint whiff of sulphur.

Dirty Work

An hour later, three burly Polish men met in the dingy surroundings of the Walworth International Café. The building had started life as an Edwardian baker's shop, but it had gone downhill steadily ever since it stopped being famous throughout South London for its éclairs and rhubarb tarts. In the past few years it had been, in rapid succession, a vegetarian curry house, a pawn-broker's and a purveyor of dirty magazines. The only significant point in its favour had been the dry humour of the dirty-magazine proprietor, who had named it, in small red letters, Onan's. This had added, in a tawdry way, to the gaiety of life, causing much sniggering on the top decks of buses taking office workers in to Victoria and Pimlico.

Now that was all past, the sign long gone. The International Café was barely a café at all. You could still buy mugs of milky instant coffee accompanied by elderly biscuits in cellophane, but the real trade was in international telephone cards, Eastern European beer and gossip about casual employment. By mid-morning on a Monday there would be a long line of tired-looking men standing and waiting for foremen and gangmasters; a side of the European project that was rarely discussed in Downing Street.

This evening, as on many others, the three thickset, unshaven and sad-looking men were occupying the plastic chairs at the table by the grimy street window. They often came here to smoke

Sobieskis and reminisce about home. They all looked alike – red-cheeked, with large noses, small ears and shaven, balding heads. Aleksander and his much younger brothers, Borys and Dawid, were from Białystok, that forest-swaddled, pine-scented city near the Polish border with Belarus. As they watched the procession of black, brown and yellow faces passing the café they would ruminate about the pleasures and miseries of following Jagiellonia, that fine if fatally flawed football club. Three of the eight children born to a chemistry professor and the lead carver of the Białystok puppet theatre, they had grown up running through the woods, playing cops and robbers in the lush parks and dreaming of escape.

Good with their hands, strong and intelligent, Dawid and Borys had done their military service and found useful trades, which they had brought to Britain. Well-read and hard-working, they hoped to go back to their families in a couple of years with enough money to build their own houses. They were typical examples of the tens of thousands of Eastern Europeans who had arrived in the United Kingdom in recent years – more ambitious and determined by far than most of the locals.

Aleksander, the oldest brother by ten years, was very different. There was a darkness about him. After serving with the Polish special forces during the communist years he had been seconded to military intelligence. Borys had been an infantryman and a poet, and Dawid a humble electrician, but Aleksander had become a killer. A good intelligence officer – ruthless and genuinely intelligent – he had gone to Moscow in the late 1970s, where he had been blooded by his colleagues in a basement of the Lubyanka. Without compunction or comment he had cleanly killed four captured Western spies, each with a bullet to the base of the skull. He had watched, though not participated in, acts of torture with hammers and pliers and lengths of electric cable. He had returned to Warsaw with Moscow's endorsement, but had been able to make a smooth transition after the fall of the communist government in 1989.

With his special forces background, in 1990 Aleksander had taken part in Operation Simoom, the top-secret Polish mission to rescue six US agents from deep inside Saddam Hussein's Iraq – for which the Americans had rewarded Poland by cancelling half its national debt. The maps they had found and brought back with them had helped the US military in the Desert Storm invasion too. As a result Aleksander had become popular with the very people he had been trained to oppose so ruthlessly. Those were head-spinning times. A man had to tense every muscle to stay standing. In the turbulent years of early post-communist Poland he had found himself working indirectly for Lech Walesa and his prime minister Hanna Suchocka, participating in plots to break up and discredit some of the new political parties. But when the files of the secret service agent Colonel Jan Lesiak had emerged Aleksander had feared public exposure, and left Poland for the last time.

He had found jobs easily enough through his contacts in Agencja Wywiadu. Most of them had been dull, low-grade work for private American security companies, sitting in the back of an SUV with a machine gun, escorting businessmen through the backstreets of Baghdad or Tripoli. But there had also been firefights in Beirut and an execution or two in refugee camps on the Syrian border. He learned to live out of a rucksack and to take his payment in bundles of currency from men who didn't look him in the eye.

But Aleksander missed his brothers, and when Dawid suggested that the three of them form a plumbing, electrical and building company and go to Britain, Aleksander felt he was ready to change down a gear. A fifth-hand van had taken them halfway across Europe to Rotterdam, and thence by ferry to Harwich.

As befitted three natives of Białystok, home town of the creator of Esperanto, the brothers had quite easily gained a reasonable command of English. But they found the people difficult. How could it be, in the wealthy and successful West, that workers did so very little work, and that everybody complained so incessantly? In Białystok they had been brought up on stories from Shakespeare and Dickens, but the modern English seemed to read nothing at all, and to have no curiosity about anywhere else in the world. It got them down.

After six months of grinding, grafting and being underpaid by the ferrety locals in small towns around Essex, Aleksander was on the point of going back to the Middle East, where there was always work. But then one day just before Christmas a Range Rover drew up at the service station they used as an informal employment bureau, a small, neat man in a camel-hair coat stepped out, and the brothers' luck changed. At first he offered them only building work on his large and – Borys insisted – vulgar new mansion. But Mr Haydn turned out to know Białystok well, and had even attended its famous puppet theatre during the communist times. He cross-examined them, seeming particularly interested in Aleksander. He began to have plans for them.

Taking them out to shoot wild duck in the marshes around his new house – adding in a News International surveillance drone from time to time – Haydn was delighted to note that Aleksander's marksmanship was excellent. He presented him with an English shotgun, and bought him and his brothers leather jackets and a second-hand Land Rover, corrected their English and asked them to carry out personal errands for him. Finally he moved them to London so he could reach them more easily, setting them up in a modest but clean flat south of the river.

Money had ceased to be a problem for the brothers, but they felt uneasy about the man Borys contemptuously referred to as 'the

English oligarch'. Indeed, Mr Haydn seemed to them to behave more like a Russian than an Englishman. Recently he had taken to asking them to follow people, hammer on doors and issue threats of violence.

This evening in the International Café they were discussing their benefactor's latest request. Mr Haydn wanted them to dispose of a body tomorrow night. Go to the pond in St James's Park and get hold of a boat, had been his first instruction. Then someone will bring you a body and you will get rid of it. This was clearly illegal, and potentially dangerous – the kind of thing that could get them deported at the very least, as Dawid pointed out. Only Aleksander was relaxed about the task. He could do this in his sleep, he said, and it could well lead to other, better-paid jobs. That was the kind of man Mr Haydn was. Aleksander's red, meaty hands lay loosely on the zinc tabletop, playing with an empty packet of cigarettes. He felt very calm indeed. Dirty work was something he understood.

The Decapitation Strategy

It was a cool evening outside, but the atmosphere in the prime minister's office was hot and tense. Amanda locked the cream wooden door. An hour earlier she had slipped across the road to the Commons and made her way to the chief whip's office. Ronnie Ashe had taken the news badly. Unlike any of those who had actually been present at Number 10, he had broken down and cried helplessly. He had poured each of them a large brandy, and then another, after which Amanda had said sternly, 'No more,' and had made it clear that if he wanted the old man's legacy to survive, he had to get cracking.

Now Ashe was back in the PM's office with her and Jason Latimer. Nelson Fraser had long gone, and was off somewhere frantically writing new speeches for the campaign; his earlier ones had already been dispatched. But minute by minute the circle was widening: they had just been joined by a heavily-built man wearing an M&S suit – Sergeant Don Hammond, the PM's personal detective. He knew everything there was to know about what went on in Number 10, and Amanda had insisted that he be let in on the secret. Also, at some point they were going to need some literal muscle.

Latimer had said of his former leader, 'Well, he can't stay here. This is where *we* have to be. We can pretty much control who comes in. We aren't overlooked, and I take it we can't be overheard, even by our own people. But he' – the foreign secretary had jerked his thumb in the direction of the man in whose presence he had formerly always lowered his voice – 'will have to go.'

'That's going to be tricky,' said Amanda. 'All those inquisitive secretaries, all those tubby policemen with a hotline to the tabloids' newsdesks. . .'

They all knew that keeping a lid on the community inside Number 10 was going to be hard, which was one of the reasons Amanda had insisted on Don Hammond, who was trusted implicitly by the regular staff. The six-foot-tall, fourteen-stone armed protection squad sergeant had looked after the prime minister, as guard, valet, adviser, late-night confessor and occasional driver, for the past five years. Amanda knew he would be deeply upset by his boss's demise, but would he agree to join the plot? The trouble was, they couldn't manage without him, just as they couldn't manage without the chief whip. Latimer had come up with the best argument to win Hammond over: 'If he can be persuaded that we're doing this as the PM's last wish, to avoid a national disaster, then his personal loyalty should sway him.'

In the end Hammond had come around surprisingly easily: the challenge, the adventure and the technical difficulties that would have to be overcome were just too intriguing to resist. He was given one of the private secretaries' desks just outside the door, his prime job for the time being to control who came into the office and who was kept out. Don Hammond was so respected inside Number 10 that few people would choose to confront him. The PM's political private secretary had felt personally affronted when he was denied access to his boss, but the fact that the chief whip, the foreign secretary and Amanda Andrews were all ensconced in his office gave credence to the story that he was embroiled in a top-secret crisis involving the Germans.

Amanda unbuttoned her cardigan, draped it over the back of a chair and slipped her shoes off. It was clear that they were all going to be there for some time.

'Well, boys,' she said, 'where are we? We still represent, one way or another, His Majesty's government. We have a certain amount of fast-diminishing authority – I'd hardly call it power, not after this – but we do at least have a window of opportunity in which we can control events. Above all, being the government, darlings, we have money. Almost unlimited amounts of money if we're not worried about the next budget or the chancellor's feelings, which I take it we're not.'

Just as she finished speaking her phone began to vibrate. It was Alois Haydn, texting that he had found someone who could help with the disposal of a headless body, but that first it would have to be smuggled out of the building.

'Why headless?' Amanda asked Ronnie Ashe.

'I'd have thought that was obvious, my dear,' replied the chief whip. 'We can get rid of the body – we have to get rid of the body – but we can't risk anyone realising who it is, or what's happened. He mustn't be identified, don't you see? You can't simply leave dead prime ministers lying around the place. So the head, and I'm afraid both the hands, will have to go. Not very pretty, but there it is. The PM would have understood perfectly.'

The prime minister meanwhile, propped upright in his chair with towels, his head tilted away from the camera towards the window, had been photographed as well as they could manage. He did not look particularly lifelike, but nor did he look obviously dead, and at least it was clearly him. Now, with the help of Sergeant Hammond, who had received the offer of a substantial cheque without apparent surprise, they tried to roll the PM up in one of the rugs from the office floor. But he was too tall. First one and then the other of his feet had stuck out, and a wisp of hair protruded from the other end of the ungainly sausage. They'd never get him out of Number 10 like that. Hammond was sent upstairs to the private apartment, and returned with a duvet and a roll of gaffer tape that had been left behind by a film crew. After a lot of sweating, groaning and cursing, the dead man had been parcelled up.

It was, on balance, a great pity that the prime minister himself was not able to take part in the conversation about his own head that followed. His deep historical knowledge, which was presumably disintegrating in his oxygen-starved frontal lobes even at that moment, would have seized on the symbolic importance of the heads of leaders. There was Charles I, of course, but more to the point perhaps was his great adversary Oliver Cromwell, whose body had been buried in the Lady Chapel in Westminster Abbey. When the Restoration arrived it proved stubbornly difficult to winkle out. Nevertheless, with his fellow regicides Henry Ireton, Robert Blake and John Bradshaw, the corpse of the former Lord Protector was taken to the Red Lion inn – not the one still standing at the bottom of Whitehall, but an older one at Holborn, from which it was dragged on a sledge to the execution place at Tyburn, where it hung for most of a day. Only then was the head severed. It was not easy: it took eight blows with a substantial axe. After that the head was placed on a spike above Westminster Hall, where it rattled and grinned for the next twenty-four years until it was blown off by a great storm in 1685 and recovered by a watchman. From then on it was passed around between private collectors and museums for nearly three hundred years, regarded as an amusing relic of the will to power. Finally, in 1960, it was buried at Sidney Sussex College in Cambridge, Cromwell's old college, where he is commemorated by a plaque, though his head's precise location is deliberately obscured.

All this the prime minister would have been able to explain, while ruminating with gusto and at length on mankind's primitive fetish for the heads of the powerful, perhaps making an aside on the pickling of Lenin and the more recent investigations carried out into Einstein's brain. On the other hand, it might have depressed him to contemplate the grisly work that was about to be performed on his own body.

The plotters remained closeted in the PM's office until the last of the private secretaries had left for the night, and the cleaners had come and gone. It was a long wait, oiled by what remained of the prime minister's private stock of malt whisky. Amanda raised a glass to 'our leader', and they solemnly drank to his memory. Then they set to work. There was a lot to do.

Jason Latimer had spent most of his adult life in government service. He had long grown accustomed to being swaddled by cars, secretaries and ambitious buffers between himself and the hard edges of everyday life, but he was neither cowardly nor squeamish. 'I'll start,' he said. His brother-in-law was a moderately successful organic butcher in Leicester.

With Hammond taking the chest and Latimer the legs, the prime minister was carried through the back door of his office into the empty Cabinet Room. There they had to make their first difficult decision. Leaving the Cabinet Room and heading towards the front of the building would take them, via a left turn, into Number 11 and the PM's private lift to the magnificent flat where he lived. That was the shortest and quickest route, but the chance of running into late-night staff was high.

So Hammond and Latimer took the long road. They left the Cabinet Room by the doors to the outside terrace and took the stone steps down into the garden. Keeping close to the wall to avoid being spotted from an upstairs window, they reached a small garden door opening onto a spiral staircase. This led them, after an exhausting struggle, directly up to the hallway of the flat. From there it was only a short distance to the kitchen, which like most of the apartment had been substantially remodelled in the time of David and Samantha Cameron.

Hammond unwrapped the PM and hoisted him onto the brushed-steel worktop beside the Britannia oven. It was large enough, just, to accommodate the body, with the head lolling over the sink. Latimer, expressionless, examined the wooden block containing an assortment of sharp kitchen knives, but none of them, he thought, was big enough. He started going through the drawers, where he found an electric carving knife that had been acquired during the Johnson era. He flicked the switch and turned purposefully towards the prime ministerial neck.

Purposeful or not, he seemed exhausted as well as white-faced when he returned to the rest of the cabal in the office downstairs half an hour later. Light pink speckles decorated his white shirt, the sleeves of which had been rolled up above his elbows. He seemed to have aged a decade since they had last seen him.

'It's mostly done,' he said. 'Beastly work, but I suppose doctors do that sort of thing all the time. The hands were easy enough; they're in the freezer, behind a family bag of McCain's oven chips – he was a great chip-pincher, the old man – so watch it if anyone decides on a midnight feast later on. The head's harder. It's the spine. He was always known for his backbone, and now I can't bloody well get through it. The knife just slides off. Any suggestions?'

The prime minister, had he been available, might have referred back to those eight blows needed for his eminent predecessor Oliver Cromwell. To her credit Amanda immediately leapt up and began scouring the premises for something that might do the job. But Number 10 Downing Street is not a museum, and headsmen's axes were in short supply. There was a tiny chopper beside a fire extinguisher and a bucket of sand, but Amanda was on the verge of giving up when she noticed the fine gilded Arabian sword on the Cabinet Room mantelpiece.

Amanda's father had been a rubber planter in Malaysia, and she was a resourceful woman. She headed upstairs, her skirt tucked into her knickers and the gold-handled weapon beneath her arm. A few minutes later she was back downstairs, a little pale but quite calm, carrying a heavily weighted Waitrose shopping bag in one hand.

'All done, boys. He was a tough old bird, but I think he'd have seen the funny side.'

The chief whip stood up, stretched his arms and yawned immensely. 'All we have to do now is honour our leader in the only way that would have meant anything to him — by winning this sodding vote and keeping this sodding country at least half relevant.'

'Right. Now, who wants this?' asked Amanda.

An Awfully Big Adventure

Haydn told the PLS executive everything – almost. They were men and women who had kept disgraceful and dangerous public secrets all their working lives, and they were hard to shock. Even so, the odd white eyebrow was raised as he explained not only the prime minister's death, but the accelerating project of deception and game-playing that was taking place in Number 10 even as he spoke. He did not describe the decapitation and disposal of the body; that was not 'need to know'. For their part, PLS were not inclined to trust a man like Alois Haydn. Admiral Jock Dalgety and Colonel Mike Patten went immediately to meet the foreign secretary and the chief whip in person, and to hear from their own mouths an edited version of the events of the past few hours.

Once the board of PLS had decided that participating in this exercise would not be traitorous, but rather that they would be attempting to fulfil the wishes of the best prime minister Britain had had for decades, they all snapped to attention and began planning. And there was a lot they could do. Five former members of the security services, led by Dame Cecily Morgan; three former permanent secretaries; two former ambassadors; a one-time head of the Met plus three senior staff; and a constellation of senior military brass (retired) now converged on Downing Street. They brought no secretaries, but a few technical specialists.

The chancellor of the exchequer was safely away in Wales with most of his team for the last frantic days of the referendum campaign. Just behind his office and private rooms is a short corridor which leads to a magnificent but seldom used dining room. It has an elaborate scalloped ceiling, and its walls are hung with modern abstract paintings; its spacious windows look out onto the Downing Street terrace and the garden beyond. Gordon Brown had held some surprisingly convivial suppers there, but during the David Cameron years it had been largely forgotten.

It was there that PLS set up shop. Flatscreen televisions, some of them linked to CCTV cameras in Downing Street and Whitehall, were arranged around the walls. Fat, ugly computers were perched on ornate old chairs and the magnificent dining table. Netting was set up to cover the windows. Jackets were pulled off and piled on the floor. Takeaway food cartons were emptied and discarded. Empty water bottles lay everywhere. On the same floor as the prime minister's office, just on the other side of the Cabinet Room itself, this would be Misinformation Central.

Jock Dalgety had rapidly taken charge. 'The first job, everybody, is damage limitation. We are all aboard a leaking ship, and bunging the holes has to start now. I want a full list of everyone who has access to this building, and I want it tonight. Get me the full roster of Downing Street staff and everyone in the Cabinet Office. I want the prime minister's electronic diary up on a screen at all times. Apart from us, the following people have access to this room: Amanda Andrews, Nelson Fraser, Jason Latimer, that Haydn fellow, Sergeant Hammond, and Ronnie Ashe. Other than that, absolutely nobody else. Is that clear? Miss Andrews is organising security passes for you all. Pick them up before you leave tomorrow morning.'

The leathery admiral glared around the room at the tousled, wrinkled, grey-headed men and women, all of whom stared straight back at him, bright-eyed and flushed, fully expecting that they would shortly be having the time of their lives.

'It's going to get pretty bloody smelly in here. And we're none of us spring chickens. But I expect you to stay in this building for as many hours as humanly possible, until the job is done. The chancellor is away for a few days, thank God. Keep away from his flat, but there are sofas next door and washrooms along the corridor.' He opened a thick leather file and leafed through it before continuing.

'Here is our cover story, straight from Mr Haydn himself. A consortium of major British banks and finance houses have presented the government with an ultimatum should the country vote to leave the EU. Unless they are granted extremely generous tax breaks, every one of them will decamp for Paris, Frankfurt or Amsterdam. Between them they contribute something like 15 per cent of the UK's corporate taxation, so without them the country would go bust.

'This is potentially a major national crisis, but it cannot be discussed publicly, because that could unfairly bias the referendum vote. It may seem Quixotic, but that is the prime minister's personal wish. We have been brought in as the negotiating team. Some of you are former Treasury people, and others without a financial background must pretend to be ex-City men and women. Because both France and Germany would be involved if these institutions moved their headquarters overseas, those of you from the foreign services will handle the continental connections. Others of you will gather information from our foreign partners, as you have been doing all your working lives. Some of you are here to keep the Americans happy.

'All this is boring enough and serious enough to convince most of the people in this building that ordinary business has been suspended. And remember, nobody who is not a member of this

organisation has the right to question any of you about our activi-
ties. We are all here for the late prime minister, and nobody else.
Any questions? No? Then, ladies and gentlemen, it's action stations.'

All around the room, heads were already bowed over telephones
and computer keyboards as one-time spooks and former Met officers
began to go through the confidential Downing Street address book.
Most of the prime minister's political team were discreetly told to
stay at home until the current crisis was resolved. Private secretaries
dealing with individual government departments were given urgent
research work to get on with, and told to deliver it to the foreign
secretary personally.

That was the soft stuff. By midnight the process of hacking phones
and personal computers to check for gossip, or the very first shreds
of information which might rapidly turn into gossip, had begun.
These defensive measures were essential, but they could not be
allowed to take up too much time before the process of active
deception started. And that was where Dame Cecily came into her
own. The media needed a strong alternative tale. She and a clever
young man from Shoreditch had already set up a series of bogus
Witter accounts to create the illusion of a news-making domestic
argument between the prime minister and his estranged wife. It
would provide bad publicity, but of a useful sort. As Dame Cecily
always said, 'In London, if you're going to create a red herring,
better make it stink like hell.'

Soon Witter was alive with breathless reports that the PM's wife
had called him a fat, self-obsessed, libidinous pig, and that someone
had replied on his behalf that he had spent far too many years
married to a raddled old cow who was shagging her way around
West London. That should catch the morning radio programmes,
and would make the papers in due course. It was possible that some
journalist would contact the prime minister's wife in person and

get a considerable flea in his ear. But it was also possible, these days, that none of them would bother. Anyway, everyone would be looking in the wrong direction.

Meanwhile the young man from Shoreditch, ground zero of Britain's high-tech community, had been in touch with some academics in the United States who were working on 3D facial mapping and animation. He wore an unappealing pair of red jeans, and his head was shaved at the sides with a long flop of hair on the top, making him resemble the hero of *Tintin Goes Clubbing*; but he had spent five years at GCHQ, and was a family friend of Dame Cecily's. His speciality was a branch of computer graphics originally designed to improve facial recognition from CCTV cameras and currently being trialled on the London Underground.

As the prime minister's head was readily available, Tintin reported, the laser mapping of his features should be easy. 'Every pimple, every wrinkle, I promise you. It's a painstaking business, but we have the kit at University College. My guys at Berkeley and MIT say that turning that into a credible animated face – I've told them it's for a Tom Cruise movie – is a lot harder, but it's doable. So I've gone closer to home. Where's the leading edge in computer anima-tion in the world just now? Better than Hollywood, better than Japan? No, not Shoreditch – it's just down the road in Soho.'

Dame Cecily pulled her spectacles off her nose and waggled them at him. 'You're not seriously suggesting, Harry, that we can create an animated prime minister good enough to fool the public? I know I'm just an old duck these days, but I simply don't believe it.'

'Well, Baroness, we have access to the very best laser-mapping techniques in the world. We've got the cameras, we've got state-of-the-art software, and the best of the Americans have been working with us for several years. Last but not least, we're surrounded by the very top private-sector computer-animation people. Some of the best games on the internet were created in Soho; even the big US film studios go there now. All I'm saying is that if we put the two together, we might get something very interesting.'

'All right, Harry. I suspect you're getting just a little over-enthusiastic, and I doubt that we'll have the time anyway, but – very well, all hands to the pump. See what you can do. Money no object. Our budget is apparently "whatever it takes".'

Expert though many of its members were in the dark arts, Professional Logistical Services usually tried, where possible, to avoid actually breaking the law. But some of the things the team now needed to turn to were plainly illegal. The recently-appointed chairman of the Commons Foreign Affairs Select Committee, who had requested an urgent meeting with the PM, would have to be directly lied to. A notoriously pompous and nitpicking man, he might well cause trouble in due course. It was also thought that one of the Number 10 policemen on duty had guessed that some-thing big was going on, and that he might have to be blackmailed to shut him up.

At this point Alois Haydn glided into the dining room. His pipis-trelle hearing picked up fragments of conversation coming at him from every direction.

'Well, get him out of bed then. There's a crisis on. I know, but it's what he's paid for. . .'

'If you even think of printing that kind of nonsense – no, even *think* about thinking of it – you'll never work again. As it happens, I was talking about you to the DG just the other night. . .'

'We've had a word with the master of his college, and between you and me poor Briskett has let the problem get out of hand. He's been found in the most unseemly circumstances. . . We just don't want him to embarrass himself at his age, so if you hear anything, here's the number. . .'

'No, you certainly *can't* ask me what it's about. . .'

'Evan, darling, it's been far too long. I need to call in that favour. Just something for the early-morning financial bulletin. . .'

'One Margherita. One pepperoni. And the one with spinach. . .'

Alois came close to a thin smile. In his hands he was carrying a thick roll of paperwork. He pulled out a chair and hopped onto it. Then, after calling for everybody's attention, he unrolled a hand-written note that, he grandly announced, was 'your get-out-of-jail-free card, ladies and gentlemen – the Royal Prerogative'. This, he read out, had famously been defined by the constitutional guru Albert Venn Dicey as 'the remaining portion of the Crown's original authority. . .the residue of discretionary power left in the hands of the Crown, whether such power be in fact exercised by the king himself or by his ministers'. Haydn told the room that in matters of national security – and what could be more so than Britain's place in the European Union? – the Royal Prerogative allowed a prime minister to waive various awkward legal restrictions concerning elections, privacy and so forth.

Baroness Tessie Fremantle, who had run the Treasury for nearly a decade, and had been in and out of Number 10 most of her adult life, had forgotten more constitutional law than the rest of them had ever known. In most arguments about British power, simply uttering the word 'Dicey' shut everyone up. Not Lady Fremantle.

'Small problem, Mr Haydn. For all practical purposes, the Royal Prerogative can be invoked solely on the authority of the prime minister. My point is – and it is the reason we are here, after all – we don't have a prime minister. No prime minister, not legal. Or am I missing something?'

Haydn allowed himself a small grimace of triumph, reached into the silk lining of his tightly cut jacket and pulled out an envelope.

'But we do have the prime minister's – the late prime minister's

— authority. I have a letter here, signed by him in his last hours, which completely covers everything we might have to do.'

Lady Fremantle scanned the letter. 'Well, it does look like his signature, though I can't imagine he actually wrote this himself. He had a much better understanding of history than to suppose that this was decent. It *is* his signature I suppose, Mr Haydn?'

'As you can see.'

'It is *his* signature?'

'Indubitably,' said Haydn, who had forged it himself only an hour earlier.

There would, inevitably, be a major parliamentary row in due course. But that worried nobody in the chancellor's dining room that long night. Parliamentary rows almost always happen too late. Their function in the British system is the creaking and banging of the stable door.

The Great Escape

The rest of the prime minister was still lying upstairs, wrapped in a duvet and gaffer tape, seeping. How do you remove a body from Number 10 Downing Street without anybody noticing?

Immediately after Jock Dalgety's opening speech, Sir Richard Greene KCB, former chairman of the Joint Intelligence Committee, left the dining room and went to meet Jason Latimer by the narrow brick Tudor corridor connecting Number 10 to the Cabinet Office.

'This way, foreign secretary,' said Dickie, who was carrying a grubby photocopied architectural plan.

At the front of the building was a security room where the Special Protection Squad lounged watching CCTV screens, and from which Downing Street's highly sophisticated central alarm system was controlled.

Tonight, however, thanks to the intervention of Sergeant Hammond, the room was empty. A locked gun rack was bolted to the wall, alongside a poster outlining the proper use of gasmasks. Everyone who worked in Number 10 was assigned to one of two groups – green and blue – for evacuation purposes. The green group was made up of those people the prime minister required for the functioning of government, and they would be brought out very quickly, via the corridor underneath Whitehall that ends at the MoD. The blue group would be evacuated more slowly.

Also in the security room were two metal wardrobes, painted a dull green, containing serge uniforms, gymwear and some stinking old shoes. Between them was a small wooden door. 'That's it,' said Dickie Greene. 'There should be another metal one behind it.' Latimer pulled out a large bunch of keys and got to work.

The map Greene was using had been drawn up by the old Department of Works at the time when Downing Street was effectively rebuilt from the ground up in the early 1960s. Concrete and steel underpinning, and reinforced connections to the Cold War network of tunnels below, had been a vital part of the work, though the media's attention focused on the renovation of the public rooms. These had been carefully dismantled, and then reconstructed to mimic the look of the old building. The attention to detail had been careful, even though the quality of the work had sometimes been shoddy.

Here, tradition was everything, even if the whole place was in fact nothing but political illusion. When the builders started work on the famous black bricks that front Number 10 they discovered to their shock that they were actually cheap yellow London bricks, widely used at the time for fast speculative building. The black was simply the accumulated filth of the ages. Rather than being restored to their original colour, they were painted black again.

By the 1970s Number 10 resembled an iceberg, in that only a fraction of it was visible above the surface; its secrets were hidden below. During the war, SOE's black ops had been run from the top floor of the nearby St Ermin's hotel; its lift still didn't run all the way up. From below the hotel a tunnel had allowed the spooks to get into Downing Street unobserved. That tunnel was still there, as were plenty of others.

Greene and Latimer squeezed through the narrow metal doorway and clambered down a steel ladder. The shaft was lit from below, and was clearly not of recent construction: its steel hoops and raw plasterwork probably dated from the Second World War. But once they were safely at the bottom they found themselves in a surprisingly spacious and well-appointed tunnel, with neat blue flooring, zinc air ducts and even a few rubber plants sitting in white plastic pots. Also accessed by lift from the Cabinet Office, after twenty yards the tunnel ended in a heavy metal blast door with a red wheel lock. Beside this was a large, pale wooden cabinet with hundreds of slots, each of which contained a laminated pass bearing the pale image of the face of a public servant. These were the physical manifestation of Whitehall's info-log distinction between those with a 'mole card' and those without. Getting your mole card was a sign of distinction as highly prized as a minor gong from the Palace or a quiet thank-you from your permanent secretary.

'That's not our way,' said Greene. 'It leads to Pindar, the socking big emergency bunker that links up to Northwood and the top military boys. You never want to have to spend any time down there, foreign secretary. It's only for when the balloon goes up. From the MoD you can get all the way to the Houses of Parliament underground, without anyone being any the wiser. But you have to have the right accreditation. In any case, we can hardly carry the prime minister into the MoD, can we?'

'No. . . Pindar?' asked Latimer, who had had an expensive classical education.

'Yes, the Greek poet fellow. Pretty unreadable, I always found him. The point is, his house is supposed to have remained intact while every other building in Thebes was destroyed after a siege. Last room standing, d'you see? Here we are, well into the twenty-first century, and we're still run by chaps who read Greats at Oxford. Funny bloody country. Sometimes in my weak moments I almost prefer the French. . . Anyway, we have to go this way I'm afraid.'

'This way' meant a much smaller brick-and-concrete tunnel

leading in the opposite direction which, once Dickie had located the switch, was lit only by a series of dim bulbs that receded into the murk. Circular steel bulwarks stamped 'Gen Post Office' and neatly-laid-out tubes carrying cabling and covered in dust were clues to the tunnel's original purpose, as part of a network of underground communications built in the early years of the Cold War.

The first steel door they reached led to 'Q-Whitehall', the tunnel supposedly designed to allow Downing Street's senior staff, the green team, clutching their mole cards, to escape the ruin of Thebes. But Dickie led Latimer beyond that entrance too. The concrete grew slimier, the warm air grew thicker, and the light grew dimmer.

'Carry on for long enough and they say you'll pop up under Buck House. But this is hardly royal appointment standard, is it, foreign secretary?'

Latimer was well aware that the former spook was being discreet. The tunnel certainly led to Buckingham Palace, with another one branching off to Clarence House. The main royal residences had a secret communications system and excellent bomb shelters, although the atmosphere inside them was curiously bland, like exclusive airport waiting lounges. The old queen mother had been down there to have a poke around, and Latimer had always wondered if any other members of the royal family ever used the tunnels to pop up in unexpected parts of the capital. He wouldn't put it past the current king, obsessed as he was with old architecture and family secrets.

By now both men, having walked bent over for a quarter of a mile, were slightly out of breath. Suddenly Dickie Greene came to a halt. 'It'll be a hell of a job lugging him all this way. . . But here we are. This is us.' With a grunt he began to turn a steel wheel below a circular trapdoor that protruded over their heads. When it finally opened a thin cascade of dirt and dust trickled down on them, swiftly followed by the clatter of a well-oiled steel ladder. 'You'll enjoy this bit,' said Greene.

After a short but stiff climb in the darkness, and a struggle with another metal door which Greene had to shoulder open, the two men clambered, gasping, out into the night air. Greene grinned with pleasure at Latimer's shock when he realised where they were. They were standing in the middle of Duck Island in the St James's Park pond, created in the time of Charles II to provide him with fresh fowl. It was unlikely that anyone would be about in the park at that time of night, but if there had been, the pair would have been hidden from view only by an angry goose and the ornate roof of the birdkeeper's lodge. Despite the seriousness of the situation they couldn't help feeling a little like a couple of boys in a secret treehouse, unsuspected by the grown-ups. But as they took in the scene, they began to feel that this might just work. If they could manage to get the body here, they could get it away.

Nelson Fraser had proposed a simpler method. There were vaults underneath Downing Street which could be reached through a small door in the garden. Now used to store gardening equipment, they were the obvious place to dump a body. But Amanda had spotted the flaw. 'They are indeed a fine and private place, Nelson. But have you forgotten what's directly above them? It's the bloody terrace. We can't have a stink there.'

Using the tunnel would mean not having to negotiate the Downing Street gates, which were protected by armed police; it would avoid all the CCTV cameras – even the vaults had them; and the locked back entrance to the garden opened directly onto Horse Guards Parade, where there was a serious risk of bumping into members of the public wandering around at any hour of the day or night. Apart from the one leading to Pindar, the tunnels were so obscure that few of the Number 10 staff were even aware of their existence. The prime minister's mutilated corpse could rest down there safely until the following night, by which time everything would have been arranged.

5

Saturday, 16 September

Referendum Day Minus Five

The Saturday Delivery

As the first grey-pink trickles of light touched the tops of the plane trees in Whitehall a hard core of PLS members were still at work. Amanda Andrews, the chief whip and the foreign secretary had bedded down in the PM's apartment. His study and the chancellor's rooms were firmly locked.

Alois Haydn needed little sleep. The shadows were still deep under the trees in St James's Park, and sunlight sparkling only on the very tip of the Elizabeth Tower, as he left Downing Street carrying a Waitrose 'bag for life', inside which was a freezer bag, inside which was the head of the late prime minister. He was pleased so far with the work of Professional Logistical Services, though he understood very well how much they all disliked him.

He had first run across PLS when one of his larger clients had expressed an interest in buying a state-owned Polish concrete business. When his client's approaches were rebuffed in Warsaw, Alois had turned to PLS for help. It hadn't taken them long to produce a dossier revealing the Polish company's undisclosed and highly sensitive defence and security subsidiaries. Haydn had paid them handsomely, and advised his clients not to proceed.

This defeat was accepted in a thoroughly civilised manner, involving several visits to Poland for dinners and meetings organised by PLS. By the time it was all over Haydn had made a new friend. Colonel Jerzy Babiński of the Polish security service was a sleek, chubby-faced and cheerful man in a well-cut business suit who was almost as smoothly comfortable with the ways of the modern world as Alois himself. Over the following years they had engaged in various small projects of mutual benefit; and Babiński had warmly recommended an old colleague from Białystok named Aleksander for any odd jobs his British friend might need doing. Haydn's 'chance meeting' at the service station with the three Polish brothers hadn't been anything of the kind.

When Dame Cecily had asked to see the prime minister's body so that his head could be digitally mapped, Alois had had to admit to the unpleasant operation that had been performed earlier that night. She had taken the news with exemplary calm. 'Yes, of course, quite necessary and right. Let's just get it over to the Soho team run by my friend from Shoreditch as soon as possible. And Mr Haydn, it might be better if you didn't mention it to anyone else. People are funny. Mustn't frighten the horses.' So Haydn had picked it up, and was on his way.

He hadn't gone far when he heard the loud steps of a large man, wearing proper leather shoes, close behind him.

'Going my way?'

Haydn jumped. Sir Solomon Dundas was the last man he had expected to see. The fabled financier was, as it happened, an executive member of the PLS board, but he had not been brought in on the plot. His area of expertise was the mysterious world of swap options, derivatives and gearing, not Whitehall power-broking and political pimping. Haydn had thought of asking for him to be included as part of the banking-crisis cover story, but the man had the reputation of being a bit of a blowhard, and slightly unreliable, so he had been kept at arm's length. What was he doing here? Haydn knew better than to ask directly.

'Sir Solomon. What a pleasure. And where are you off to so early this morning?'

'Well, I have some pretty big clients in the upper chamber, Mr Haydn. These days I seem to divide my time between the Lords and Lord's. Flash Harrys in ermine, flash young fellows in whites. . . Although I have to admit that the old bacon-and-egg tie means a lot more to me than trinkets with portcullises. But I'm rambling on. In answer to your question, I'm on my way to a small private bank in Mayfair. Early birds and worms, you know.'

'We may as well walk together then,' responded Haydn.

Sir Solomon was not far short of seven feet tall, and heavily built with it. Skipping along in his efforts to keep up with him, Haydn found himself almost out of breath, and the surprisingly heavy contents of the plastic bag he was carrying bounced unnervingly against his thigh. But he was not one ever to let an opportunity pass him by. Sir Solomon was well known as an opponent of the EU – he was an old friend of the one-time chancellor Nigel Lawson, and had helped to fund the UK Independence Party during its glory days.

'Solly, knowing your views, I have to ask you something,' panted Haydn. 'Do you think that if Olivia Kite pulls it off and we leave the EU, the markets really will tumble?'

'Bound to,' growled Sir Solomon. 'It would be fabulous news for our democracy, and good for all of us in the long term – but in the short term, investors are going to take fright about the uncertainty, if nothing else.'

He sucked on a small cigar, blowing fragrant clouds as he walked.

'So be careful of your portfolio, Mr Haydn. Government bonds will take a battering, but the first wave of selling will hit our blue chips – Rolls-Royce, GEC, the pharmaceuticals and so on. British Airways is an obvious target. I'd expect the FTSE to fall 20 per cent — and that, by the way, is double the technical definition of a crash. If the fellows in Number 10 haven't been worrying themselves about how to handle that, they don't deserve to be in office.'

Haydn flushed. 'It's a big organisation. Even I don't know everything that goes on. . .' But then he fell silent. He was thinking, hard. The question of the dither fund was bobbing around the front of his mind. Most of his money was safely ferreted away in the Middle East, and the rest of it was securely held but readily accessible, in case he should need to get away and disappear completely at any time in the next few weeks. But what a prize it would be to take the bulk of the dither fund and do something really spectacular with it. Alois Haydn, who always thought fast, was thinking very fast indeed just now.

After a short time, Sir Solomon halted. Nestling between a shop selling Eastern antiquities and a Parisian shoe designer was a small, yellow-painted building with a heraldic shield swinging in the breeze over its front door. Sir Solomon announced that this was his destination.

As they parted, Haydn said, 'It was good to talk to you at long last, Solomon. I hope we meet again soon.' And, still skipping, he headed on towards Soho, where he would deliver the prime minister's head to the Tintin lookalike and his friends — a group of paunchy youths whose heavy-metal T-shirts encountered soapsuds only rarely.

Alois Haydn was not a man much bothered by the inner voice of conscience. His last words to Amanda Andrews and Ronnie Ashe, both of whom were now visibly tired and nervous, had been to promise them that their role in this business would never come out; that the secret would hold, and Britain's awesome official-secrecy mechanism would close over the whole episode once the referendum was over. And yet it struck him inescapably that if he leaked everything to Olivia Kite and the 'No' campaign – in return for a promise of a personal amnesty – he could make a fortune. Could there be a bigger piece of market-changing information than that the great European referendum was going to go the way few people expected?

You can short a huge private company. Why couldn't you short an entire country? The conversation with Sir Solomon had fired Haydn up. By the time he turned into Old Compton Street, the package he was delivering seemed almost insignificant.

A Little Politics

Out in the real world, that Saturday was going to be a long day for every MP in the country. Peter Collingwood was very unhappy. He had left three or four messages the previous night for Ronnie Ashe, the chief whip. He needed an answer before he began his surgery, which was imminent.

Earlier that morning he had slipped in the shower of his rented constituency house while fulminating about the matter, and had – he thought – broken a toe. The pain was agonising. But he had not given up. He owed it to the constituency. He had pulled on his socks and shoes with considerable effort. Just as he was putting the kettle on his daughter had called from London, in a furious mood. She had come in at 3 o'clock that morning, drunk and stinking of cigarettes, and her mother had ordered her to call him. 'Mum says it's your duty to act as a father for once. The *cow*.' The conversation had not gone well. Peter could not find quite the right tone of command. In the House of Commons he was a decisive voice. He was known in the press for his strong and traditional moral views. He had a chiselled chin and dark eyes. But none of this cut any ice with his daughter.

It was too early in the morning for a call like that. She had been, frankly, rude, saying he was just full of the same old shit. He was going to make her cry again, she told him – she could feel it. Her voice was going wavery. Why were daughters so completely impossible? The conversation had gone on just long enough – 'Why don't you get a life, you poor, sad old man?' – for Peter, who was forty-nine, to miss his breakfast. By the time he hobbled to his car and set off for the school annexe where his constituency surgery was held, he was in a bad mood.

Waiting for him, he knew, would be two or three hopeless whingers, smelling of damp wool, the kind of men and women who infested doctors' surgeries day after day. They'd want him to do the impossible – resurface their road, amputate a neighbour's tree, deal with the impertinent manager of their local Tesco. Then there would be the same hard case he saw every week, a raddled ex-serviceman who had been thrown out by his wife. For good measure there would be at least one entirely insane constituent, possibly violent.

But none of this – not the pain, not the hunger, not his daughter, nor the prospect of the predictable and dispiriting hours ahead of him – was the source of his unhappiness. No. The real trouble was that a dozen, or perhaps two dozen, intelligent and friendly constituents would also be waiting for him, and would ask what he thought about the referendum and how he was going to vote. Among them would be his constituency party officers, eager to spread the word.

'Collingwood says. . .' But Collingwood did not know what to say. All his life he had prided himself on having strong views, if weakly held. But now, on the most important national question of his lifetime, he did not know which way to turn; and he suspected that if his constituency party realised he didn't know, his political career was over. 'The worst are full of passionate intensity, and the best lack all conviction,' he comforted himself. But in politics it was a meaningless truism.

Sophie, his constituency secretary, greeted him with the dispiriting news that eighteen people, most of whom were all too well known to him, were awaiting him in one of the science rooms. A formidable young woman, she stood guard by the glass door leading into the school office while he hastily grabbed a bite to eat. Ever since a Labour MP had been attacked by a constituent armed with a kitchen knife, security even at these humble surgeries had been taken very seriously. Sophie had laid out the usual selection of cheap biscuits, and the tea urn was hissing. Peter was munching his third biscuit, his mouth dry, when his phone started vibrating. He looked down to read: 'Whips' office'.

'Peter,' said Ronnie Ashe. 'You've always been a sound man, loyal but nobody's fool. I can't believe you're even thinking of not voting for us in the referendum. What *are* you playing at?'

Peter hurriedly washed out the paste of biscuits in his mouth with a swill of tea.

'Ronnie, my constituents hate Europe. They don't trust any of us. They can't understand why I would vote for more regulations, more red tape and more immigrants. This is what it's like at the sharp end, Ronnie. In two minutes the door of this room is going to open, and it's going to be the same conversation time after time.'

Ronnie, who was leading a ring-around from the whips' office at the House of Commons, started to run through the familiar achievements of the prime minister, beginning with his dramatic meeting with the German chancellor, David McAllister, and the 'Hanover Pact' which offered the prospect of a lighter-regulation and more conservative inner Northern European group in which Britain would feel more comfortable.

Nobody really knew whether this would actually lead to anything concrete – the French were dismissive, and the commissioners in Brussels were claiming that such a pact was illegal under European law. In Britain the newspapers had been divided between those which, noting the prime minister's gaunt face, had christened it the 'Hangover Pact' – a fairly friendly nod to his obvious personal exhaustion – and those that preferred the 'Handover Pact', a cynical manoeuvre which would only lead to more powers going to Berlin rather than Brussels. The facts that McAllister had a British father, had proposed to his wife by the banks of Loch Ness and spoke perfect English cut little ice: wasn't he really a Scot, after all?

But the truth remained that only this prime minister could have got German, and therefore Northern European, backing for a radical rewriting of the existing treaties. There was certainly a fight ahead in Brussels, but nobody since Margaret Thatcher had managed to change Britain's relationship with Europe so dramatically: 'Trust the prime minister and vote "Yes" ' was by far the strongest argument the whips' office had.

In Peter Collingwood's constituency that didn't feel like quite enough. Peter met, of course, a disproportionate number of voters who were full of passionate intensity, but even so it appeared that the pact was widely unpopular here. Elsewhere around the country the opinion polls showed that the prime minister was still just about winning the argument: the last-minute concessions from Berlin were seen as a dramatic and unexpected triumph. In return, the PM had given chancellor McAllister his personal pledge that the British would vote to remain in the EU.

'In the end it comes down to this, Peter,' said Ashe. 'Do you trust the PM, or don't you? You know he's the best thing that's happened to this party in years. Without him you wouldn't be an MP at all. Show him some bloody loyalty.'

Peter sighed and switched off his phone. Like most MPs, the only thing that really mattered to him in the end was getting re-elected. Whatever they thought in the South or in Scotland, here he simply couldn't risk being on the wrong side. He'd caught the look in his constituency officers' eyes. If he faltered, they'd kill him. Perhaps literally.

At that point there was a knock on the door, and the first constituent on his morning list was walking towards him. She had a pleasant, ruddy face and a shock of almost white hair. Stifling the pain from his foot, Peter managed a broad welcoming smile and mentally rehearsed his pro-European arguments. She sat down, leaned over and picked up his last biscuit.

'Now,' she said, 'here's the thing. Some plausible bastard's got me pregnant, and I don't believe in abortion. What I want to know is, *what are you going to do about it?*'

6

Sunday, 17 September

Referendum Day Minus Four

Rosy-Fingered Dawn

Had the Germans known that in the early hours of that
Sunday morning the British prime minister's headless corpse would
be carried, swaddled in an old duvet, along a subterranean tunnel
from Downing Street to a goose-dung-smeared island in the middle
of a public park, they might have begun to have second thoughts
about the Hanover Pact. The chief whip, who had been conscripted
to help carry the body, said a short prayer over it. Amanda Andrews
placed some roses on top of the grubby bundle, but there was little
time for leavetaking. A creak of rowlocks and the weak glimmer of
a torch revealed where Aleksander, Borys and Dawid were waiting
in a rowing boat they had liberated from the park's boathouse. Alois
Haydn's instructions had been clear: get rid of the body as completely
as possible.

A few hours later, a homeless alcoholic man, 'Chicken George'
MacDonald, still shaking the night-time cold off his bones, dropped
the cigarette he was lighting. Mortlake Cemetery offered security
from passing police and the shelter of a public convenience which
never closed, but at this time of day, as dawn began to colour the
early-morning river mist hanging over the gravestones, it could be
an unsettling place. Chicken George was staring at a large grey
tube, or worm, with six legs, that was moving steadily towards him
along one of the gravel paths between the headstones. The worm
stopped. Its tail and front part sagged. It seemed defeated, but then

it began to talk from both ends, and moved on again. Chicken George decided that either he was hallucinating, or this was some kind of student prank. He chose not to be frightened. He could still choose that much.

But Aleksander, Borys and Dawid, if not frightened, were at least seriously worried. They had succeeded in taking the prime minister's body from the island to the boat, and then into the back of their VW van, without being spotted. However, disposing of a heavy corpse wrapped in a stained duvet in the middle of London was proving nightmarishly difficult. The council-run refuse dumps and recycling centres were all locked up for the night. There seemed to be no pull-ins or backstreets that didn't have CCTV cameras or idle, slouching English people in them. The brothers felt vulnerable. What would happen to them if they were found with a dead body – a mutilated dead body at that? Whatever it was, it would not be good.

Eventually Borys had suggested trying a cemetery. 'If you have to hide a fish, take it to a fish shop. Dead body, cemetery. Find a hole, job done.' Mortlake, however, proved unwelcoming. Even at this hour of a Sunday morning it was home to a surprising number of council employees in yellow vests trundling about in small mechanical diggers.

By the time Dawid spotted a small iron gate leading out onto the dank, gravel river path the brothers had had more than enough of heaving and sweating. Fending off a wire-haired terrier, they dragged their burden to the bank of the Thames by a straggle of boathouses. The brothers' burden looked nothing like a boat, but, led by Aleksander, they carried it down the nearest slipway and pushed it out into the current.

'Which way will he go?' Dawid wondered as they turned to walk away.

'Up to Richmond, I think,' said Aleksander. 'The tide is coming in, and it will push everything up the river.'

But in fact the prime minister's body, kept afloat by the air in the duvet and rotating in the current, drifted at some speed towards the centre of London. It bounced off Putney Bridge, and was still afloat when it reached the globular glass monuments of the financial centre and the span of Tower Bridge. It might have ended up in a salty marsh somewhere en route to Holland, but just then the tide turned. One bare arm, on which there was a faded blue tattoo but no hand, had come clear of its wrapping, and seemed to be making a defiant gesture as the prime minister made a final ceremonial pass by Westminster. Shortly afterwards the duvet was torn off him by the current. He reached the bank of gritty slime at the foot of the formidable Victorian stonework that lines the river at Battersea, and there what was left of him came to rest at last.

7

Monday, 18 September

Referendum Day Minus Three

The Voice of the Nation

Back in Downing Street the following morning Rory Bremner was feeling that he hadn't had so much fun since John Prescott had left frontline politics. Britain's impressionists had gone through a dark period during the years when a succession of bland, smooth, professional politicians who all looked and sounded much the same had taken over with the mission, apparently, of boring the country to death. Even if you could distinguish your Cleggs from your Camerons from your Milibands – which wasn't easy – there wasn't a lot of fun to be had. At least with this prime minister there was an old-fashioned character to get your teeth into. Unfortunately, by the time he came into office the public's taste had turned so far away from politics that it was hard to elbow one's way past the game shows and endless quiz programmes.

Bremner had spent most of the previous twenty-four hours hunched over the desk he had been given in the prime minister's private flat upstairs in Downing Street, playing back TV and radio downloads to get that voice exactly right, with its undercurrent of Lancashire and its slightly mushed syllables, the knowing hesitations, the half-chuckles after a well-delivered line. But this was not for the purposes of entertainment: as well as the general public, Bremner would also have to speak in private to people who knew the prime minister well. No easy gig.

Earlier that morning the chief whip had passed him a thick folder containing scripted answers, private in-jokes and ideas for deflecting dangerous questions which had been prepared for Bremner's first outings – a telephone conversation with the king, closely followed by Dermot Murnaghan's radio phone-in.

Soon enough there was no more time to prepare. The foreign secretary, Jason Latimer, and Amanda Andrews were sitting on either side of him, pens poised. The phone was set to speaker, and there was an audible gasp from the trio when the king's voice came through the plastic grille.

'Prime minister.'

'Your Majesty. I really must apologise for my discourtesy this morning.'

'Yes, you really must. I may be a poor, weatherbeaten, ridiculed old fellow, but I am still your king. Dare I say, you'd do well to remember it.'

'Come, come, Your Majesty. Surely we are not merely a humble subject and his monarch, but two old friends . . .'

'I never wanted to be king, you know. Who wants to be gagged? You know the Wordsworth thing, prime minister? The very prison walls, and all that – suit of shabby grey, cricket cap. "And his step seemed light and gay; But I never saw a man who looked so wistfully at the day." I do feel a bit wistful. Doesn't help when I'm ignored as well.'

'Oscar Wilde, sir, I think you'll find. But your point is very well taken. The truth is, I consult you in my thoughts all the time. Nobody else has stood up to the brutalities of the modern world quite like you. And your words stick. Nobody knows as well as you, sir, how invaluable your advice has been these many years. That familiar handwriting on your letters has always made my heart lift. . .' Bremner wondered if he was laying it on a bit too thick. For years the king's 'black spider' letters had been notorious throughout Westminster. Virtually every minister had cursed them at one time or another. But the monarch took the bait.

'Well, prime minister, you are very kind. Some of your – erm – more – aah – jumped-up colleagues have not been. I do worry so very much about whether the national thingy is not, as it were. . .'

'Education? Schools?'

'Exactly. I feel we need to see a more holistic. . . return to curiosity, and wonder, and so forth. Wendell Berry. The Lake poets. Wonder. That's the thing. Do you read the Koran?'

Without pausing a beat, Bremner replied, 'Every morning, Your Majesty.'

'Well, prime minister, that is a great relief to me. But when we weave together we must surely choose harmonious colours, and cut our cloth, as it were, to the shape of our ancient fields. Do you not agree?'

'Beautifully put, sir.'

'So that is my poor, old, out-of-date and I am sure highly unfashionable problem with this European business. I have drawn up some notes. Some few pages of notes. I had hoped to have time to discuss them with you personally. Given, aah, that you are my first minister and so forth.'

Bremner decided he'd had enough of this. 'Why don't you send them in the box, sir? May I speak openly? If we leave the EU now, your government will be rendered virtually bankrupt by the flight of capital and the financial institutions moving overseas. I will have to jack up taxes. And perhaps even extend them to hitherto unthinkable parts of the nation.'

'Unthinkable parts?'

'Yes, hitherto unthinkable. Tearing up ancient and historic compacts between the Treasury and, for instance. . .'

'Prime minister, you are not suggesting. . .'

'So long as we stay in, everything can carry on much as it has done. But make no mistake, sir, leaving the European Union would have unavoidable consequences for – and let me put this delicately – the established ways. As your most loyal and devoted subject, I could not feel easy in my own mind unless I had spoken to you plainly.'

There was a brief silence before the king's voice came down the line again. 'Well, prime minister, you have always been a good friend to my family. I cannot deny that. And you have certainly spoken very plainly indeed. I will bear what you say in mind. May we turn to the question of phosphates?'

At this point Switch, alerted in advance, intervened to say that His Holiness the Pope was on the line, and Bremner was able to put an end to the call.

The feeling in the room was that the conversation had gone more smoothly than any of them had dared hope. A delighted and relieved Latimer said to Andrews, 'Well, Amanda, you were quite right. This chap's a genius.'

'Merely a professional, my loves,' Bremner murmured, though he was quietly rather proud of how well the call seemed to have gone. He was also beginning to glimpse the seductive power that had, however briefly, been offered to him.

Things started to go a little awry with the radio phone-in.

'It's good to have you with us at the beginning of such an important week for Britain's future – and, if I may say so, for your own – prime minister,' said Dermot Murnaghan. 'Our first question is from Caroline in Twickenham, and no surprise here, it's about Europe.'

'Good morning, prime minister. Caroline here. You've been campaigning relentlessly to keep Britain in the EU. What will you do if the result goes against you? You can't carry on, can you? So what are your personal plans in that event?'

Latimer wrote the single word 'Deflect' on a piece of paper and passed it to Bremner. But he was already replying.

'Good morning, Dermot, and good morning to all the listeners. Well, Caroline, you're absolutely right about one thing. If the electorate decides to leave the European Union – I hope and believe that they won't, but if they do – I would immediately step down as leader of the government. What happened then would be determined by how the parliamentary arithmetic stacks up.'

'Yes, that's pretty clear,' said Caroline from Twickenham. 'But my question was really about you. Would you be like David Miliband, and leave politics altogether? Or would you stay in the House of Commons?'

'Caroline, I have no hesitation in telling you now that should the result of this referendum go against me, I will immediately resign my parliamentary seat and leave politics. I simply could not bear to have a ringside seat at the decline of this great country. But I would like to take this opportunity to assure you, and all the listeners, that I am quite fit, and' – Bremner found himself saying – 'I have always rather wanted to face the music and. . . dance.'

By now Latimer was doing a dance of his own, waving his arms, shaking his head and making zip-it gestures. But Bremner seemed not to notice.

Huffing with excitement, Dermot Murnaghan broke in: 'Dance, prime minister? Dancing how? Dancing on ice? Are you being serious?'

'Now now, Dermot, you are just being malicious. I was thinking of course about ballroom dancing. I am of the foxtrot and quickstep generation, and I'm still pretty light on my toes. I imagine there are many patriotic British ladies who would be happy to pay for a dance with a former prime minister, don't you? I have after all spent most of the last ten years dancing – dancing on thin ice.

Perhaps I could demonstrate my talents on a cruise liner or something. Or surely there's a BBC television show?'

Latimer and Amanda were both staring at him aghast, but Bremner was concentrating so hard on getting the PM's voice right that he was almost unaware of what he was saying.

The next caller, Jane from Ealing, surprised him with a question on housing, and apparently achieved an unexpected minor alteration in government policy. Latimer slipped him a note that read 'You've just changed the government's position!' Bremner gave him a small smile.

Another light on the phone, another caller on the line.

'Polly from Chalk Farm, prime minister. I don't know if you've seen the latest numbers on university admissions from state schools, but I'm outraged, and I think the time has come to look again at tuition fees. I know it would be expensive, but —'

Bremner broke in. 'But it's an investment in the future isn't it, Polly? I have to say that I too am shocked at the drop-off in admissions. So yes, you have a point. We are going to look at this again, and at the very least we will prune back current charges. The universities will simply have to cope.'

Another note from Latimer: 'Have you any idea how much money you have spent in the last ten seconds?' Bremner smiled and shrugged. He was trying to calculate how far he could go. He could hardly change nuclear-defence policy, or move the seat of government to Stoke-on-Trent, but he might, he felt, be able to exert a modest benign influence. So when Reg Dwight from Pinner pleaded for an increase in arts funding he found the prime minister surprisingly receptive; and when Sarah Harris from Oxford demanded a ban on plastic bags she got a clear pledge that it would be enacted by the end of the year.

All around the country junior ministers were gaping at their radios in disbelief. But then Bremner wrapped up the phone-in with a long prime ministerial lecture on the importance of staying inside the European Union that was so larded with literary quotations and obscure historical allusions that any suspicions faded away. Even so, it had been the most expensive phone-in in British political history, and Bremner had enjoyed himself hugely.

His thoughts were interrupted by a tinny rattle as a little green light began to flash on the phone. Amanda picked up the receiver then turned, ashen-faced, to Bremner.

'Your wife wants to speak to you.'

'*My* wife? Or *his*?'

'His.'

'Oh fuck.'

It turned out to be a close shave. Bremner teased the prime minister's estranged wife about her taste in shoes, and invited her to join him for his final speech of the referendum campaign. She retorted that she was going to be away on holiday. This was followed by an uncomfortably long silence, at the end of which she said that he didn't sound quite himself. Was he all right?

'All right? I'd be a lot all righter, my darling, if you were alongside me in the biggest crisis of my life instead of chucking bottles from the street.'

'You were the one, sweetie, who put me out on the street, remember?'

'Let's not go over all that bloody ancient history again. . .'

'Do you think I have the slightest intention of humiliating myself by slinking back into that building and seeing tart-face, with her skirt up to her knickers?'

'Of all the stupid, paranoid accusations you've made over the years, sweetheart, that's about the lowest.'

'Oh for Christ's sake, everybody knows. The fact that she looks like a boy only leads people to speculate about your real urges. God, you disgust me.'

'Not half as much as you disgust me, darling. I hope I never see you again. Just keep out of my way. Go and give yourself a melanoma on some celebrity-crawling strip of grit. I'll make my own arrangements once this is all over. Goodbye.'

'Ta ta, you pathetic plonker.'

Although this was a private call, Professional Logistical Services were listening in from their headquarters next door in Number 11. It was decided that it would be going too far actually to leak a recording of the conversation to the press, but calls to a couple of spectacularly untrustworthy bloggers meant that yet more stories were running within the hour about the prime minister being distracted by a blazing row with his wife.

That was just a minor bit of opportunism. Thanks to PLS, nobody was now going to accuse the prime minister of not being active enough. The minister for further education, who had long been worried about tuition fees, was contacted by his former permanent secretary – now working for PLS – who told him that it was vital, to fend off an irate Treasury, that he immediately tell the media that the change of policy on the issue had been agreed at a meeting between himself and the prime minister the previous day. No, strictly speaking it hadn't happened, but that was merely a technical matter, as a result of the PM's overloaded diary. In strategic terms it *had* happened, and the minister would be well advised to make that clear. He would have the full backing of Number 10, and the chancellor would be unable to reverse the change. PLS then brought in the chief whip, to phone the angry chancellor in Wales and persuade him that in order for him not to appear humiliated or overruled, it would be advisable for him to say that he had prior knowledge of the change, and had discussed it in cordial terms with the prime minister that morning.

Working closely with Nelson Fraser, PLS issued a series of remarkably eloquent short addresses – 'stump speeches' that the prime minister was giving during a series of brief, impromptu 'regional tours' in places just a little too out-of-the-way for the television crews to reach in time. Constituency chairmen were tipped off: the PM is coming to your area, and it would be good publicity if he spoke locally. Sadly, his diary's completely manic, so would you mind if we just issued a press release saying that he said the following in Marbury Magna, or Dimbleby Parva? The local party officials, delighted to be able to drop into the lunchtime conversation that Number 10 had been on the line again, were uniformly obliging. So the prime minister's interventions – witty, waspish about Olivia Kite, warning against complacency – were faithfully reported on radio bulletins and in local papers. Inert and dismembered though he may have been, the man was a whirlwind.

In this he was only following a long-established, if rarely admitted, tradition in British politics. Every Friday when the House is sitting the long, polished wooden table where hacks gather in the lower press gallery at Westminster is littered with speeches. Journalists on the weekend rota browse through them like shoppers at a market stall of dodgy fruit before selecting some from the dozen or so strewn before them to carry away and 'write up'.

Each speech carries a self-important rubric at the top of its opening page explaining that it is to be delivered by the leader of the opposition, or the minister of state for defence procurement, or an ambitious backbencher 'at a meeting in his constituency', or in some obscure school hall or industrial unit. And each one comes with a health warning: 'Check against delivery.' Nobody ever bothers to do this, or ever will. No newspaper has the staff any longer to actually send somebody to trek off to hear these speeches being given. Audience-less, they may nevertheless generate plenty of comment, criticism, applause and editorial reaction over the days to come.

The team in Downing Street understood this very well, and had been exploiting the laziness of British journalism quite ruthlessly. In fact, thanks to Nelson Fraser's industry, in the twenty-four hours after his death the prime minister gave more speeches than he had done in an average fortnight when he was alive. His attacks on what he called Olivia Kite's jingoistic scaremongering became ever more pungent, personal and borderline offensive. His warnings about the terrible impact on the City and on British exports if the country voted to leave the EU were familiar, but were now delivered with an added urgency.

8

Tuesday, 19 September

Referendum Day Minus Two

The Campaign

What a man. What a leader. Over the weekend, as Whitehall insiders knew, the prime minister had been working flat out in Number 10, talking to bankers across Europe about the possible consequences of a 'No' vote. Yet now, exhausted as he must be, he was finding time for a succession of media broadcasts and flying visits to far-flung regions.

And on it went, the scattering of chaff. On Tuesday morning the PM trounced the cantankerous Welsh presenter of the *Today* programme, being perhaps a little funnier than usual in the process, but also entirely in command of the arguments in the final run-up to the vote. Some listeners, concentrating unusually hard, thought they detected a literary exuberance in his use of words like 'sapient', 'pharisaical' and 'prelapsarian' that they hadn't noticed before, although hardly anyone thought it worth mentioning, even across a kitchen table or on Witter.

Back in Downing Street, however, there remained the huge problem of visibility. Digitally, it turned out that there was a surprising amount that could be done. A couple of computer wizards in a windowless basement studio in Old Compton Street – if wizards can look too young to shave – had subjected the PM's head to an advanced scanning process, and the resulting computerised images had been stored on a USB drive and were being digitally manipu-

lated by an aged goth who had been installed in the by-now rank
and airless Treasury dining room.

Dame Cecily was padding impatiently around this genius of
computer animation, seemingly oblivious to his numerous tattoos
and piercings. She made him feel nervous, but he got on with his
work, playing about with an increasingly realistic simulation of the
prime minister's face. Using 3D digital mapping the PM's head was
spliced into footage from old press conferences and election
hustings. The resulting images gave a convincing impression that he
had been out and about at a succession of events in the Birmingham
area. He was glimpsed only in flashes, never in close-up, but no
one looking at the footage would doubt that the PM had been
present.

Dame Cecily's team used old video clips, stored in the private
office archives, of the prime minister seen at a distance or from
behind, and overdubbed them with Rory Bremner's vocal mimicry.
The PM appeared to be haranguing a crowd, just out of vision,
about that morning's headlines (PM 'DISTRACTED' BY WIFE'S
ANGER). They had a stroke of luck when a burst of heavy rain
lashed Downing Street, meaning that Bremner, wearing a wig and
one of the prime minister's trademark pinstripe suits, could carry
a big umbrella which hid him from the single TV camera stationed
there as he climbed into the back of his official car before being
driven off at high speed.

For added security, on Sunday afternoon some of the PLS
personnel had been relocated to the COBRA emergency room –
the secure committee room used for major government crises.
From there a small convoy of limousines with motorcycle outriders
was easy enough to fix. Sir Dickie Greene, rubbing his long hairy
ears and snorting with impatience, cornered the Met commissioner
to demand extra security for reasons he couldn't go into. 'Lots of

the boys on bikes, chief, if you don't mind.' The commissioner, who remembered Sir Dickie from tense COBRA meetings in the old days, didn't even think of saying no; and so, wherever Bremner went he was accompanied by more sirens and BMW R1200s than the flashiest third-world dictator could hope for. 'It's the noisiest bloody undercover operation in history,' said Sir Dickie, clapping his hands.

The plotters quickly came to understand just how thin these confected photo-opportunity visits really are. When the politician arrives, almost nobody actually sees him in the flesh. People rely for their impression of the event on glimpses provided by the television cameras, which combine to produce a common false memory. News bulletins and press photographs reassure the public that the events they see on television or read about have actually happened; a willing suspension of disbelief spreads like mist. With or without a living prime minister, the odder, sharper, slightly more inexplicable three-dimensional world of reality is pumiced and reshaped every hour of every day.

Prime ministers exist partially as background reassurance that the world is not entirely disorderly, that someone somewhere is taking responsibility. Laziness and habit, a weary assumption by the public that they know the news before they see or hear about it, made the job of hiding the prime minister's death easier than the cabal had believed would be possible.

Hiding it from the general public, at least. Lord Briskett was sniffing about, and if he somehow stumbled upon the truth he could become the single biggest problem of all. When Amanda had rung, full of apologies, to tell him that unfortunately the PM would not now be able to make their rearranged meeting, he had seemed entirely unsurprised − in fact even a little pleased, as if priding himself on his famous nose being thoroughly vindicated. The ruse about the king's Europhobia had bought the plotters a bit of time, but Briskett was clever, determined and gossipy. PLS had managed to smear him just a little, with a few words dropped into editorial ears about his fondness for a drink, for getting above himself, exaggerating his contacts. But Briskett was too respected, just too damn good, for this dirty work to neutralise him completely. PLS were listening in to his phone messages, and were following him too, as he buzzed around London like a hiveless bee between various bookshops, his club and his flat.

Alois Haydn confronted Dame Cecily. 'I brought you people in because you can do anything – at least that's what I told Number 10. Now we have a hairy-suited, polished-brogued, nasal-voiced potential fuck-up, and you have no plan?'

'What do you suggest, little man? Bribery? Blackmail?'

'Well, some sort of . . . *inducement* might be worth considering, Dame Cecily.'

'If you think that Trevor Briskett, a man I have known and not entirely liked for more than twenty years, can be bought off, then you are not the judge of human character your reputation suggests.'

'You mean he's rich enough and famous enough already?'

'No, I'm afraid it's much worse than that. He may have his ridiculous side, but at heart he's honourable.'

Haydn felt himself beginning to sulk. 'People drop dead every day. Why can't it be the right people, at the right time?'

That afternoon, drawing all the wizards' tricks together, the plotters succeeded in carrying off their greatest achievement. The prime minister, it was announced, would be visiting the Bluewater shopping centre in Kent. Bremner, protesting hotly, had been persuaded to get back into his wig and the prime minister's suit. By means of some brief glimpses of his back and a 'security alert' which allowed the release to the media of a blurred CCTV image, plus the insertion of a month-old clip which had not been used by the main bulletins, a thoroughly busy and plausible prime ministerial day was confected.

To all intents and purposes this *was* a visit to meet a group of shopworkers who were worried about the effect leaving Europe would have on their jobs. It had heft, movement and colour. Everyone *knew* the PM had been there in person – although nobody, if pressed, would have been able to say quite *how* they knew. He was always just around the corner, just leaving, or just a little delayed. There was a real cheer of triumph in Downing Street when two teenage assistants from the Gap store spoke on camera to Sir Nick Robinson about what the prime minister had told them. It was another unexpected bonus when an elderly shopper popped up to tell the cameras that she had given 'the old fraud' a blast of English common sense. He had looked, she said with considerable self-satisfaction, 'like I'd whacked him across the face with a wet fish'. This gave rise to a second delighted cheer in Downing Street.

As so often, the British public was playing an active, even enthusiastic, role in its own deception.

A Coffee Break

After the cancellation of the previous day's interview with the prime minister, Ned Parminter had stayed on in London. All night he had tossed and turned in an overheated and clammy Paddington hotel room thinking about Jennifer Lewis. He had an ideal Jen firmly stuck in his head, a lissom, prancing faun with jade eyes that cut through his dreams.

At exactly the appointed hour he arrived at the branch of Caffè Nero near Piccadilly Circus which she had suggested for their rearranged meeting. Looking around, he felt a stab of disappointment that he could see no sign of her.

He joined the queue at the counter. In front of him was a honey-skinned, voluptuous Italian girl with cascades of glossy black hair. Ned barely noticed her. Jen, he was thinking, would want a skinny medium cappuccino, extra shot, and no pastry. Feeling a spasm of tiredness even though it was only mid-morning, he ordered for both of them, choosing a latte for himself and a muffin, making a mental promise that he'd only eat half of it. When, he wondered, did we start thinking that a lump of cake and a polystyrene cup of hot milk constituted a wholesome breakfast?

He'd paid and was waiting for the coffees when he saw Jen, more street urchin than faun, rapping on the window and pointing at a table outside, just under the horse statue. She didn't smoke, but she knew that he did, and he gave her a little nod of thanks. He had forgotten how she always took charge of things. There was just enough sun to make an outdoor seat possible.

After a bit of small talk Jen confirmed that Olivia Kite was still on board with Lord Briskett's book, and would be happy to fill in the 'No' campaign's side of the story of the last days of the campaign. She mentioned that the latest polling was mouth-watering, but Parminter couldn't help noticing that she didn't seem her usual bright self. Her long, pale hands were shaking a little, and she kept brushing her hair out of her tired green eyes. After she'd finished her coffee she cleared her throat, reached into her bag and drew out a thick plastic folder.

'This is the stuff I mentioned. I'll also email it to you as usual, but it's easier to read this way. It tells you exactly what we make of the latest polls. I've stuck in the minutes of yesterday's steering-committee meeting; you'll get one of those every day from now on. And printouts of Olivia's emails from the leader of the opposition, UKIP and the Scottish Nationalists, and hers to them. She's on fire.' But Jen's tone was curiously listless.

'That's fantastic.' Parminter paused for a moment, wondering if he should say something. This didn't feel the way it had in his early-morning dreams. Could he perhaps rest a hand on her arm? Brush his fingers down her pale cheek? He so badly wanted to kiss her, to tell her that he would protect her forever. But Ned Parminter prized his dignity. He trembled, but he did not make a move, and kept the conversation briskly facetious.

'You're a complete star and a fine human being. And what's the verdict? What does Olivia Kite think it all adds up to?'

'Well, it's bloody tight, Ned. It's tighter than the PM's letting on, or any of them. We're still behind nationally, though we're ahead in the Midlands, the West Country and the South-East generally. They've got London sewn up, and Scotland and the North. We're ahead with C1s, C2s, older men and women and – get this – with students. They're doing as well as ever with younger women. But we think their lead's under one per cent overall now.'

Parminter broke his promise to himself and finished off the last of the muffin. He could feel himself shaking with excitement, and pulled out a cigarette.

'And that's down to the PM, right? If it wasn't for him –'

'Exactly. If the public didn't still love him deep down, we'd be cruising to victory.'

Despite her apparent tiredness, Jennifer's excitement provoked her to do something uncharacteristic. She leaned over, pulled Ned's cigarette gently from his lips, took a deep puff, and replaced it.

'I think I like the beard, by the way,' she said. 'Anyway, people may hate the PM for what he's doing in the Middle East. They may laugh at that mane of hair and the plonking Lancashire-variety-club jokes. But there's still enough of the old magic, I'm afraid. In some funny way they still love the old sod. People admire Olivia. They stop talking and listen when she's on the telly. But they don't love her.'

'And Olivia's afraid that he'll pull victory from the jaws of defeat one more time?'

'She's a clever woman. Even though I don't exactly love her, I really admire that brain. She doesn't fool herself, Ned. Olivia Kite can be scary and hard, but she knows it, and she knows her own limitations. She's fighting like fury against a great, loveable, incoherent, charismatic, contradictory, sexy. . . *blob*. And it drives her nuts.'

'Still,' said Ned, 'all the PM has to do now is throw himself into these last few days – really get out there among the voters and remind them why they followed him even when they were laughing at him.'

'Yes, yes. . . but he's being so slow about it. There are only two days to go. I can't think why he's leaving it so late.'

Ned Parminter buttoned his coat and slipped the folder neatly into his briefcase.

'Clever tactics, I guess. The later he leaves it, the more impact it will have. He always was a brilliant tactician. But that's exactly the sort of thing we need to ask him. What Briskett needs to get.'

He stood up. Jen, suddenly looking about seven years old with her short green skirt and bright red hair, remained sitting.

'You OK, Jen?'

'Mm. Sure. . .'

'I mean, I know we need to talk. . . about the other stuff. And about that crazy man Lucien McBryde. You don't half pick them, girl.'

'Yes,' said Jen, shaking herself and managing a smile as she rose from her chair. 'But this isn't the time. It's just. . . Lucien and I had such a bad scene that I was really frightened for him; and now, although he's left me a few text messages, he's not answering his phone. He's really upset, Ned. Really upset. He has been for months. I'm worried about him.'

They stood for a moment, staring into each other's faces. Then Ned leaned down, cupped her face and kissed her, holding her tightly against him. She must have felt him harden. That she didn't pull away kept him warm for the rest of the day.

Syntax and Sincerity

'**I'll call this afternoon. Promise,' said Ned. With that he** left her, dodging the Piccadilly taxis before striding down St James's Street towards the park.

Jen collected the empty coffee cartons and the paper plate, deposited them tidily in the bin provided, and then, after confirming the last text from McBryde, headed off to the London Library. She went straight to the British history section, pulled out a book by Dominic Sandbrook, extracted a white envelope and put it firmly into her bag. Once she was back out in St James's Square she hailed a cab and clambered in, patted her pocket to check her mobile was still there – it hadn't vibrated for at least ten minutes – and asked for Falkland Road in Kentish Town. She checked her emails as the cab dodged its way through the tourists and cyclists. (What had cab travel been like, she wondered, before the relentless, uninvited display of Lycra-bagged masculine arse?)

Feeling slightly queasy, Jen tried to stifle her thoughts about both Lucien McBryde and Ned Parminter – clever, sussed, grown-up Ned Parminter, who would have fucked her in the café's loo if she'd given him the slightest encouragement. Ned Parminter, who wasn't frightened by commitment, indeed seemed to be wordlessly urging it.

If she could just stop. . . *thinking*. . . Could give her brain a rest.

But Lucien McBryde would not allow that. Jostling his way into her mind, past the emails from campaign HQ, Politicshome,

Editorial Intelligence, Coffeehouse and the rest, was the pleading, floppy-haired, chaotic, unreliable, manic, coke-encrusted journalist with his irresistible lopsided smile.

Just then an 'urgent'-flagged message pinged in from Essex. Had she seen the new polling from YouGov? Another: could she speak to the US ambassador, who was asking for a personal briefing from Olivia, and put him off until tomorrow? Yes, and yes. More messages in bold in her inbox: her mother was already starting to worry about next summer, and whether she should book the cottage.

But still no word from the one person Jen actually wanted to hear from. She texted McBryde yet again. Her thumbs seemed slow and witless today. It wasn't really a question of what to say, it was the tone. Kind, concerned, regretful – no, not regretful – a little tough. Stupid emotions. . .

By the time she'd composed and sent the text, the taxi was halfway up the grimly predictable parade of Kentish Town High Street. Jen scrabbled for her keys. £15 and twenty-five minutes poorer, she opened the turquoise-painted door in Falkland Road and stooped to pick up her mail before delving into her bag for the object that had been haunting her ever since she had picked it out of the book in the London Library. There it was, a white envelope with her name written on it in a spiralling, once-familiar script. *Handwriting* – from him? She hadn't seen that for months now. 'Jen', with a huge, long, curling J. Her heart jumped in response.

Putting the envelope down next to the sink, she switched the kettle on. Four-fifths of the art of learning to live alone was self-discipline, imposing order even when you didn't feel like it. So, coffee. Then jacket off. Then check the answerphone. Check the milk in the fridge. Only then. Sit down. She tore the envelope open like a madwoman.

Dear Jen.

You know, first, I'm so sorry. I'm really sorry. I'm sorry for being an arsehole. I'm sorry for what I said the other night.

This is weird. I haven't written to you like this for so long — really written, on paper. I'm going to slip it through to you in the old way.

I'm really sorry for being a moron the other night, and for what I said. You can see who you want. I know I don't have any right to tell you who you can see. I've screwed up big time, and there's nobody to blame but me.

But I just have to say that without Jen Lewis, Lucien McB is absolutely fucking nothing. I'm desolate, Jen. I'm going out of my fucking mind.

But that's not why I'm writing this.

For the past day or so I've had an odd feeling that something's up at Number 10. Then, yesterday evening, I had a call from that weird, creepy PR guy who's always hanging around in the shadows, Alois Haydn. I'm sure you must have met him. He said he wanted to see me, and that it was urgent.

I've sent you, enclosed, what he told me. If it's true, it's the biggest political story imaginable. But the thing is, it's just killing me. It's really wrong.

He said I should do with it what I thought was right, but that I couldn't just put it in the paper, because it was too big. Jen, he said I should talk to you, and that you'd know who to take it to. (Her, I guess.)

Well, Jen, I don't think we're talking at the moment, are we? So, being a bit paranoid and everything — but not, I swear, even a little high — I thought I'd get it down on paper and slip it between the sheets.

And one last thing, Jen. No — doesn't matter —

X M

Enclosed with the handwritten letter was a single typewritten sheet of paper. Jen read it.

Then she read it again, forcing herself to concentrate, sentence by sentence. When she had finished, she gasped. This was impossible. It would change everything.

Double-Cross

Alois Haydn agreed entirely. It would change everything.

Professional Logistical Services had chalked up some notable successes. The prime minister (in the person of Rory Bremner) was still broadcasting, and his speeches were being widely praised. Amazingly, nobody from Number 10 had gone public with any suspicions. But a clutch of private secretaries were causing real difficulties; a meeting with them, Dame Cecily, the chief whip and the former Joint Intelligence Committee chairman had been arranged for later that day in COBRA. The plotters' tactics for that meeting – tell the truth and try to win them over, or tell the big lie and keep their fingers crossed – had yet to be agreed.

Only one man never faltered or flinched. Alois Haydn had put his arms around Amanda Andrews and promised her – and Ronnie Ashe, who was with her – that this would never, *ever* get out. Everyone just needed to keep their nerve for two more days. Haydn had the ability to mesmerise people into calm, into acquiescence.

From there he went directly to meet Sir Solomon Dundas and Charmian Locke, to make damn sure that if the entire plot was leaked just before the vote, he would indeed become an extremely rich man.

They met in Mayfair, three shadows in the back row of the Curzon cinema. The location had been Sir Solomon's idea.

The cricket-crazed father of eight and former private banker did not quite fit into the social world of the rest of PLS. At sixty-six he was a little young, and a great deal too flamboyant. Described in 2014 as 'the best egg of all good eggs' by the insurgent UKIP leader Nigel Farage, his long arms dangled from an ungainly body, encased in purple and green tweed. But Sir Solomon brought to PLS a deep knowledge of the London financial world, dating back almost four decades, which the organisation's former civil servants greatly valued.

When his toothy subordinate Charmian Locke had first told him about the exotic Alois Haydn, a man Solomon knew only by reputation, he had been intrigued but cautious. He had left Whitehall early on Saturday morning purely to follow Haydn and strike up a conversation: the 'private bank' into which he had gone turned out, to his considerable embarrassment, to be a 'gentlemen's club', or upmarket brothel.

So where should they meet for a sensitive discussion, one neither man wanted anybody else in PLS to know about? As he did on most things, Sir Solomon had consulted Charmian Locke. It was a surprisingly tricky dilemma. Where in London could a chap arrange a meeting with absolutely no danger of being seen or overheard? Lord's? No good. Wouldn't want to spoil a good morning's cricket. . . Any decent restaurant might have an acquaintance in it; any ordinary restaurant was, well, unthinkable. Parks were full of members of the public with mobile phones and cameras. Almost every street, underpass and underground station was covered by CCTV.

'Culture! That's the ticket. Blasted bloody stuff,' said Sir Solomon. His secretary, who loyally arrived at his private office at four every morning so that Sir Solomon's desk was clear for him to start work at seven, tracked down a morning screening of a Shakespeare season by a no-longer-fashionable Russian film-maker.

The Curzon was quiet, certainly, but it had the disadvantage that the three men had to sit awkwardly, twisted towards one another. As the usher swept her torch around the auditorium, Charmian's teeth gleamed briefly back at her, like the cliffs of Dover on a moonlit night.

Alois Haydn was speaking.

'You have to believe, gentlemen, that I have market-changing information which I cannot divulge to you just now. This referendum is not going to go the way that everybody thinks.'

Sir Solomon shifted in his seat and growled, 'I devoutly hope you are right. I hope we are going to get out. But you, sir, may *think* it — you cannot *know* it.'

'Trust me, I do.'

'The polling companies tell us. . .'

'I *know* it.'

'And your friend the prime minister is giving the performance of his life, Mr Haydn.'

'*I know it.*'

'The question ish, Sholomon,' broke in Charmian, 'in these circumstances, how could our friend here make a *leetle* money?'

Now that the real subject of their clandestine meeting had been put to him squarely and openly, Sir Solomon came to life.

'There is no doubt that serious money could be made. If you genuinely have sensitive, market-moving information that is big enough, and that is known by no one else, you have a golden key. You have equities, gilts and currency to play with. All are going to be affected. There will be a considerable shock in the City.' Sir Solomon paused and performed some rapid mental calculations. 'At a stroke, sterling would lose its reserve status, and as I mentioned during our previous chance encounter, I would expect the FTSE to drop by 20 per cent. So then. Equities. Simple and clear. You buy "put" options to short them, then they plummet, and three or four weeks later, at the bottom of the market, you clean up. Your targets are obvious. The big exporters and transporters, and the financials, who have to be inside the EU to trade in euros. They will all take a big hit.'

Charmian could see that Alois was eager, but was hazy about the details.

'Sho what you have to do ish buy options to sell BA at, shay, £4.50 in a month's time. They're a fiver now. If they fall to £4, you're up 50p a share. Get in big enough – and all this is hugely leveraged, remember – and you will be filling your boots. Right, Shir Sholomon?'

'Wrong, I fear,' said Solomon. 'But it's a bold thought. In effect you are shorting not just a few companies, but the entire UK. However, equities are no go, not at this scale and at the speed you propose. Warning lights would flash right across the City. You'd have to get out of the country, clear out quick. And even if you got your profit wired overseas you'd be charged with insider trading and extradited. Mr Haydn, you'd end up being buggered senseless in jug. Not my idea of a happy ending.'

Charmian twisted on his seat. He was smiling hugely. 'There'sh a much easier way. Gilts are too tricky to be sure about. But currenshy! Short the pound against the dollar. Shell a month forward and you can trade as much as you like, with makshimum anonymity.' In the darkness of the cinema, a huge shadow moved: Sir Solomon was nodding his agreement.

Increasingly excited, he and Charmian began to talk numbers. 'If the UK does leave the EU – well, the dollar is 1.55 to the pound now. Sterling will no longer be a reserve currency, so it will fall to, say, 1.35. Probably lower than that. You'd want to sell a hundred million dollars of sterling forward for a couple of weeks. You buy the right to sell at 1.50, and sterling falls to 1.25. So you're making twenty-five, and it costs you 1p or 2p per pound max.'

Sir Solomon paused. Haydn was desperately trying to calculate his profit, and failing.

Charmian butted in. 'But if you buy forward for jusht two weeksh. . . That would only cosht you half a penny a pop. If your margin is 20p, then you've multiplied your inveshtment' – he tapped the calculator on his iPhone – 'forty times over. But you'll have to move very fast. You do have an offshore account, don't you?'

Forty times over.

Forty times over.

They sat in silence, entranced, as Russian kings and princesses pirouetted across the screen.

Solomon turned directly to Alois. 'And the extraordinary thing is this. I'm pretty sure that, by a curious anomaly of British law, shorting sterling on the basis of confidential inside information is entirely legal.'

'Legal? What do you mean, legal?' Alois asked.

'I mean legal as in not being illegal, Mr Haydn. Not against the law.'

Alois was thinking of the lengths he'd gone to in the Middle East to hide his wealth. He was thinking of his increasingly elaborate plans to vanish. 'So shorting the currency on the basis of private information which the rest of the market doesn't have is entirely legal? I can scoop that forty times over, and no one can say anything about it?'

'They can say what they like, and I'm sure they will. But no one can touch you.'

'That's extraordinary. It's a loophole, is it?'

'A loophole, Mr Haydn, is exactly what it is.'

Haydn laughed. Solomon chuckled. Charmian silently bared his enormous teeth.

'Now, gentlemen,' said Haydn, 'this is something anyone can try. I am not. . . narrowly exclusive. I am happy to aid my fellow man. If a Sir Solomon Dundas or a Mr Charmian Locke should wish to dip into the pot, I am no loser. In addition, Solomon, you get the political outcome you long for. However. Alternatively. Nevertheless. The whole thing depends on timing. It requires the contacts and the credibility for maximum impact – first the purchase, then the explosion, tick-tock. And that's my talent. On this you must trust me. If not, gentlemen, you may end up losing a great deal of money. I never knew her as a child, but – mum's the word.'

Charmian's teeth waggled. Sir Solomon wobbled.

Alois Haydn Can Fly

Haydn left the cinema and found himself walking through Green Park almost on automatic pilot. He was thinking fiercely. As his small, leather-clad feet padded swiftly across the grass, he appeared to be gliding. His eyes were dark, spongy sultanas; they almost vanished into his face. It was time to take the plunge.

So – the prime minister was dead. That was the first thing.

The public did not know this. That was the second.

The third thing was that when they heard about it, it would change the referendum result. It would have to. It was the prime minister's personal agreement with the German chancellor that was the sole basis for the current narrow majority in favour of a 'Yes' vote. But if the public discovered he was dead, and not only that, but (the fourth thing) that his death had been covered up by the same inner cabal of politicians they already blamed for lying to them over the years about Europe and so much else. . . Well, the reaction would be spectacular. The vote would certainly go the other way.

And then they would string up Amanda Andrews, the chief whip, the foreign secretary and all the rest of them.

He, Alois Haydn, was not the only person who knew that the prime minister was dead, of course. But (the fifth thing) he was the only person who knew both that he was dead, and that the plot to conceal his death was going to be exposed before the vote. He knew this because he would shortly be heading off to Essex to tell Olivia Kite himself. He had intended that Jennifer Lewis would do this job for him, but that was now too dangerous. Why? Because (the sixth thing) being the only person with this knowledge could make him one of the richest men in England, but only if he was able to short sterling before the news became public. Fingertip control of the timing was all.

Assuming that Lucien McBryde – who, thankfully, was now dead – had told Jennifer Lewis, and that she intended to tell Olivia Kite, there was a risk that things could move far too fast, and spin out of his control. Olivia must not learn that the prime minister was dead until Alois had bought his currency options and was well prepared. Nothing must go wrong with the timing. And nothing must damage his relationship with Olivia; she was going to rise to power, and he had to jump from the dead old horse to the frisky new mare.

But the truth was, Olivia Kite scared him. From the first time he had met her, shortly before the PM elevated her to the cabinet, Alois had detected something in her that caused him a spasm of unease. Chalk-white skin, high cheekbones and depraved lips. . . What was it Mitterrand had said about Thatcher? 'The eyes of Caligula and the mouth of Marilyn Monroe'. Others saw Kite as a dead-eyed, sexless political automaton. But Alois looked deeper, and she, just once or twice, had looked deep into him too, penetrating his secret dread. He had squirmed, turned to water, but said nothing. She had risen in fame, flame-haired and commanding. And then her husband had betrayed her.

The last time Haydn and Kite had met was her last time in Downing Street, after that final brittle and ill-tempered cabinet meeting before the ministers departed in different groups to fight the referendum on opposite sides. Haydn had of course been outside the room when she and the PM had had their very unpleasant confrontation, but he was standing in the lobby as they all came out. Olivia had paused as she passed him. She had leaned close to him and seized his flesh, high up on his chest, twisting it between finger and thumb – she always wore gloves, even indoors – until he gasped.

'Sordid little turncoat,' she had said very quietly. 'Contemptible little worm. Come down and see me some time. At' – short pause – 'my' – longer pause – 'pleasure.'

Then she had walked on as if nothing had happened, expressionless. Haydn had felt he was about to pass out.

As he relived that moment, Jennifer Lewis began to seem a very serious problem indeed. She had been close to Lucien McBryde, who had known far too much about what was going on; and Olivia Kite depended very heavily upon her. Yes – the more he thought about it the clearer it was that this girl, who even now might be careering about with too much information, was the weak link in his otherwise perfect plan.

Looking back over the past few days, Haydn reflected that so far he had done nothing irreversible. True, he would eventually be implicated in covering up the prime minister's death, but after all, he himself had initiated nothing. He had merely been a cog, spinning between the big wheels – the cabinet ministers, financiers, ex-security-service bosses and former admirals.

So far, so remarkably good. However, it was possible that Lucien McBryde could still blow things sky high from beyond the grave. Charmian Locke had let it slip during their meeting at the cinema that he had known McBryde since their schooldays. Haydn had kept a poker face, but he had been shaken.

Running through all these considerations, Alois came to the decision that he must do something from which there was no turning back. He would have to have Jennifer Lewis killed. It was unfortunate, but it was absolutely necessary. He felt a pleasurable shudder run through him.

Then, calmly and deliberately, as he let his gaze rest on the hydrangeas, roses and languid willows, that haze of green, wet leaves, Alois thought about Professional Logistical Services. He had drawn them into the plot. Could he trust Solomon Dundas not to fill them in further? It was unthinkable that a man like Sir Solomon would be content to remain a mere bystander. But no, thought Haydn. Faced with an opportunity like this, he would plunge in and fill his boots. He wouldn't blab.

As to the rest of PLS, he'd like to see them humiliated. There they sat, well-fed and honoured old spiders. Like the prime minister's inner circle, they had a secure place in the world, a snug little trapeze from which they could scuttle about and sneer at the doers and the fixers like himself — the *staff*. Well, now they would find that the lower orders were striking back. What must be done, must be done.

Alois left the park and walked up St James's Street, veering east to the London Library. He left without taking a book with him.

The Quarry

Jen was becoming angry with herself. This sunlit Tuesday was running away from her. Ever since she had absorbed her former lover's final message about what was really going on in Downing Street, she had been entirely unable to concentrate. The truth was, she was badly frightened. Still no message from Lucien. She'd called his office; they seemed equally worried and baffled. The news editor had come back to her, and had been most odd. Given the astonishing nature of what Lucien knew, she began to wonder if he was already dead. When she tried to summon up an image of his face, or to hear his voice, nothing came back. And if somebody had cared enough to silence Lucien, then somebody would care enough, she supposed, to silence her too.

What to do? Where to go? Who to talk to? As she stumbled around her bedroom, pulling on a T-shirt and some jogging bottoms, she realised that the final two questions, at least, had obvious answers.

The safest place to go would be to her mother's – no one would expect her to go there. And without question the person she needed to talk to was Olivia Kite. She would know how best to make use of the information. But who was the villain? Who should she be scared of? It had to be Alois Haydn, that mysterious man she'd never met, but whom Lucien had seemed obsessed by. He must be behind it. Lucien had almost told her as much. It was most unlikely that

Haydn knew Lucien had been passing messages to her. How could he have known about the London Library system, still less have infiltrated it? And yet Jen felt in fear for her own life. Panic was overtaking her.

She did not feel like eating, and when she tried to make herself an instant coffee her hands shook so much that she spilled the milk across the kitchen worktop. She kept needing to pee. Half a dozen times she picked up her phone and called Olivia, hanging up as soon as she heard the recorded message. Half a dozen times she picked up her phone and was about to call her mother, but, not being able to envisage the conversation that would follow, she put it down again.

She returned to the bedroom upstairs, stripped off her clothes and began to run the shower.

As she stepped out, dripping with water, she saw a thin, girlish figure, small-breasted and hardly fledged, looking back at her from the full-length mirror: the very image of the victim. At just that moment there was a hammering on the door downstairs. Her heart began to race.

'Just because you're paranoid. . .' she muttered. She ignored the banging and began hurriedly to fill a small suitcase – clothes, laptop, cables and toilet bag. She dressed for a journey: jeans, boots, cable jumper and a thick woollen coat, topped off with a fur hat. 'A bit much for September,' she thought to herself, but she was shivering. She had to move, she had to get outside and hear normal voices.

Edging over to the bedroom window she peered down to the street below. A thick-set, Central European-looking man with a bald head and dark glasses whom she'd never seen before was standing on her front steps. She jumped backwards before he could see her. Quietly she took her suitcase and slipped downstairs, unlatched the kitchen door and hurried through the garden, climbing over the small fence at the end into her neighbour's property, which led to a small gate and an exit by some garages into the next street. Head down, she walked briskly towards the bus stop. She thought she heard a shout behind her, but forced herself to keep walking and not to break into a run.

Mercifully, a bus was just pulling up at the stop. Jen jostled her way to a back seat, where she wedged herself between a Russian man talking into his phone and a large Jamaican woman with a small, wriggling infant on her lap. From there she could see that nobody had followed her onto the bus. As it slowly eased its way out into the traffic she glimpsed the same Middle-European-looking man staring through the window at her with a blank expression.

The next hour felt to her like something out of a bad spy novel as she launched herself from bus route to bus route, then down into the underground, changing lines three times before emerging back into the sunlit world at Sloane Square and making her way towards her mother's flat in a gloomy Edwardian mansion block. She rang the bell, but, getting no response, let herself in. Inside, the blinds had been pulled down against the light. A small colour television murmured in a corner, and in front of it Jen's mother was lying on a reclining chair, chain-smoking.

Myfanwy Davies-Jones's loathing for successive governments – Blair, Brown, Cameron, Johnson, and now this lot – had been transmuted into a single-woman campaign against 'the nanny regime' which took the form of militant tobacco use. The novelist had decided to smoke the government to death as a form of suffragist direct action – or so she considered it. She smoked with a dogged, martyred air. The general effect was of a Rosa Luxemburg or La Pasionaria, mummified and then incarcerated in a kipper factory.

Much of the room was taken up by piles of cuttings from the financial pages of the newspapers, stapled together and neatly arranged on the carpet, the table and most available chairs. Myfanwy had tried many things in her old age to avoid the chore of writing novels. She had started to learn French, German, Spanish and Russian. She had joined a bridge club. But she had a talent for none of those things.

What she could do, she discovered, was invest. She had a natural aptitude for numbers which had lain dormant since her school days. Now she took delight in decoding the hints and warnings in the densest briefings from investment companies or financial editors. She had the courage to plunge in, and the even greater courage to pull out when everybody else was still plunging in. She had made a surprising amount of money simply sitting in her chair and smoking. She was, in her way, even more a woman of the world and a woman of her times than she had been in the 1970s.

Jennifer had expected her mother to be sceptical and dismissive about her fear of assassination at the hands of anonymous government goons, but Myfanwy was surprisingly receptive.

'Dear heart, you know I'm not one to cast nasturtiums, but this is positively the first time you've ever come here without boring me dreadfully. I'd begun to think life was passing you by. There's been barely a casual fuck, not a single piece of thoroughly poor behaviour. What have you been doing all this time?'

In short, Myfanwy did not think that Jennifer was hysterical. A government that was prepared to stamp all over the individual liberties of smokers, and steal from blameless investors of a certain age, was capable of anything.

Myfanwy closed her eyes and thought about one of her racy early novels. 'They sound like terribly dangerous men. If they catch you, make sure they torture you just a little bit first, before they kill you. Too thrilling.'

Then, tactful as ever, she sprang into action – or at least as much action as was compatible with continuing to lie flat on her back, chain smoking and watching the television all at once.

'What we need, dear, is help from someone who really knows what's what. I have a friend, a darling man who can come in a jiffy. He mostly does. . . What, I wonder, really is a jiffy? Anyway, if you pull out that leather book by the phone, I'll call him.'

'Myfanwy' – Jen could never bring herself to use the word 'mother', even now – 'that's a kind thought, but I really just want to stay here and lie low.'

'Nonsense. You can't stay holed up here with me forever. We'd bore one another to death. We should be *screaming* in half an hour. Besides, I'm expecting company.' A minute later the elderly agitator-novelist was calling Gregory Lime, a former SIS officer with a literary streak who was now working for Professional Logistical Services. He said he was in a meeting, but he took the call none-theless, and listened intently.

'What does she know? Or rather, what does she think she knows?' he asked. Myfanwy told him. He whistled.

'I'll come right over,' he said. 'I'm just with some people.' He hung up, then turned to Alois Haydn and Dame Cecily Morgan. 'You'll never guess what I've just heard,' he said.

Back in Myfanwy's flat, the novelist had finally clambered up from her recumbent position and was rummaging in a haversack hanging by the front door. 'I'm not going to lend you my pistol, dear, I'm afraid. It's practically antique, and of sentimental value. But you might find this useful.' She handed her a heavy steel wrench.

'Now push off. And good luck.'

The Chase is On

Frightened as she was, Jennifer was beginning to think more clearly. Expecting to find useful advice, still less a place of safety, in her mother's flat had been foolishly naïve. Had she stayed there, she imagined that it wouldn't be long before a procession of elderly men in loud tweed jackets with grey, dandruffed hair and faces which had long ago surrendered to whisky and paranoia – ancient retired majors, one-time spooks, the owners of specialist bookshops – would be banging on the door and offering dangerously impractical suggestions about what she should do next.

So she accepted the wrench, kissed her mother's powdery cheek, and hurried down the stairs and out into the street.

If Jennifer had known what had taken place in Downing Street earlier that morning, she would have been even more scared than she already was.

After their work disposing of the prime minister's body, Dawid and Borys had both decided to wash their hands of the whole business. Dawid had more than enough building work coming in to keep him going, now that the Irish had all become accountants, and Borys just wanted to go home. More importantly, the two of them had become thoroughly frightened of their older brother.

Aleksander had been sent by Alois Haydn to sit in the prime minister's office, and make himself useful to Ronnie Ashe and Jason Latimer.

'He'll do anything you want,' Haydn had promised them. 'Just ask. He's completely reliable.' The chief whip and the foreign secretary had assumed, wrongly, that Aleksander was working for Professional Logistical Services.

A literal man, Aleksander had been sitting in his place on Tuesday morning when the time came for an unavoidable confrontation with the most difficult of the private secretaries. He accompanied Latimer and Ashe to the ground-floor video-conferencing room. Around an oval walnut table were a dozen leather chairs which were occupied by secret-service chiefs or military men whenever the PM spoke to the White House situation room, the Élysée Palace or the Kremlin. Behind the prime minister's chair were a British flag and an artistic rendition of the Number 10 front door. The vast flatscreen at the other end of the table was the only evidence of the room's real purpose. Above all, like COBRA, this room was a Faraday cage – no electronic signals of any kind, other than the main connection, could penetrate or leave it. No phones or electronic devices would work here; there was no way of overhearing what went on inside.

'In space, no one can hear you scream,' Aleksander quoted when he was told this.

At around the usual time for mid-morning tea or coffee, Francis Fieldfare, the prime minister's senior private secretary, arrived in the room. He was bristling with suspicion. He had left half a dozen urgent messages which required a decision on the top of the papers in the prime minister's red box the previous evening, but he had neither seen nor heard from the PM. Other prime ministers in his experience had been dilatory. But this one, like David Cameron before him, was normally punctilious about returning his red box first thing in the morning with every page duly initialled, every decision taken, accompanied by scribbled explanations which would later be worked up into statements and speeches. But the flow had suddenly ceased. In Downing Street, paperwork was life. Its absence was deeply unsettling. Fieldfare didn't believe a word the chief whip had told him earlier about a mysterious banking crisis.

Though still only in his mid-thirties, Francis Fieldfare was already a near-legendary figure in the Civil Service. It was he who organised what the prime minister would read, who he would see, where he would go – in effect, running his daily life. Amanda Andrews had suggested involving him in the plot earlier on, but the others had thought it would be just too dangerous. Fieldfare was notorious for both his intemperate outbursts and his rigorous sense of public duty. He considered Number 10 Downing Street his personal territory – even Don Hammond had flinched from trying to stop Fieldfare entering the PM's study. And, particularly dangerously, since he knew all the pass codes, there was nothing to stop Fieldfare from entering the private apartment upstairs and discovering everything.

So when he confronted Latimer and Ashe in the video-conferencing room, they felt they had no option but to admit the truth. Fieldfare sat immobile, rigid with disgust, as Ashe awkwardly mumbled his way through his explanation.

'The thing is, Francis, this is about a lot more than the referendum, you know. The PM's whole legacy hangs on it. And the country's prosperity. Its prosperity, Francis. The FTSE will crash if we leave the EU. Crash. A lot of British companies will go under. Under. You can kiss goodbye to your pension pot, too. Goodbye. It's a ghastly situation. Ghastly. And extreme danger requires extreme measures.'

Fieldfare placed his hands flat on the table and drew his shoulders back, so that he appeared to be sitting to attention. 'Unless you have told the king about this disgraceful scheme – which I rather doubt – and if you are misusing the prime minister's authority – which I don't doubt – then it is my considered opinion that you are committing treason. I'm not a legal expert, so whether it's high treason or mere run-of-the-mill low treason I cannot tell you off-hand. But in either case it's totally unacceptable. You should be bloody well ashamed of yourselves.'

He rose to his feet. 'I can't stand here and promise you I'll keep my mouth shut. It's a long time since we've had an impeachment in Westminster Hall, but frankly you're asking for nothing less. Count me out.'

Francis Fieldfare was an honourable and passionate man. In his formal suit and with a red, pinched yachtsman's face he looked much older than his thirty-five years. In Downing Street he had the authority of personal integrity. Even Jason Latimer, holder of one of the great offices of state and his elder by a quarter of a century, quailed a little.

But Aleksander slowly stood up from his chair by the door. This, he thought, was what he was there for.

'You want me to help, Mr Ashe?' he asked.

Ronnie shrugged.

That was all it took. With shocking speed and force Aleksander reached forward, grasped the private secretary's neck, jerked his head roughly back and clamped his free hand over Fieldfare's mouth and nostrils. He had clearly done this before. Fieldfare kicked out his legs and lost his balance, so that Aleksander was holding him aloft. Gagging, he swung his arms back in an effort to reach Aleksander. His face purpled. A dark stream ran down his trouser leg.

'You will keep your mouth shut,' said Aleksander, finally snapping the neck. 'And here, anyway, there is no one to hear you.'

Latimer and Ashe stared wordlessly at one another. There was nothing to be said. Extreme measures. They felt very close.

But there was now a second body to deal with. Guided by Latimer,

Aleksander dragged Fieldfare along the corridor, past the room that housed what Churchill had dubbed the 'garden girls' — those essential women who type (and sometimes compose) the prime minister's letters, emails, reports, requests and refusals, and who keep him going when he travels, providing him with fresh information, clean clothes, including a black tie for bad news, and anything else he might need. No keyboards were clicking as Fieldfare's slack heels bounced past the closed door. The garden girls, did the plotters but know it, had guessed that the prime minister was dead; but they were utterly loyal, and besides, they had nobody to tell.

It was too dangerous to carry Fieldfare openly across the garden in mid-morning. Summoned by the chief whip, Don Hammond unlocked the vaults and returned with a wheelbarrow and a tarpaulin. Aleksander bundled Fieldfare in and trundled him round to one of the vaults, where he laid him under an arch of limewashed brick.

The foreign secretary told the staff in the prime minister's private office that Fieldfare had agreed to take personal control of the financial crisis, and was now working with the PM in his flat upstairs. He knew it wouldn't keep them quiet for long, but it would have to do. It was somehow fitting that Fieldfare, who had been a kind of human switchbox at the very heart of modern British power, a link between the monarchy and Parliament, and who had actually felt that Whitehall was his spiritual home, should end up being left under Number 10 Downing Street itself. But his next resting place would be grander by far.

Scrambled Eggs at the Wolseley

Aleksander had gone straight from Downing Street to have brunch with his former secret-service controller, Colonel Jerzy Babiński, at the Wolseley – the colonel's choice. They attracted curious glances as they sat eating their scrambled eggs: the sleek, shiny and cheerful middle-aged man in an English blazer and striped tie, his hair pomaded and his cheeks freshly shaven by Alfie from Trumper, and the dishevelled, beetroot-faced old thug with his huge nose and large meaty hands, wearing a badly stained leather jacket. They were talking confidentially, old friends.

'Aleksander, you were always a strong man. I liked you. That is why I told Mr Haydn about you last Christmas. Whatever you do now, you must stick with him and please him. He is a very important man, to us at home as well as here in London. Now, whatever happens, he will be on top of the pile. So if anything he asks you to do makes you unhappy, remember *me*. You will be completely safe.'

Aleksander, his mouth full of toast and egg, took some time to reply. When he did, he sounded angry.

'What do we do here, all of us? We look after them when they are sick, we wipe their arses when they are old, we keep their houses clean, their gardens neat and their children safe. They don't make any buildings here any more, but when they do it's us who build them. We brush their teeth and bake their bread and carry

away their rubbish. We do all the things they cannot do for themselves any longer. What people. I am no different from the rest of
us. Just another Polish service industry, eh, Babiński?'

The colonel shrugged, and brushed the crumbs off his cheeks
and trousers. He was calling for the bill when Aleksander's phone
vibrated. He looked down at it. 'It's a text for you,' he said to
Babiński in surprise. The message was from Alois Haydn, who knew
that the Polish spy chief was a man of discrimination and learning.
It read simply: 'LL as explained. Piers Brendon, Dark Valley.' The
colonel turned to Aleksander.

'It's started already. I think I'm about to receive your orders.
Follow me, we're only five minutes away.'

As they walked to St James's Square the two men kept to opposite sides of the street — a remnant of the old basic tradecraft — so
as to avoid being photographed together. Babiński entered the library
by the back door, checked on the computerised system and quickly
found his way to the history shelves.

Sure enough, pressed inside the unappetising volume Haydn had
chosen was a typed card. Babiński pulled it out. It read: 'Alex. Get
the girl. She is probably on her way to her mistress's. They must
not meet. Dispose of her. Fast. Money in the usual place in the new
house. I will meet you there. Tear this up.'

Babiński slipped it, and a small photograph of a young woman
getting into a bus, into a pocket, walked briskly back outside and
gave them to Aleksander, who asked, 'Does nobody in this ridiculous
country use email?'

'Apparently not,' said Babiński, then hugged him, kissed him on
both cheeks and went off to work.

Aleksander returned to his flat. He knew his shotgun would not
fit into the pannier on his motorbike, so on the way he called into
a DIY store and bought a small hacksaw. When he arrived home

he carefully cut the gun down to the length familiar from American gangster films. It would blow a head to pieces. He loaded it, and was just filling the pockets of his leather jacket with extra cartridges when he had a call from Haydn. They were in luck. Thanks to the girl's mother's call to Gregory Lime at PLS, Haydn knew exactly where she was, and directed Aleksander to Myfanwy's flat in West London. He was just half an hour behind her.

Jennifer could think of only one thing – she had to get to Olivia Kite as soon as possible. The thought of being stuck on a slow, empty train out to the wilds of Essex terrified her, but she didn't own a car. Then she remembered that the lovestruck Ned Parminter had once told her about his proudest possession, a vintage Mercedes – was it? She knew nothing about cars – which was garaged in Mayfair. She called his number as she walked. If she had known how close Aleksander was behind her, she might have run.

Aleksander had reported straight back to Haydn when he found the novelist's apartment empty, his quarry gone. His new instructions were 'Find the old lady, then. She'll know where the girl's heading.'

Immediately forgetting her arrangement with Gregory Lime, Myfanwy had left soon after her daughter for her regular session in a nearby gymnasium, where a 'falls club' for elderly local residents who had had a dangerous slip, or merely teetered, fearful of one, provided her with a never-failing source of amusement. Jogging pants and a pair of orange-and-silver trainers protruding bizarrely from underneath her fringed Liberty dress, she took her place in a large ring of old people, arranged as for a country dance, many of them leaning on walking frames or sticks. Scattered amongst them were a small army of white-uniformed physiotherapists, supporting aching backs and wobbly knees.

A preparatory hum of conversation filled the room: 'I'm so sorry.'

'I do apologise.' 'I'm terribly sorry, I nearly fell. . .' 'I feel really lucky, you know, I'm so lucky, I just feel enormously fortunate. . .' These remnants of the wartime generation greeted the indignities and pains of old age with chin-up cheerfulness and smiling apologies for their frailty and dottiness. They waited patiently and listened to the old Elvis songs and stamped their weak feet when they were told to, meekly accepting the tellings-off from the athletic young Romanians and South Africans in charge. There was nothing else they could do. Soon enough their children, and then their grandchildren, would themselves enter this no-man's-land of petty humiliations and early-morning aches.

Myfanwy was, as ever, unimpressed. 'All this politeness,' she muttered to herself. 'All these apologies and this cringing Galilean niceness. How did these pathetic people ever build an empire?'

She had been speaking slightly louder than she realised, and not everybody around her was entirely deaf yet.

A man in corduroy trousers the colour of crushed strawberries, a neat white shirt and a silk cravat smiled at her. 'Sorry, sorry, sorry. But my dear lady, I think your history is slightly awry. We are the ones who *lost* the empire. But we're quite happy about that, aren't we? Bloody useless thing, an empire.'

An apple-cheeked grandmother added that she wasn't interested in politics, but she thought nobody in Britain worked any more. Except the 'Easterns'.

Myfanwy harrumphed, took the man's outstretched hand and performed some desultory knee bends. On her third stoop she felt her left leg turn to jelly, and was about to fall across the strawberry corduroys.

'Ah. . .I am sorry,' she gasped as she grabbed at him.

'There you are,' he said smugly.

A few bars of Vivaldi rang out from Myfanwy's pocket. Her

mobile phone was ringing. It was good old Gregory Lime, wondering where on earth she'd got to. She hurriedly apologised and told him where she was.

Ten minutes later a rough-looking man in a leather jacket was standing on the edge of the group. He was clearly neither a frail client nor a trim, well-meaning physiotherapist.

'You'd better take your jacket off,' said the man in the red trousers. 'It's a bit hot in here. Would you like a cup of tea?'

Aleksander ignored him.

'You are Mrs Davies-Jones?'

'And you are?'

'Gregory Lime sent me. He says he was sorry to miss you at the flat.'

'You don't look like one of Gregory's friends.'

'Lady, I am not. I am working for Mr Lime, and for the others.'

'Others? Reggie? Ally? Rupert? Hugo?'

'Yes, of course. And for Mr Haydn too.'

Myfanwy froze. This was not part of the script. Could Gregory really be mixed up with a shit like Alois Haydn? She'd been light-hearted with Jennifer, but it seemed the poor little mouse was right to be afraid. Myfanwy reached out gently and touched Aleksander's raw, callused hand.

'She's not really in any danger is she? She told me she was in some kind of trouble, but she's always been rather a bland and timid girl, you know. I suppose you're going to have to torture her.'

Aleksander groaned to himself. The old woman was clearly demented. He was about to give up, but then Myfanwy's chin lifted and she glared at him.

'You're above your pay grade here, chum. My daughter works for Olivia Kite, who is at least the second most powerful politician in the land. Try to get anywhere near her place to get your hands on Jennifer, and you'll find out what protection really means in this country. Be on your way, young man.'

Aleksander, who hadn't been called young for at least two decades, grinned. Of course, that was it. The girl would be going to Essex, to hide with her Mrs Kite. He'd follow her there. Mr Haydn was, he knew, a friend of Mrs Kite's. He'd know what to do.

At this moment a large, white-tunicked woman with a haulier's face and Doris Day hair marched over to confront the intruder.

'These are NHS premises!' she barked. 'Where are you from, and what do you want?'

'Lady, I am from Poland,' said Aleksander, 'and I have got what I came for.' He pulled himself up to his full height and strode towards the door in as dignified a fashion as he could manage.

'I love all the foreigners,' one nice old lady said to his departing back. 'I hope we haven't been any trouble, have we?'

Outside in the street, Aleksander clambered onto his motorbike, felt in the pannier behind him for his gun, and adjusted his testicles before kicking the starter and roaring away from the kerb.

On the Road

Ned Parminter was in love. He assumed it must be love, because it felt like indigestion – or, to be frank, Irritable Bowel Syndrome – but in a good way. When Jen had rung him he experienced a strange coldness in his feet, his inner organs billowed and his palms moistened. Now, when they met and he leaned forward to kiss her, multicoloured birds rose from the London pavement and performed aerobatics, while rousing bars of Elgar burst from taxis passing in the street.

He had been moving closer for days, light-footed and nervous as a cat stalking a pigeon. Jen, conscious of a squirm and a tremor around him, was relieved when they stopped at an expensive grocer's to pick up some food. She was famished.

They ate as they walked. Ned, wolfing down sandwiches, watched Jen's pink little tongue probing her sushi. A mixture of sauce and juice ran down her chin. She allowed him to lean over and dab it off, and made no comment when he sucked his finger. Ned kept a Portuguese custard tart for last. He bit off half of it, the yellow goo and flaky pastry coating his beard, and pressed the other half directly into Jen's mouth, nearly causing her to trip. Then he kissed her powerfully, grinding his face into hers. For the second time that day she did not push him away.

Passers-by saw an oddly matched couple: Jennifer, with her long red hair and white, pointed face could have passed for eighteen;

Ned, with his unfashionable black beard and academic sports jacket, could have been forty. As they clutched each other, as if for support in a gale, Jennifer found herself feeling oddly protective of this gangling, clever, nervous man who had nearly bitten her hand off when she asked him to drive her away from London in his Mercedes. She had dismissed the idea of ringing Olivia. Lucien McBryde had taught her that phone calls can be tapped, and phones can be tracked. Anyway, she'd get more credit if she told her face to face.

In fact Ned didn't own a Mercedes. It was a matter of principle. He hated their ubiquity, their bland ugliness, and the people who drove them. He was actually the proud possessor of a Bristol; and not just any Bristol, but a two-litre 402 drophead cabriolet, a piece of magnificence, and as lovely a symbol of vanished British values as a Mark II Spitfire or Horatio Nelson's bloodstained undress coat.

Ned's mother had died the year he embarked on his PhD. He had sold her south coast flat and spent a considerable part of the proceeds on the Bristol. Much of what was left over went on keeping it warm and safe in a lock-up garage in Mayfair, out of the Oxford rain and safe from child vandals. The car, he reflected, was warmer, better-housed and more expensive to maintain than his mother had ever been.

His previous car, a Jason Cowley, had been slick, tinny, noisy. But this machine, solid and shining grey, had the fingerprints of the Bristol Aeroplane Company all over its dignified lines. It growled. Sometimes it snarled. Inside it smelt of wood, leather and motor oil. This, he had imagined, was where he would tip Jen up on the back seat, hoick her lean white thighs apart and explore, Mungo Park in a world of fragrant mystery. He'd thought too about disrobing her in the garage and having her on a pile of rags; or after a frolicsome country picnic, with the Bristol gleaming by the side of a sunny field.

Ned took the car out only rarely, and savoured every occasion. He didn't drive, but 'motored', planning his route carefully in advance, using a 1939 RAC atlas to pick out scenic back roads between obscure country towns, often losing his way in counties now sliced up by motorways. That, for him, was the price of the difference between motoring and merely driving from A to B.

In truth, Ned's automotive nostalgia was in danger of becoming a mania. It ran to a wickerwork picnic hamper with heavy stainless-steel cutlery and china plates, home-made sandwiches and a tartan-decorated Thermos of hot, strong, sweet tea. Not only did he not want a Mercedes, he certainly did not want Britain to remain in the European Union. He and Jen, therefore, shared certain values. He hoped they would soon be sharing rather more than that.

The thought of driving her away from nameless dangers, safely out of London to Olivia Kite's country house had, he felt, the authentic Bulldog Drummond ring to it – the long snout of the Bristol's bonnet nosing through leafy B-roads, the silent girl in a headscarf beside him, while unnamed German aviators tracked them from between scudding clouds. He could see it all. Bring back Kenneth More.

And then there was their objective – Danskin! Ned the historian had long known about Danskin House. He had written an under-graduate thesis on Sir Stuart 'Blackie' Mountstewart, its original builder, who had made his fortune on the bleached bones of African slaves in his Jamaican sugar plantations, feeding the English sweet tooth before buying his way to a seat in the Lords and considerable influence in the Navy Office, bleeding that dry and thus contributing in no small part to some years of unexpected French successes on the high seas. Facing impeachment, and widely suspected of raping the then prime minister's son, Blackie had fled London for faraway Danskin, and turned, with immaculate timing, religious.

Ned had read the poetry anthologies. Wilmot Mercer's 'Ode to Danskin House' celebrated an estate that was both lavish and wicked:

Garden of England; your transported beauties grow
From half the Earth on English soil, steadily and slow,

it began, before going on to refer to Mountstewart's rapacious trading reputation:

Pluck'd from Carib isle and Indian plain,
And tended here — where once the Barb'rous Dane
Rais'd castle rude; but now with Temple, Fane
Column and Pilaster glorified — all forg'd
from noble trade.

Before concluding, accurately enough:

— where swoll'n cucumber, gourd engorged
Proclaims the manhood of fair Danskin's Lord.

Last but not least, at Oxford Ned had enjoyed hearing Lord Briskett's stories of visiting Danskin House in more recent times, when it was owned by Sir Rufus Panzer, from whom Olivia Kite's father had bought it. During the Thatcher years Panzer had gathered right-wing politicians, journalists and academics there for long, argumentative dinners.

Briskett had recalled that one of Panzer's favourite tricks was to invite first-time visitors up to the top of Danskin's central tower. From there, one of the architectural oddities of the house stood out — literally. A freestanding slate wall protruded some sixty feet from the main building. Presumably it had originally been built for a planned extension of the tower which had subsequently proved unaffordable. Now it remained in eerie isolation, with a sheer drop on either side. Along the top a narrow pathway of rough brickwork, slimy with moss and grass, could be traversed by anyone with a good sense of balance and nerves of steel.

Panzer, a bottle of Saint-Émilion inside him, would put his hands in his pockets and saunter along the top of the wall to the very end, gazing carelessly down at the geese in the pond before spinning on his heel and walking slowly back. Then he would languidly address his guest with a lizard smile.

'Funny thing. Windy fellers don't much like this exercise. Lovely view, though. Margaret was here once. Did it after a couple of whiskies and *in heels*. Fancy a stroll, old boy?'

And the junior minister, or *Daily Telegraph* commentator, or Oxford historian, would feel obliged to take a deep breath and stride out, running the serious risk of a broken neck. If his guest was teetering and sweating, Rufus would wait until he had reached the furthermost point, where the bricks were especially slippery, chipped and easy to lose one's footing on, before telling the story of a former visitor, a backbencher whom 'we lost, poor chap. Panicked. Windy. Came down the wrong side.' For one side of the wall overlooked a stand of rhododendrons which would have broken one's fall, though not enough to prevent a considerable smash. On the other side, however, was bare soil, with a row of spiked railings running parallel to the wall, only a few feet from its base. Sir Rufus had erected them himself. They were intended to prevent local boys from climbing the wall, but from above they seemed designed to maim and impale.

Those who acquitted themselves well in this ordeal would be lavishly entertained and amused for the rest of their stay, for Sir Rufus could be a very genial host. But he had an abhorrence of

'bores', in which category he included physical cowards. The reputation of the wall, which circulated quickly through the lobbies of
Westminster, ensured that those who accepted his invitations tended
to be men and women of his own sort.

After hearing this story from the insouciant wall-pacer Briskett,
Ned had always asked himself whether he himself would be able to
walk the walk. He hoped he would never find out – not now that
Sir Rufus had fallen to earth himself; and if his reputation was half-
merited, to a darker and hotter place.

But still, all in all, Ned could think of nowhere he would rather
visit than Danskin House, which now found itself the rebel capital
of the patriotic insurrection. Where better to win the hand of
Jennifer Lewis, humble servant of its current mistress?

As they walked north from Piccadilly to where his car was stabled
(this car deserved to be more than merely parked) Ned mentally
re-clothed Jen in a fawn coat, leather driving gloves and a silk print
scarf. He pulled a pair of dark glasses from his jacket pocket and
put them on. They had the desired effect of turning the whole world
sepia, though combined with his beard, they left very little of his
face visible.

An hour later they were sitting in almost motionless traffic, easing
east out of the capital. They had another few miles of constipated
East London roads to go, but Ned didn't mind. He had been listening
to Jen's breathless explanation of what had probably been going on
in Downing Street, and he was agog.

'I am Gog and Magog, old thing' – for he liked a phrase. 'I hang
on your very voice. I gape.'

Briskett would never forgive him for getting the story first, of
course. That might be a problem, because Ned would need a good
word from him when he applied for a proper teaching post of his
own. But what a tale it was! Ned could see that it was easily big

enough to change the result of the referendum, and thereby the country's destiny – perhaps the whole of Europe's too. Jen was quite right to be taking it straight to Olivia. She would know just how to use it to the most deadly effect. So this journey was therefore historic, in its own small way. One day television or movie producers would be phoning around to try to match his Bristol in order to recreate this very trip.

Ned Parminter was a man of honour and scruple. So when he turned in at a service station to fill up with petrol, his conscience dictated that he call Lord Briskett to fill him in. His timing could not have been better. His timing could not have been worse.

'Boss?'

'Ned! *Enfin!* I've been worried about you. There are some things I need to talk over with you. Suspicions. . .'

'You can forget those. I'm with Jen. You remember her boyfriend used to be that journalist Lucien McBryde?'

'Hmm. Perhaps. Rackety sort of fellow. . .?'

'Yes, but thick with all sorts of people. And someone told him – and now Jen's pretty sure he's been killed, but just before he disappeared he told Jen – and now she's told me – you see. . .'

'Told you what? You sound not quite yourself, Ned.'

'That the PM's dead. Snuffed it. Heart attack. But they're covering it up. Keeping it quiet until after the vote. . .'

'Jesus. Who's covering it up, Ned? Did the Chinese whispers tell you that?'

'Not exactly. But I guess it's all of them. Downing Street. Amanda.'

'Fickle girl! But what a story, Ned. . .'

*

In the Number 11 dining room the PLS operator who'd been monitoring Briskett's calls pressed a button to mark the recording as top priority, and called Dame Cecily and Dickie Greene over.

'We have a situation.'

They listened silently to the recording.

'Point one,' said Cecily at last, 'we need to shut this down. Now. Briskett and Mr Parmesan, or whatever he calls himself. And the girl too, obviously. Point two, who's blabbed? That's dirty business. It's all dirty. So, point three, without shuffling off our responsibility, we need to get that foul castle-creeper Alois Haydn onto this. He can do things we can't.'

'Hush, old girl,' said Dickie quickly. 'No need to spell things out.'

'Quite,' Dame Cecily replied, putting a callused finger to her lips.

The Tea Game

Lord Briskett, armed with certainty at last, had rapidly decided where he needed to go. At that moment he was sitting on a leather sofa in the reception area of the *National Courier*.

Upstairs on the first, editorial, floor of the building, the long afternoon was being enlivened by the tea game. Editors, subs and correspondents would take it in turn to wander into the editor's office and ask Ken Cooper, in the politest way possible, if he would like a calming cup of tea. For he was losing it. Visibly. And even by his standards, quite fast.

'Cuppa, Ken?' asked the deputy editor.

'Nah, thanks. Busy.'

'Like a cup of tea, boss?' asked the man who wrote about new media.

'No. Get out.'

Then the obituaries editor, a polite and elderly Old Etonian, sauntered in with two china mugs in his right hand.

'Cha, Ken?'

'Go and fuck yourself.'

In desperation the staff sent in the sixty-something fashion editor.

'Ken, dear, time for a cup of tea?'

Cooper rose from his chair, buttoned up his suit jacket, walked to the window, turned around, unbuttoned his suit jacket, sat down again, and said, 'No, thank you.' He then glanced around suspiciously at what sounded like a quiet round of applause from somewhere out in the newsroom.

The next to arrive was the junior crime reporter, who knocked on the door and opened it with a plastic cup in one hand. Ken did not look up. 'You're fired,' he said.

All his adult life Ken Cooper had thrived on stress. He was addicted to it. He took stress – fried, diced and with béarnaise sauce – for breakfast, lunch and supper. But over the last couple of days he had been a man possessed. Of all the people he had hired onto the *Courier* over the years Lucien McBryde had been his favourite. His death had shocked Ken, and he had dedicated himself to solving the mystery. But even with the help of the young police-woman who had found the body he hadn't got far. No CCTV images of McBryde entering the building. No sign of a break-in. Now, however, since Lord Fucking Briskett – who was probably sitting downstairs right now – had rung him and babbled out his theory that the prime minister was dead, and that it had been covered up, Ken was beginning to put things together.

McBryde had had a political secret. He'd said so. He'd also told Ken that he was meeting Alois Haydn the day before he died. The death of a reporter may have seemed a small matter at a time when the country's future was at stake. But perhaps Ken now had – motive.

He was sketching out a sidebar front-page piece about the polit-ical murder mystery. He'd put McBryde's byline photo at the top. Next to it would be the main picture, showing Alois Haydn leaving Downing Street. Thus Haydn and McBryde would be visually linked in the reader's mind. Stage one.

He simply had to insert Haydn's name, delicately, into the murder story – a reference to his clandestine meeting with

McBryde, perhaps – and, stage two, the fucking cat would be among the fucking pigeons, blood and feathers, giving them a good fucking over. Fucking pigeons, serve them right.

It was all a question of fine lines. At last Ken was finished, and threw down his marker pen. Knowing that he was skating close to the most libellous front page he'd ever drawn up, he called for the office lawyer, a burly, ponderous man in a shiny pinstriped suit who remembered the glory days before the internet and the Leveson inquiry into press misbehaviour. Ken could feel his heart thumping. Breathe out, boy. . .

'Ah, Mr Cooper. Busy afternoon,' said Gerald the lawyer. 'Perhaps we should start with a nice cup of tea?'

Downstairs, Lord Briskett was startled by a scream of rage from somewhere above his head.

Shortly afterwards an off-white-faced young man – the trainee himself – arrived to apologise that the editor was unable to see him this afternoon.

As he left the building Briskett took his phone out of his pocket. He was in no mood to give up. If Ken Cooper wasn't interested in hearing the truth about what had happened to his young reporter, and why, then he might as well stick it up the craw of Dame Cecily Morgan, the supercilious old bat.

'You are completely barking, Briskett,' she said after he had outlined the story to her. 'You've absolutely lost it. Alois Haydn told some journalist that? Impossible. If you believe it you must be mentally ill.'

Quietly and calmly he took her through the whole story, step by step. McBryde's meeting with Haydn. His messages to Jennifer Lewis. His mysterious disappearance.

'Which bit of that, Cecily, with your long history of skulduggery, do you not credit? I'd be fascinated to know.'

'Almost every bit. First, your missing reporter was an alcoholic, drug-addled maniac. I'm sorry to speak ill of the dead, but there's nobody working in Westminster who wouldn't agree with me. Second, you have not a shred of evidence linking Mr Haydn, a man I dislike as much as you do, with the unfortunate death of young Mr McBryde, whose demented scribblings to his girlfriend have about as much credibility as a poison-pen blog. All the rest is speculation. You have a fevered brain, Briskett, and I would take it off somewhere for a quiet rest before you air this nonsense and find the world divided between those who ridicule you and those who simply pity you.'

As a young woman, before the Service had called, Cecily Morgan had wanted to go to RADA. And she was very good. In fact, she had almost planted a seed of doubt in Briskett's head. Yet all the while her focus had remained on calculating between the options that were open to her. Was it really possible that Haydn, of all people, had let the secret out? Why would he? And could she trust him to take care of Briskett and his little team? He'd do more than threaten them. It felt like a big moral choice. But without Haydn the whole carefully constructed edifice would come tumbling down. For the first time in years Dame Cecily didn't know what to do.

9

Saturday, 16 September

Referendum Day Minus Five

Rewind. . .

Ned Parminter's adventure had really begun the previous weekend — although he was not to know that — because Lucien McBryde had been bored and at a loose end early on Saturday evening. McBryde may have been uncontrolled and wayward, but he was not stupid. He understood himself well enough to know that for him, boredom was an exceptionally dangerous condition. But Westminster was dead. All the campaigning and the action had drained away elsewhere, to the marginal parts of the country. Hardly anyone was left to gossip to, or be briefed by. The PM seemed to have disappeared from the scene altogether. So McBryde — the self-proclaimed porcelain conduit, the raffish magician of minor scandal, the maker of five or six from two plus two — felt himself a man brimming with talents in a world that no longer needed them; an itchy-palmed electrician, as it were, during the New Stone Age.

He found himself mooching through Soho, eyeing the tarts and the gays, peering through windows at pornographic magazines, rare whiskies and the few traditional shops and cafés left in the area. Squinting through one window he spotted Ian Hislop of *Private Eye* earnestly and very solemnly working his way through a huge cream cake, waving his hand from side to side as if he were participating in some obscure religious rite. But McBryde was still bored, bored, bored. Perhaps he should try to get in touch with Jen. He changed direction, heading south-west towards Piccadilly Circus and the London Library. As he did so his phone began to vibrate.

He was surprised but pleased to hear the unmistakable sibilant lisp of Alois Haydn, the political legend in person. McBryde's boredom evaporated at once. He had texted him a few weeks before, suggesting a profile, although with no real expectation of an answer. Ken Cooper had told him, 'Understand Alois fucking Haydn, McBryde, and you understand modern fucking Britain. Trouble is, nobody does. Now get a fucking move on.' To be asked to meet him was an unexpected break.

McBryde dipped into the nearest pub, avoided the barman's eye and went straight to the toilet, where he took fifty quid's worth in two loud sniffs, one up each nostril. Then, blinking and buzzing, he set off for Whitehall, feeling like a fisherman with a baited hook.

Alois Haydn did not want there to be any record of Lucien McBryde entering Downing Street, so he had suggested that they meet in the old-fashioned café opposite the Cenotaph. It was sometimes used by journalists after prime ministerial press meetings, but it was mainly a tourists' place, and was quiet and anonymous. Haydn ordered a couple of cappuccinos and sat back, waiting for his prey. He didn't look much like a fish that was about to be hooked.

After McBryde joined him the two men talked for twenty minutes about exactly how he would structure his profile, who Haydn would allow him to talk to, and what 'line' the *Courier* wanted to take. But then McBryde, whose slightly watering eyes and raw nose had been observed by his companion, was alarmed to hear Haydn say, 'You know, I don't think I want to do this after all. Like you, I'm a creature of the shadows. We need to keep the limelight for the elected ones, don't you think? The fact is, I'm going through what in someone else would be described as a crisis of conscience, and

I want to tell you something. But you must put that notebook away. And no recording either.'

McBryde rubbed his eyes, shrugged, closed his small notebook and jammed it back into his suit pocket, which had already begun to fray. Haydn then told him about the prime minister's demise the previous day, and how the foreign secretary and the chief whip, backed by a mysterious group of mainly pro-European establishment figures called Professional Logistical Services, were conspiring to keep the whole thing a secret until after the vote on Thursday. McBryde asked a few questions, struggling to concentrate on the key facts he'd write down as soon as Haydn left. His excitement was tempered by a strong suspicion that he was being wound up.

'You have got all this, haven't you, Lucien?' Haydn had said sharply. 'You're not just going to go off and have a swift one, and end up slumped on the pavement somewhere with piss down your pants?'

McBryde was offended. That was all long ago. 'Yeah, I've got it. I'm just wondering what your game is. If I go to the paper and this all turns out to be bollocks, then that's me finished, the laughing stock of Fleet Street. Imagine the smirk on Hislop's face. Imagine *Have I Got News for You* next week. How can I be sure you're telling the truth?'

'Fair point,' smiled Haydn. 'Perhaps you're a little more on the ball than I thought. Well, I can't prove a negative, sitting here. Nor do I suggest that you break the story straight away. You'll have to take my word that you won't be scooped. Why not pass it on to your little friend Miss Lewis, and then she can pass it on to her boss, and you can make it public just before she does, passing the burden – or should it be the honour – on to Olivia Kite?'

McBryde rubbed his itchy scalp and tried to ignore the prickle in his armpits. He squirmed in his chair. 'That doesn't work any better, does it, Mr Haydn? That sounds to me as if I'm being used as the patsy in a plot to make Olivia Kite look ridiculous and help you get a "Yes" vote in the referendum. Do you think I'm an idiot?'

'Of course I do, Lucien. Everybody does. But you can be a useful idiot if you choose, and a successful idiot. I'm not surprised that you have your suspicions. All I suggest is that you try to find our dear prime minister. I assure you, you won't be able to. Then, if you like, you could air his curious non-availability in your fine newspaper. Sprinkle question marks like pepper through your copy. Ask some awkward questions. Do your job, for Christ's sake. People like you always wait for people like me to do it for you.'

With that Haydn, giving quite a good impression of a man in a petulant huff, stood and walked away. Later he would curse himself for allowing the story to drift out in such a haphazard way. But that was only when he realised how critical the timing was for his financial coup. At this moment, it seemed a perfect operation in deniable leaking, a textbook case of the real British system at work. As he walked out onto the Whitehall pavement, still crowded with tourists, he allowed himself a smirk. Job done. He imagined a fizzing line of black gunpowder in a cartoon.

After the meeting McBryde had visited one of his favourite watering holes in London, the artistically grimy Gordon's wine bar by Embankment station. There, perched at a wobbly table, he had drunk a full bottle of Barolo and composed his letter to Jen. For clarity, he typed out Haydn's story on his laptop, printed it in a copyshop, and popped it and the letter in an envelope. That really was his work done for the day. Then he had delivered the envelope to the London Library, shimmying through the evening party; the walk cleared his head.

But, as Ken Cooper occasionally observed, whatever else he was, Lucien McBryde was a proper fucking journalist. He sensed that something was wrong. Alois Haydn was no real contact or friend of his. He was clearly part of this Downing Street plot, so why the hell had he spoken to him? What was his motive? It couldn't be about power, since power appeared to be shifting, almost minute by minute, to the prime minister's rivals, primarily to Olivia Kite. So it had to be about something else. Could it be money? What was Haydn really up to?

During his long night drowning the sadness that had welled up as he wrote Jen's name, McBryde texted his old school friend with the enormous teeth and the genius for numbers. If anyone could get to the bottom of this mystery, it would surely be Charmian Locke.

10

Sunday, 17 September

Referendum Day Minus Four

Boys' Stories

Charmian's first thought was that Lucien hadn't changed much in twenty-five years. At the age of nine he had already been tall, raffish and handsome, a boy equally quick to attract admiring glances and to pick a fight. Charmian, by contrast, had been pudgy and awkward. He was slow with words because he was embarrassed by his speech impediment, and the other boys said he smelled. Break time was hell on asphalt. Charmian would linger in the classroom for as long as he could, and then skulk at the edge of the playground, where the dusty plane trees gave some protection, watching the other boys run and laugh and throw things, or just stand in easy circles, their hands in their pockets, talking like adults.

Charmian had tried to approach them, offering to share chocolate and the football coins everyone was collecting. The occasional shin-kicks and kidney-punches did not hurt nearly as much as the cold, averted faces. Indifference, though he didn't yet know the word, was the hardest thing to endure. After a while he targeted other unpopular boys, and actually made one unkempt, dwarfish friend for a while. But eventually even the other outcasts would form little circles or new boy-colonies, turning their backs on him, and Charmian would be left by himself again, a grey bundle of misery at the edge of human noise. Lucien McBryde had not persecuted him or singled him out. He had simply ignored him.

Charmian came to believe that the other boys were right, and that some original disaster must have cursed him from birth; he was an outcast because he was disgusting and pitiful, and there was nothing more to be said about it. His parents were oblivious. He never spoke of it, never cried.

So when, years later, as they were toiling up the lower slopes of A-levels and Lucien came to him for help – Charmian was no more popular than before, but he had discovered hitherto unsuspected talents for maths and science – he felt emotions he had never felt before. He was even, once, invited round to Lucien's house, where his father, a journalist, treated him with apparent respect, and Lucien himself was affable in a lordly kind of way. For the first time Charmian's world sparkled a little. Sometimes it even glowed.

The two boys never became close friends – that would have been impossible – but Charmian continued to hero-worship Lucien from a distance. They went to the same university, where Lucien was as popular and glamorous as ever. If he almost stopped acknowledging Charmian Locke, Charmian understood why. What he could never understand was Lucien's failure to live up to his brilliant promise after he left university – the stories of drunken and scandalous misbehaviour, the succession of disappointing, mediocre jobs. Charmian felt personally affronted, almost like a spurned lover. The two men did meet up very occasionally for a curry or a beer, but afterwards both would find themselves wondering why they bothered.

At 9 o'clock on this Sunday evening McBryde was back at Gordon's wine bar, at an outside table this time, finishing a bottle of claret and smoking a cigarette, with Charmian Locke sitting opposite him. When McBryde told him about his conversation with Alois Haydn just along the road in Whitehall, Charmian put out a long grey tongue and licked his large yellow teeth with it. He smiled. McBryde tried not to look.

'Shhh. . .assshh. . .tonishing. The old man'sh no more? And the world doesn't know? Ooh, Lucien, you're going to be a famous man. What'sh keeping you from writing about thish in your paper, old friend?'

'Charmian, think it through. Think like a hack. Why was that lying bastard Haydn telling that story to *me*? What's in it for him? It doesn't add up. I've told Jen about it, so even if I'm wrong, at least something will come out. But until I've worked out what Haydn's really up to, I won't sleep. I suppose it could be power – if he thinks he's been backing the wrong horse in the referendum. But my hunch is that it's money. We're talking about some pretty serious inside information here, aren't we?'

Locke found it hard not to blurt out that he knew Alois Haydn very well. But he realised that he had to stay close. If the PM really was dead, then some great game was surely in play; Haydn would have had his reasons. But this blabbering wreck of the boy he'd once almost loved was now a very loose cannon indeed. Once before, long ago, Charmian had confided in McBryde. He'd been led on to boast – in this very wine bar, in fact – about some inside information he'd received. He'd read a ridiculous account of it in the *Courier* two days later, and an hour after that he'd lost his job. McBryde disclaimed all responsibility, but when Charmian had checked out the byline of the financial reporter who'd ruined him the man had turned out not to exist, and he'd never discovered who'd hidden behind the pseudonym. Now, as he listened to McBryde grandstanding, it was all so obvious. Sprawled in a chair before him was someone who'd do anything for a story.

Charmian had a motto: 'Forgive your enemies, but never forget their names.' Now he had a name, and he was feeling increasingly thin on the forgiveness side. The more he thought about it, the more it felt like a peculiarly personal betrayal. So he talked on, flattering McBryde with jargon-laced theories, his pebble eyes growing stonier as he enjoyed the journalist's rapt attention.

McBryde, in truth, understood very little of the financial jargon and the percentages, but he did grasp the essential point – advance knowledge of a change in the likely outcome of the referendum could make someone very rich indeed – and jotted down a few notes.

What he had told Jen in his London Library note was meaningless, he realised, without this last piece of the jigsaw. He felt he now understood Haydn's motive.

Two *Courier* colleagues were finishing up at another table. As soon as Charmian headed for the gents McBryde went over to them, with his note carefully folded over.

'Fenton. Price. Not your normal hangout. But a piece of luck for me. I'm on a story, guys, not just on the piss. Could you take this to the London Library? Whack it into the latest Dominic Sandbrook?'

'Lucien. Greetings, you dirty fucker. No prob. Girl trouble?'

'Something like that.'

Jammed in a queue in the gents, waiting his turn, Charmian thought back to his childhood and the infuriating, charming figure of Lucien McBryde. He had no intention of angering Sir Solomon Dundas, or bringing down Alois Haydn. And he certainly saw no reason why he shouldn't make a little money himself. But Lucien was in danger of getting in his way.

So when he returned upstairs, instead of saying goodnight he suggested that they move on to the American Bar at the Savoy, just around the corner. There he drank tonic water while McBryde sank one whisky sour after another. Then they went for cocktails at Christopher's. Charmian drank tonic water. McBryde drank cocktails. After this they headed east, McBryde walking like a man recovering unsuccessfully from a stroke. By the time they arrived at the Cheshire Cheese in Fleet Street he was becoming sentimental.

'Wrgg. Gaaah. . .aabbia. Nnnn. 'nifer. 'ucked up. Gaagh,' he said.

'I think we need something solid inside us, don't you old friend?' said Charmian, leading McBryde by the elbow into the Golden Cockerel. He got them a table outside, on the smoking terrace – McBryde was loudly grateful – where they sat alone in the cool late-evening air. Charmian ordered steaks for both of them, and another bottle of red wine. McBryde, he noticed, was well beyond taking any notice of the food, though he managed most of the bottle.

McBryde clearly thought he was talking, since his mouth was moving, but only a thin, incoherent trickle of sound came out. By the time Charmian's prodigious teeth had devoured his steak, his friend had laid his head on his plate and was fast asleep.

Charmian, who knew the restaurant well, quickly went inside, dodged behind the bar and removed a key labelled 'Terrace'. He returned to their table, undid McBryde's trousers and yanked them down to his ankles. Then he went back into the main restaurant, locking the door behind him. From inside McBryde was invisible, concealed behind a row of yew bushes. Charmian paid the bill and left.

'Goodbye, old pal,' he said. 'I wish I could say good luck.' Strangely, there was no hint of his famous lisp.

This was, Charmian thought, in no real sense murder. He believed that those who raised themselves did so by climbing, while those who destroyed themselves did so by flinging themselves off the ladders – or the restaurant terraces – squandering their gifts and embracing destruction. Should it happen that McBryde was left alone and unnoticed when the restaurant closed, and should it further happen that, with several litres of alcohol inside him, he woke up at some time of the night in urgent need of relief, and should it further happen that in the dark, with his trousers around his ankles, he should stumble and topple over the low railing that was the only barrier between the terrace and the street below – if all of this should happen, who would be to blame but McBryde himself?

*

Lying with his face on his plate, Lucien McBryde was dreaming of Jen, her pale arms around him and her tongue in his mouth. Then the dream faded, and he began to shudder with the night's chill. He needed a piss. Christ, it was dark. . .

I I

Tuesday, 19 September

Referendum Day Minus Two

Virtual Reality

From the start the conspirators had known that there would be some things over which they would have no control. When asked about his biggest problems in office, the languid old showman Harold Macmillan had memorably answered, 'Events, dear boy, events.' And so it proved.

The American ambassador in Rome was travelling home from a short break at his rural villa when his car was stopped by two motorbikes. Five bullets took out his driver, the sixth killed him. His wife sustained serious internal injuries. The gunman and his two accomplices, captured by the Italian police after trying to escape on foot, turned out to be British Muslims from Manchester. Not surprisingly, the White House was on the line almost at once: the president insisted on talking to her good friend the prime minister face to face, via their video-conferencing rooms.

Dickie Greene, the former chairman of the Joint Intelligence Committee, had been working for PLS for four years. Noisy, rasping, garrulous and opinionated, he had fallen out badly with Tony Blair, and had never fitted in with the smooth atmosphere under David Cameron. He had been a very important hiring for the company, but there was a general feeling that up to now he had, frankly, not quite earned his keep. Today, at last, he did so.

When the president, flanked by her national security adviser and the director of the CIA, flickered into life on the screen, she saw no British prime minister in front of her. But the Americans did recognise most of those seated around the table in London: Sir Richard Greene had been back and forth to Washington during the Iraqi and Afghanistan wars; the foreign secretary, Jason Latimer; the former chief of the Defence Staff, Admiral Lord Jock Dalgety.

'Good afternoon, gentlemen,' said the president. 'Where is my old friend the prime minister? This is a grave day for both of our countries. . .'

'You'll remember me, I'm sure, Madam President,' replied Greene. 'And I'm glad to see two other old friends with you. I'm afraid the fact of the matter is that this is a graver day in London than perhaps you realise over there. The men who were apprehended in Rome were not working alone. We have uncovered a very serious threat to the life of the prime minister, which was planned to take effect today. For that reason, as I'm sure you will understand, we have decided to move him to an entirely secure location. Nothing but the gravest concern would have led us to take this step. He has asked me to give you his personal apologies for not being here this afternoon.'

The president, stony-faced, gave the briefest of nods. A short, businesslike exchange of information, followed by a discussion of pan-European security protocols and an agreed statement of apology and sympathy on behalf of HM government, drafted earlier by Dame Cecily Morgan, took up the rest of the meeting.

The plotters had got away with it again. But they were very close to panic. The press were beginning to ask some awkward questions. And Briskett was still on the loose.

And then there was the ever-present vigilance needed in Number 10 itself. As Amanda had predicted, one of the biggest problems for the plotters was to limit the number of those inside Downing Street who became aware of what was going on. More than 150 people had access to the complex network of rooms that sprawled through what had originally been three shabby terraced houses.

With Francis Fieldfare out of circulation, Number 10's chief of staff, Chris Tickell, the political operator responsible for the PM's relationship with the rest of the parliamentary party and the opposition, as well as writing most of the jokes for his speeches, was the greatest danger.

In the basement of the building, directly below the prime minister's study and the private secretaries' office, a constant scrum of people bustled up and down the corridor leading to the secure office, with its paperwork and its secrets, and the kitchen and laundry. The buzz down there was a questioning hum, puzzled but not angry. From the Russian specialist on secondment from the Foreign Office to the man who replenished the vending machines with chocolate bars, everybody sensed that something was wrong. The hive had no queen, and the bees were beginning to notice. Self-importantly elbowing his way along the narrow corridor, Chris Tickell found himself pressed against Sam Mulligan, the cheerful, red-faced diary secretary. In a world where status was measured by proximity to the PM, the two men felt themselves equals.

'Rum business, Chris.'

'Damn shady, Sam.'

'Seen the old man lately?'

'Not a flash or a feather of him. All of these oldsters around the place suddenly – high security clearance and all that, but I don't quite understand what they're doing here. Have you spoken to Fieldfare?'

'Yesterday, not today.'

'Pompous long email from him this morning, rambling on about a big crisis in the City, plus the German thing, and now this shooting in Italy.'

'Yes, I got that too. That's why we haven't seen the PM. Have to be patient, keep our heads down and keep the machines rolling, all that stuff. Everything clearer after the referendum's done.'

'That's the one. Convinced?'

'Not at all. I don't like the mood in here, and I don't like those people crawling about upstairs.'

'Nor me.'

'Going to do anything about it?'

'If I could think of something.'

'We could try finding a way of getting into the flat to speak to him.'

'Yes, I did think of that. But what if he's up there, all busy and angry? What do we say? "Oh, prime minister, just wondering if you were still alive"? He wouldn't be a happy bunny. We wouldn't be working here much longer.'

'That's more or less what I thought too. Don't fancy it much.'

'Nor me.'

Two floors above them, Ronnie Ashe was reflecting that as chief whip he may have been an expert in the ways of the House of Commons, but he was less well-versed in those of Downing Street. Nevertheless, even he couldn't remain unaware of the questioning, almost pre-mutinous mood in the building. He finally managed to pin down the foreign secretary.

'This isn't going to hold for much longer, Jason. Half the private secretaries know something's up, and I think the garden girls as well. Then there's our rogue historian.'

'All right. So what do you suggest?' said Latimer.

'Well, we can't go around bumping more people off. We're surely accessories to murder already, after poor Fieldfare.'

'You're right, Ronnie. We certainly don't need any more bodies lying around. But I've given that Polish chap some thought. He was brought in by Haydn. It's his fault. If we stick together, we can load the blame onto him. Where is Haydn originally from, by the way?'

'Iraq, I've heard.'

'You sure? I always thought he was a Kraut.'

Ronnie, his mind slightly more at ease following this conversation, nevertheless thanked his maker that Parliament was not sitting, and that most cabinet ministers were safely out of London. Even so, there were still just too many people here – all the wonks and advisers, never mind the secretaries and the secretaries' secretaries. At least the clock was ticking. They were now only two days away from the vote, and there had been a gleam of hope from the digital weirdos that they just might be able to deliver a full, face-on, speaking PM. Maybe they would get that final speech after all.

But the tension was taking its toll on all of them. Ronnie was feeling trashed. Amanda looked shattered, and Nelson Fraser stank like a recently disinterred mammoth. Ronnie had found the pair of them stark naked in the prime minister's well-appointed small study upstairs – the room in which Samantha Cameron had once designed her dresses. Their exhaustion was not just post-coital.

Reptiles

And then there were the gentlemen, and the ladies, of the press.

There had been a sticky meeting of the parliamentary press lobby at its daily briefing, moved for the duration of the referendum campaign out of the usual tiny room up a spiral staircase in the Commons to more spacious surroundings in Number 10.

On parade in the overheated pale-wood-panelled room, crammed onto plastic chairs and having been ordered to surrender their mobile phones on entering the building, the cream of London's political journalists felt penned and frustrated.

PMOS – the prime minister's official spokesman, Nelson Fraser – was parrying some lacklustre attempts to turn that day's supposed incident at Bluewater into a 'Prime Minister Insults Pensioner' story when the veteran reporter Simon Selfridge rose from his seat at the back of the room.

'Fraser, all very interesting, as usual. Many thanks. But we'd like to *see* the prime minister. We'd like to talk to him. We've been dragged over here, day after day, in the middle of this huge crisis which we're told is tearing the country in two, and without wanting to be pompous about it, I think the PM owes it to the free press to come occasionally and make his case in person. So where is he? Can you go and get him?'

Nelson Fraser smiled, and shrugged, and shook his head, and

made deflecting gestures, but there was a hubbub of agreement throughout the room. He leaned forward over the baize-and-hardboard podium. 'He's just along the corridor, working like a maniac as you'd expect, Simon. He's a very busy man.' But the grunts and exclamations of protest only grew louder. Several of the hacks were claiming that they refused to leave the room until they had seen the PM.

The exhausted Fraser decided that the moment had come to take a calculated gamble. A lobby lock-in would be a major story, and he would have to head it off, whatever followed. He took a deep breath.

'All right, I'll go and get him. Would the chairman of the lobby like to come too?'

Fraser, who had had a distinguished career working for the *Guardian* and *The Times* before being poached by the prime minister, had no idea how he was going to get out of this one. Alois Haydn, who he knew all too well had never liked him, would have his guts for garters. And Amanda. . . But he had to keep his mind off her. Still, accompanied by the fat and self-important figure of the lobby chairman, the long-standing political editor of the Leeds and Halifax newspaper group, the PMOS walked confidently enough down the corridor and rapped on the prime minister's door. There was no answer. He pushed it open. The room was empty. That was odd, since he had left Bremner there immediately before taking the briefing.

Then he heard a cough from behind the closed door of the annexe to one side: the prime minister was in the bathroom.

'This is a little embarrassing, Simon,' said Fraser to the chairman of the lobby. 'As you can see, the prime minister is – engaged.'

Just then, from behind the door came the unmistakable voice of the man himself. 'Who's that out there? Is that you, Nelson, you

Caledonian maniac? And there's someone with you. Simon Selfridge, our esteemed lobby chairman, I think.'

'Yes, prime minister,' said Selfridge. 'It's good to, ah, come across you in person. The lads were hoping you'd be able to give them a few minutes on your final thoughts before the country actually goes to vote. . .'

There was a long pause from behind the door. Finally the silence was broken. 'I'm, as it were, rather *engaged*, Simon. Have you heard the one about Churchill and Sir Stafford Cripps? True story. . .'

'No, prime minister, I don't believe I have,' said Selfridge, with a sinking feeling that he was losing control of the situation. The prime minister's stock of anecdotage was legendary – as was his use of it to deflect uncomfortable questions.

'Weelll. . . Cripps had just come back from Moscow, all vinegar and socialism, and Churchill loathed him as much as ever. It was 1942, I think, and Winston was rather on his uppers. We tend to forget that he lost popularity at times, even in the middle of the fighting. Well, Churchill suspected Cripps, who was then lord privy seal, of being after his job. He wasn't far wrong. Cripps came to see him, and was standing more or less where you are now, but he found the prime minister then in the same condition that the prime minister is in today. So he got the official messenger to knock on the bathroom door. "Sir Stafford Cripps insists on seeing you immediately," Churchill was told. Winston's growl came back straight away. "Tell the lord privy seal that the prime minister is on the privy, and he can only deal with one shit at a time."'

There was a long, guttural laugh, then Bremner put an end to the conversation. 'So go back and tell your girls and boys that we had a nice chat, and that you did your best for them, but the circumstances were not propitious.'

Simon Selfridge waddled back down the corridor, hugging to

himself a story and a meeting that he knew he could never use in print, but that would buy him more than one whisky and soda at the parliamentary press bar.

And so that crisis, too, had passed.

Old Flames, Flickering

Lord Briskett had started to feel uneasy almost as soon as he put his phone back in his pocket, even though he was in Paradise – a good bookshop. He had half a dozen hardbacks under his left arm, a credit card in his teeth, and his briefcase dangling from the other arm. He was at Hatchards in Piccadilly, talking to the manager about a rare first edition he was trying to track down. The bookshop was on the verge of closing for the night, and his legs were tiring after a day spent wandering around London.

Apart from that, the more he thought about what had been going on in Number 10, the more troubled he felt. Was Ned in danger? From the tone of his call he had certainly thought he was running a risk in taking Jennifer Lewis out to Essex. Briskett suspected there might be aspects of this whole affair that he didn't yet fully understand.

He put down his briefcase, pulled his credit card from his teeth and paid, having entirely forgotten about the elusive first edition. His eyes drifted over the tempting tables of new books, coming to rest on a florid design in purple, pink and gold that read *Kafka in Kensington – A Novel*. By Myfanwy Davies-Jones.

Briskett had a brainwave. He'd known Myfanwy back in the seventies, when he was a radical young academic with permed hair. Hadn't everyone? He also knew, because Ned Parminter had told him, that Jennifer Lewis was Myfanwy's daughter. Her only daughter.

So they must be close. If anyone knew what was going on, and could help him to put anything right that needed putting right, it would surely be Myfanwy Davies-Jones. She had always been game for an adventure.

Using his charm with the bookshop manager, Briskett obtained the name of Myfanwy's publicist, and even as he was walking back up Piccadilly he heard her voice on his phone – a voice that had only become deeper and sexier in the past thirty years.

'Dear thing,' he said.

'Dear heart,' Myfanwy replied.

'Sweet girl.'

'My *lovely* man.'

'It's been too long.'

'Dear, *dear* heart.'

'You sound just the same.'

'Darling, special man.'

'I have a small favour to ask,' said Briskett, preening.

'. . .All right, I'm foxed. Who exactly *is* this?' said Myfanwy.

But eventually the dim memory of a rather sexy young don bounced to the surface of Myfanwy's lightly sherried brain, and she agreed to meet him in a café overlooking Sloane Square an hour later.

By the time he arrived Myfanwy had clearly been sitting at the outside table for some time: Lord Briskett noticed an ashtray filled with lipstick-smeared butts, a nearly-empty bottle of wine and a sentimental look on her face. He still felt offended – all those years of letting it be known at high table that he'd been 'very close to' the famous, mysterious Myfanwy Davies-Jones, and the wretched woman was too sozzled to remember him. He'd been pretty good, he'd thought. They'd connected. He'd thought.

'How now, old cow,' he greeted her, not entirely nicely.

'Sorry, sweetie. But you were a long time ago.'

'So much to talk about at any rate, now we're here. One of your children, to start with.'

Myfanwy roused herself. 'One of? I only have poor little Mademoiselle J. Wren. That's the lot, you tweedie barbarian.'

'Oh Myfanwy, Myfanwy darling, I'm a historian. Or had you forgotten? I *remember things* for a living. I even remember people's voices.'

Briskett gestured wordlessly for a second bottle of wine, took one of Myfanwy's Camels and lit it, barely pausing for breath.

'So I remember full well your *first* child, the little boy, even if you affect not to. Lots of speculation at the time about the father. Lord Croaker, *Requiescat in pace*? I rather fancied that it might be Rufus Panzer, the lecherous old maniac. Always liked Rufus myself. But you gave the boy away, didn't you sweetie? Who was it? Camden social workers? Or the nuns?'

'Don't be vulgar. So many good friends one had, who offered. . . He's much better off than he would ever have been if he'd stayed with me.'

'Ah,' said Briskett, with the expression of a man who's just looked down and seen a winning hand. 'But I seem to remember the rumours at the time. That you'd actually held a dinner party and *auctioned* him.'

Myfanwy stared at the traffic wordlessly for a full two minutes. 'Balls.'

'Thank God for that,' Briskett sighed. 'It was a ghastly little story.'

'I don't give dinner parties. Never have. I auctioned him at a luncheon.'

A longer silence followed. Briskett felt that he'd had his revenge. In any case, Myfanwy had moved on.

'So what were you going to tell me about Jenny? The poor dear girl has got herself into trouble at last,' Myfanwy said eventually. 'Actually, it's the first interesting thing that's ever happened to her. For a long time I could hardly believe she was mine. So little blood in her. There are only two things that matter in life, Lord Briskett of Bollocksy College, Oxbollocks. They are sex appeal and a generous heart. Poor little Jennifer never had either. Or so I always thought.'

Briskett, who'd forgotten Myfanwy's robust conversational style, but was fast recalling how much he'd once enjoyed it, explained that his young researcher had telephoned, and that he seemed to be carrying Jennifer away from the jaws of danger, but that he'd sounded dazed, as if he needed help.

Myfanwy, who seemed hardly to have been listening, now embarked on a philosophical diversion. Wasn't it interesting, she said, that the only real impulses of humankind were lust and love; and they were not siblings, or even related, like red and pink – but deadly foes. Nobody stood up for lust in a cultural sense. Who ever had? Silly little Lawrence, *The Rite of Spring* and a small platoon of ridiculous literary pornographers. Love – purer, less selfish – had on its side all the religions, the great poets and novelists, the lawmakers. 'But in a fair fight, Briskers, lust wins every time. Culture and religion add up to diddly-squat. The warnings of hell, the happy endings, mean nothing compared to the sight of a shapely bottom walking down the street.'

Briskett, who found himself enjoying her company more every moment, replied that Myfanwy had always thought like a man, not a woman.

'Secret of my success,' she replied, unaffronted.

Briskett dragged the conversation back to business. In order to keep the 'Yes to Europe' movement ahead in the polls, he said, the death of the prime minister had been hushed up. Jennifer had heard about this, and that was why she was on her way to Olivia Kite's house at that moment.

'I know all that,' said Myfanwy. 'She told me some of it, and a rather crude man – Russian, I think – working for that foul little splodge Alois Haydn confirmed it.'

'But what I don't understand, Myfanwy, is why your daughter is in danger, and why Haydn, of all people, should be after her. He must know that the plot's failed. The news is going to come out, one way or another. Surely at this point he should be thinking about leaving the country. He's not British, after all. From Alexandria originally, according to my sources.'

Myfanwy looked a little disconcerted.

'He is certainly not from Egypt. He is from. . . around here' – she waved vaguely at the King's Road before draining the last of the bottle and continuing. 'Dear heart, what Alois is up to now is pretty obvious once you think about it. But that's not the point. It's probably true that Jennifer is in danger. I didn't really believe her to start with. But I believe her now.'

Briskett raised his eyebrows questioningly and offered her one of her own cigarettes.

'And I'll explain every single last thing, m'lord, if you agree to come with me. This has all gone on for long enough, and Alois must be stopped. The time has come for you and me to pay a visit to that dreary house in the country and sort things out. The old way.' Myfanwy reached into her battered Chanel handbag and pulled out a small ebony-handled pistol.

'We are going prepared. Dear, sweet Lord Croaker gave me this when I was quite a young thing. I've never had occasion to use it, not properly. Perhaps this adventure will be different. . .'

Briskett flinched. He had an appetite for a story, but none for violence. Weakly, he pointed out that he had no car.

'Don't be a big girl's blouse, professor,' said Myfanwy. 'It's far too late to set off now. We'll go together, first thing tomorrow morning. And in the meantime you will come and stay, and we'll get to know one another better once again. I confess it, I couldn't quite remember you at first my dear, but there are certain little details I would like to refresh my memory about.' Briskett had gone the colour of poached salmon. He remembered very well. He stood and bowed slightly.

The following morning, with Lord Briskett following in her wake, Myfanwy Davies-Jones walked down the stairs of her apartment block and straight into the street without pausing to check the traffic. She raised one hand, let her jacket fly open and called, 'Taxi!'

On the Verge

They should have driven faster. By the time her mother was giving Lord Briskett that brief glimpse of her pistol, Jennifer was on her own.

The A12 had begun life ringing to the clatter, curses and alien commands of sweating Roman legionaries as they built what was first known as the Inter V, a dead-straight spear jabbing out north-east from Londinium. But it had been badly mucked about with by the locals after the Italians with their German work ethic had gone home.

No hills around here, no West Country knolls or northern moor-land – just flat fields, their dark, almost black ploughed soil sprouting barley, with pylons and occasional grain silos like dark, upraised fingers on the horizon. Almost every roadside sign was covered in graffiti; blunt, dwarf words, limping refugees from the language of Johnson, Dickens and Orwell. And the hedgerows and grass verges were bestrewn with strips and rips of plastic bags and discarded fast-food containers. This was countryside designed for bleak weather, short days and low cloud.

The road grew narrower, and a high drystone wall made a grey serpent alongside it for several miles, interrupted only by a pair of pillared gates. Somebody's fine house, and no sign of a National Trust logo. The sky was that impenetrable almost-white with hints of green and purple that you normally only get in eastern England at the end of an interminable winter. Yet it was mid-September, and the weather was warm.

After many miles of companionable silence Ned slowed and parked at the point where the estate wall ended, then he and Jen got wordlessly out of the car and began to kiss again. Tongue under tongue. Ned had never thought he would be much good at whatever he knew must now follow. He always carried with him the burden of rejections and the harrowing sound of mocking girlish laughter. But instinct took over as he began to ease Jen's tight blue jeans gently downwards, lifting her almost off her feet as he tugged them hard over her small white bottom. She reached around behind his shoulders, gasping slightly. The jeans became snagged on her boots.

She grunted, leaned over, resting one hand on the car door, and violently kicked off both jeans and boots, leaving herself bare from the waist down. Ned, shaking, took the opportunity to unbuckle his belt and hoick at his trousers. Jen could feel the damp leaves and clay under her feet. She reached up again, ground herself into Ned's chest and dug her sharp fingers through his wiry hair. She put both arms around his shoulders and lifted herself up, impaling herself most successfully. Ned, pleased as he was by this development, was simultaneously wondering if his legs would give way. Both of them had been thinking about this ever since they had got into the car in London. And the sex worked; they bucked like deer and squirmed like eels. And after that, vice-versa.

'What on earth do I see in him?' Jen had asked herself an hour earlier, looking at the strong, pale fingers resting on the gearstick and the guarded face staring through the splashes of rain and muck on the windscreen. The answer, she eventually decided, was a musky, reliable, old-fashioned manhood, romantic but stable. Here was somebody who would never not turn up, a man you could lean upon. Hardly beautiful. In fact a clumsy, nervous male animal. But it was the thought that making love with him was so incongruous, the thought of him looking down at himself in bemusement, that made the prospect of it so exciting. She had no idea what was going on in his mind. She liked that too. Most men were grimy windows: a quick rub and you could see everything inside. Not Ned Parminter.

Ned's thoughts at that moment were not, as it happened, particularly elevated. He was thinking hard about her nose, the way she wrinkled it when she was thinking, and about her legs, the way she had stayed pressed to him after that ambrosial coffee that morning. Ripeness is all. Ever since she had dumped Lucien McBryde, an event which had briefly been the talk of Westminster, Jen had been at least theoretically available. Ned had never been put off by her famous chilliness. To him she seemed interestingly tensed, or primed, rather than cold. Nor was he distracted by her fiercely-held political views, above all her loathing of the European empire. He himself was also politically conservative, nostalgic for an emptier, kinder, less frantic England. And people who are interested in politics tend to be interested in people who are interested in politics. Flinty, he needed a spark; and Jennifer Lewis, though cautious, was whetstone-hard.

Jen was, however, by now melting and finished, and had held Ned inside her for as long as he could manage. The two of them were kissing lightly on a patch of damp, clean grass. Lust gone, Ned was becoming aware of a twig pressing into his left buttock, while Jen's shivers were now from the cold only. Soon they were doing the ungainly hopping dance the English – and only the English – perform when getting hurriedly dressed out of doors. The old car hid them from the occasional passing traffic.

So the mood was broken. Guiltily, Jen turned her mind to what lay ahead of them. If she could convince Olivia that the prime minister was dead, Olivia would then be able to shock the country into a last-minute reconsideration of just how this old, cynical, corrupt political game was being played. It was unthinkable that the voters would not turn on those who had deceived them. The entire future of the British Isles hung in the balance, a balance which could be tipped by a few words from her, Jennifer Lewis. Yet here she was, thinking about none of that, delayed and distracted by a man she hardly knew, like a pilgrim seduced. He had been after her for weeks. Well, now it had happened. That was that.

She suddenly felt intensely weary. She really didn't fathom Ned. How could she ever have thought of trusting him? He was some sort of academic. . . He must have his own interests. He wasn't a friend, perhaps not even an ally. She had simply run to him, in a mixture of blind panic and blind faith, to take her away from London and the threat of Alois Haydn — whom she had no doubt would have her killed if he thought it necessary, just as she had no doubt that he had somehow had Lucien McBryde killed. Yet here she was nevertheless, only a few miles from Olivia's house, on the verge of changing England's long history.

But now, weak and confused, Jen's intense need for order kicked in. She could not afford all this. Without thinking more than instinctively she refastened her bra, leaned into the back seat of the car and felt her fingers rest on a heavy object — Myfanwy's wrench. She swung round and brought it down hard on Ned's tousled head. He said, 'Hmm. Ahh?', slumped to his knees, and toppled over. He didn't move. There wasn't much blood.

Jen finished dressing, then wrapped her arms around his chest for the final time and dragged him away from the car towards a line of larches. In their shadows was a green plastic bin attached to a concrete pillar, which she had not noticed before. A sign on it read 'East Ness Borough Council. No general rubbish — dog mess only'. She gently propped Ned Parminter, BA Oxon, against it, and climbed back into his car.

As she sped away she looked in the wing mirror, and glimpsed a leather-jacketed man in a motorcycle helmet watching her closely from the opposite side of the road. Still distracted by the thought of what she had just done, she didn't see him slowly pulling a gun from the pannier of his motorbike.

Over to Olivia

Olivia Kite was also feeling distracted as she paced the library of Danskin House, her heels making tiny indentations on floorboards that had been laid when William Shakespeare was newly dead. She peered through the half-open door: her advisers were clustered around a television screen, clucking away in despair. The prime minister's final broadcast ahead of the vote had just finished, and they were all agreed that it had been a masterpiece – a master-piece of malice and innuendo, but of political genius too. He had barely referred to his German triumph, as if it were simply taken for granted. Olivia supposed that he had scheduled some Olympian pressing of the flesh for the next day, floating confidently above the battle.

The broadcast had started with the prime minister staring out of a window of Number 10 into the Downing Street garden, the sun playing on his face and hands. Then the picture dissolved into grainy black and white, as viewers were invited to imagine the United Kingdom's dystopian future outside Europe, a land of pinched, Soviet-style poverty, with London an echoing relic of its current glory. The PM's voice-over had been lugubrious and reflec-tive, the man at his very most persuasive as he sketched out a vision of life in the Backwater Islands, a land too bewitched by its own history to dare to play any meaningful role in the modern world. Olivia herself featured as a kind of Wicked Witch of this Winter

Kingdom, the Cruella of contemporary conservatism. With grinding Shostakovich music punctuating the prime minister's words, it was a shocking, brutally effective little film.

It ended with the prime minister standing at the end of the cabinet table, around which, thanks to computer wizardry, were seated not just a few of the more eminent faces of the current cabinet but some famous figures from history – a slight, long-haired Horatio Nelson; an imperturbable Winston Churchill; Margaret Thatcher poking through her handbag – 'Margaret in this?' spluttered Olivia's press officer. 'Quite disgraceful! Is there nothing the man won't stoop to?' Finally the prime minister gestured around the table, stared at the camera – albeit from a long way away – and concluded: 'Please, ignore some of the ridiculous rumours you may have heard in recent days. Believe in me, as you always have done. And vote to stay part of a *Great* Britain.'

The reference to the rumours about his health proved conclusively that the prime minister was still active.

Back in Number 10, Dame Cecily Morgan turned to the three men with whom she had been watching the broadcast: Nelson Fraser, who had written most of the words; Rory Bremner, who had spoken them; and the awkward-looking goth, who had created the images. 'Gentlemen, for all your preposterous conceit, that was a masterwork.'

'Thank you, Baroness,' replied Bremner. 'But I can't help wondering whether the old PM was really such a genius after all. That was the best, most eloquent speech he ever made, and he didn't write a word of it.'

Nelson Fraser, whose Hunting Tadger kilt now hung like creased curtains from his waist, shook his gingery head. 'Now, we can't say that. The words were mine, but the inspiration was all his. I pride myself on being able to turn a phrase, but all that was nothing more than the higher plagiarism.'

Looking in particular at the goth, Dame Cecily put an end to the conversation. 'Well, remember, none of you can *ever* discuss this. The PM doesn't die until after the voting finishes on Thursday. So my "well done" is the most you will ever hear. Now piss off, the lot of you.'

As they left they passed Amanda Andrews standing in the corridor. She applauded them, her eyes full of tears.

That business concluded satisfactorily, Dame Cecily phoned Haydn again. She didn't need to explain what she was calling about. She'd resolved her moral dilemma by telling him about the leak – he'd seemed blandly unsurprised by the news – but had made him swear that no violence would be used against Briskett, who was after all a decent enough man.

'Any sign?'

'None. He turned up at the *National Courier* office but didn't get to see anyone, and now he's vanished again. We haven't been able to trace him with CCTV cameras, although I'm pretty sure he hasn't been onto the tube or to any of the main train stations. And he hasn't been back to his flat. I have limited resources, of course. It's time for you people to pull your fingers out and help. We absolutely have to shut His Lordship up.'

'But not for good, Alois. That's absolutely not necessary.'

'Analyse the word "necessary", Cecily. Don't hide behind euphemisms.'

'I've been hiding behind euphemisms all my professional life, you silly little man,' said Dame Cecily, and ended the call. She regretted her closing words immediately. Whatever one thought of Alois Haydn, he was not a man to offend, still less to disregard.

But it was too late for regrets. Haydn had been speaking to her from Essex. He had a contract with one of the smaller private companies operating out of Battersea heliport, and it had only taken a single call and a short taxi ride before he was lifting off from the tiny concrete curtain beside the Thames. Getting in and out of London by helicopter was becoming harder every year – a string of near-misses and a crash into a crane had made the route ever more convoluted – but it wasn't long before, headphones clamped over his ears, he was staring down at the long, grey wash of East London as it straggled towards the North Sea. The ride was cold, and Alois could feel his teeth chattering, but as they headed north along the coast the sun came out. He could pick out Danskin House with its turret and flag, surrounded by trees. Then there was the crazy-paving maze of wetland and, still looking raw and unfinished, his own house, Rocks Point.

Haydn was afraid of flying, and he was still shaking slightly when he was greeted at the door by Ajit. They kissed on both cheeks, then Alois pulled himself away.

'No time to lose, darling. I have to get over to Danskin House. Meeting I can't get out of. . .'

Olivia licked her lips when she saw him. Haydn had heard the phrase, of course, but he had never actually seen anyone lick their lips in quite the way Olivia did.

'You are the mistress here,' he said. 'I have some news for you which will make you the mistress of everything.'

'I am the mistress. What does that make you?'

'Today, your humble servant, a mere messenger.' Alois felt himself breathing more heavily. But he made himself sit down, and continued to speak calmly enough.

'The prime minister is dead. He has been dead for several days. Everything that's come out of Number 10 since then has been a fiction. A confection. A lie.'

Olivia moved not a muscle. She was so still she seemed mineral.

Not the blink of an eyelash. Not the faintest movement of nostril or lip.

'We – that is, the inner group at Number 10 – felt that you were bound to win the referendum if it got out. So we panicked, Olivia. It's a massive cover-up. Now you can reveal the truth and change everything.'

Olivia laid her thumb against her mouth. She grimaced so that her perfect teeth were visible. Then she bit herself, hard.

Shaking her hand, she asked, 'Proof? Motive?'

'You know how to get proof. Half a dozen telephone calls, half a dozen shaky voices. Come on Olivia, don't insult me. As for motive, whatever you think of me I'm a patriot. All I want is to be as welcome on board as the first recruits who clambered up the rope a year ago.'

'You want to be mine.'

'I want to be yours.'

'You may find that more arduous than you imagine,' said Olivia, turning her back on him. Within moments she had called half a dozen aides to her side and was orchestrating a flurry of arrangements. Haydn found himself feeling both aghast and admiring as he watched her. He had always thought of himself as a player. He was nothing. *This* was a player.

Meanwhile, the first reverberations from the PM's broadcast were beginning to be felt. Political editors and a handful of anti-Europe government ministers immediately got on the phone to Danskin House for Olivia Kite's reaction. The general view was that the broadcast was devastating, and everyone wanted to know how she would respond to it. They couldn't understand her cheerful and dismissive answers to their questions. But she knew exactly what her public riposte was going to be. The guy was dead. If his final appearance had been achieved merely by clever trickery, so much the better: the British people would be all the more offended by the cynicism of the ghouls in Number 10. Very soon she was going to blow this whole referendum sky high.

Very soon – but not quite yet. Her instincts told her that Haydn was holding something back. His story didn't quite add up. If he was wrong, or if he wan't telling the whole truth, she could still be left looking like an idiot. She continued to ponder as she paced the flagstones in front of the old grey orchard.

The political crisis and her own private crisis merged in her mind. She had not forgiven her husband's adultery; but he was a weak man, and she was not a woman to look behind her for long. And at this moment she felt herself suddenly becoming interested in a man she had known for years, and who, despite his well-known homosexuality, had often eyed her with a look she could not misread.

Yes, to reel in Alois Haydn, the prime minister's most notorious apparatchik, at this moment of all moments, would cause widespread amazement, as well as prurient speculation. She'd like to see him on his knees. If only she knew what was really going on in his mind. But the one thing everyone knew about Alois Haydn was that he always found himself on the winner's side. That in itself could be useful. Yes, that was it. That was the answer.

At the moment she chose to tell the world about the deception being practised in Downing Street, Haydn should be standing along-side her. He would admit his early complicity, name his fellow villains, and pledge his loyalty to her. This would send an unmistak-able message. As an added bonus, it would humiliate and infuriate Reeder. It would also, however, mean that she would be leaning very heavily on the slight figure of Alois Haydn, who even then was waiting in the pantry for her decision. He had his part to play. Meanwhile, he might be in for an uncomfortably long wait. She had to know everything about this situation. And she didn't, not yet.

Olivia walked indoors and across a vaulted hallway to the house's dining room, now the buzzing nerve centre of her campaign, where sugar plantations had been bought and sold, merchant ships paid for and their voyages plotted, complex petitions drafted to a succession of monarchs, and where the Kite family cats now prowled and mewed in confusion. The old oak table had been cleared for maps and handwritten charts marking out the last twenty-four hours of campaigning. Olivia lit one of her rare cigarettes, picked up a riding crop and began to prod the papers, glancing at printouts of the latest polling.

She felt broadly satisfied. Everything that could be done was being done. Jimmy Cardigan, the trade union leader and Labour frontbencher, once fanatically Europhile, had agreed to appear alongside Matthew Aron, the most ideologically pure of the Tory free marketeers, in Leicester. Both Sky and the BBC had promised to cover the event, and she had a big clutch of MPs in Birmingham – all local, but no real newsmakers. This referendum was going to be all about the undecideds. Boris had taken a while to come off the fence, and she had been trying to persuade Isabel Ashley, the stand-up comedian, and Lord Osborne, the former Tory treasurer, now a crossbencher, to come over to what she had tried to convince them would be the winning side, but neither seemed keen. She shrugged. Everything would change with tomorrow's press conference. To that she now turned her formidable attention.

In the slackening breeze the Union Jack hung limply from the central tower of Danskin House.

Enter, a Bear

Just a few miles away, Ajit Gupta had taken one of the racing bicycles that were kept outside the kitchen for the use of visitors and was vigorously pedalling through the dusk towards the nearest village. Sand martins darted above and sea lavender brightened the grey-green marron grass, but Ajit kept his eyes firmly on the narrow, winding track. Here England and the sea were interlaced. Salt water could uncurl at the speed of a whip cracking, and cut a man off from the shore. Away from the track nothing was certain, no foothold reliable.

Ajit was daydreaming of a new start – lemon groves and fresh papaya, with the sound of breaking waves in the distance. What did breadfruit taste like? It sounded horrible. No matter. He imagined himself tapping away at his computer, stories pouring out, uncurling in the heat. Naipaul and Graham Greene. As his legs pumped the pedals the bicycle's back wheel threw up a fine spray of water and clay, leaving a long stripe of filth, like a heckle from the soil of Essex, running from his nape to his buttocks.

He freewheeled the last few hundred yards towards the post office and general store, where he was going to post an urgent letter to his bank. But then his sunny, escapist mood was rudely interrupted by the sight of a large, grim bear of a man. Wearing an old leather jacket, frayed jeans and heavy motorcycle boots, he was standing in the shadow of the store, but making no real attempt to hide himself.

'Aleksander? What are you doing here? Are you on your way to the house? But Mr Haydn isn't here.'

Aleksander edged out of the shadows and gestured towards his motorbike. 'I am here from London now. I have been following people for Mr Haydn. They are not good people. They behave like dogs. One of them may be dead. I hope. I am trying to find the other. I almost had her, but then I lost her in these ridiculous narrow English lanes. The girl. Jemima.'

'Jennifer?'

'Yes. Jennifer.'

Ajit wanted nothing to do with this monstrous creature, this sweaty Caliban. Olivia Kite would know how to deal with him, and anyway, Danskin House was probably where Jennifer was headed. If Alois was there too, and would be embarrassed by the uninvited arrival of his creature, that was too bad. Let him take responsibility for once.

So Ajit gave him directions to Danskin House. Aleksander grunted his thanks and clambered back onto the machine.

Jen Blows It

With a crunch of gravel and a squeak of protest from its
ageing suspension Ned Parminter's Bristol came to a halt in front
of the pillared entrance hall of Danskin House. Jen scrabbled through
her handbag, pulled out McBryde's envelope and reread the typewritten account of his meeting with Alois Haydn. It was short on
detail, gory or otherwise, but it was specific about the timing and
the identity of the plotters. To her surprise, a folded piece of paper
that she hadn't noticed before fell out of the envelope.

'Addendum' was written in pencil, heavily underlined, at the
top. 'Jen,' she read, 'there's a bit of a twist, though I can't properly
stand it up. . .' So, she thought, just more speculation. Stuffing it
in the back pocket of her jeans she promised herself that she would
read it carefully later. But first she had to find Olivia. She headed
straight for the dining room.

Her boss's greeting was not as warm as Jen might have hoped.
Olivia stood up without a welcoming smile, and turned to the few
workers who hadn't yet left for the evening. 'It's an Americanism,
I know, but would you mind giving us the room?' Jen stood ramrod
straight in front of her, hands behind her back, a schoolgirl before
the headmistress. Olivia fingered her riding crop.

'So you've turned up at last. I was wondering how long you'd
linger in London. We've been managing rather well in your absence,
dear. I find I have a few questions for you.'

Jen held her ground. 'You'll want to hear what I have to say. I haven't been wasting my time, as you'll see. So the first question goes to me. Who are we fighting here, really?'

Olivia trotted out the words Jennifer had expected, and had heard scores of times before, but always in private.

'Number three, apathy – the British people's fundamental lack of seriousness. Number two, the big-business and banking cowards who would happily sell our democracy for a little more influence over the regulatory gnomes in Brussels and Strasbourg. But number one, as you well know, is the prime minister himself, that slippery, honey-voiced old hypocrite. The people love him. . .' But Olivia seemed distracted, almost bored.

Jen stepped nearer, staring fiercely into her eyes. 'What would you say if I told you that our number-one enemy is no longer with us? That the prime minister died four days ago in his office. *It's true.* They've hidden his body and managed to keep the whole thing secret. Quite an achievement. That disgusting Alois Haydn's involved. He confessed it all to Lucien McBryde, who's since been killed. It might seem nuts, Olivia, but I think they're after me too.'

Having carefully removed the firing pin and thrown the grenade with a girl cricketer's forearm lob, Jennifer took a full step back, waiting for the blast. A shout? Laughter? Amazement? Incredulity? But Olivia merely smiled tightly.

'So, Jennifer, your ex-boyfriend came through for you in the end, just before he committed suicide. It may surprise you, but out here in the sticks we've known about the prime minister's death for ages. So don't you dare come here and start throwing around stupid accusations about one of the most important allies we've got – who, I'll have you know, also happens to be a good personal friend of mine. "Disgusting"? I'll tell you what's disgusting: trailing around London smearing good people, wittering on about murder and delaying, for many hours, telling the woman who employs you a vital piece of information.'

Jen flushed and opened her mouth to speak, but Olivia cut in. 'Don't protest your innocence. Don't you dare. A little bird has told me everything.' And then she raised her voice and called, 'Oh, little bii-ird!'

The pale oak door behind her swung open, and through it came dark-eyed Alois Haydn. Jen gaped. Beelzebub himself. The killer alongside her queen. She could not have been more surprised had Olivia revealed that a pet Siberian tiger was living in the kitchen.

Behind her, the door leading to the entrance hall creaked open and Aleksander entered the room. He began to raise his gun, but when Haydn gave a slight shake of his head Aleksander shrugged, reversed his grip and brought the butt down hard on Jen's head. She dropped to her knees, hovered there for a moment as if praying, before sliding gently to the carpet.

If even a tenth of the things Alois had told her about Jennifer Lewis were true, Olivia reflected, the girl deserved a very sore head indeed, and probably a lot more than that. Olivia felt almost hurt.

'And so. In this way. Is poetry justice,' said Aleksander as he bent down and picked Jen up under the elbows. Alois took her feet and the two of them lugged her up the stairs to a bedroom, where they laid her on a bed. Aleksander produced a thick roll of tape from the pocket of his leather jacket, covered Jen's mouth with a strip of it, then bound her feet and hands tightly. He glanced around the room. The window was too high to jump from, and there was an old-fashioned lock on the door. After Haydn had gone through Jen's handbag and removed her mobile phone the two of them left the room. She was safe enough for the moment, a problem that could wait.

Some time later Jen came to with a raging headache. She may not have felt it, but she had been remarkably lucky. Had Alois or Aleksander taken the trouble to rifle her pockets and found the crumpled note she hadn't bothered to read, they would have killed her there and then.

Speaking Plainly

Overlooking the circular lake in the grounds of Danskin House was a small white replica of the Temple of Artemis, with Doric sandstone columns and a roof of wooden tiles. Its present function was to house a collection of lawnmowers. Lounging on the seat of the largest of them, his motorbike propped against the back wall, Aleksander, who had just told Haydn about Jen felling Ned Parminter, was being briefed by his employer.

'That girl knows more than enough to ruin me, and that means to ruin you too,' said Haydn.

Aleksander yawned. He did not want to appear overly enthusiastic. Money was involved. Wait and listen.

'If everything turns out as it should, I will become — comfortable. I've been generous to you, haven't I Aleksander? So let me make this clear. If that girl blabs to Olivia and screws things up for me, she screws things up for you as well.'

'And so you wish me to do what?' As he spoke Aleksander took his mobile phone from his jeans pocket, held it towards Haydn and pressed a button on it.

'What are you doing?' said Alois.

'This I think is a dangerous business. I am making a recording. We are men, we trust each other. But just so you do not drop me in the toilet, Mr Haydn, this is my insurance. Do you object?'

Alois did object, but he also knew that he would not be able to do this on his own.

'No, of course not. And you're quite right, this is all very unfortunate. You want me to be specific. You want leverage. I'll give it to you. Unfortunately, the girl must be finished off. There. I wish there was an alternative, but there isn't.'

Aleksander showed no sign of surprise, but merely grunted and scratched himself. He felt a sneeze coming. Alois continued in a low monotone he hoped the phone would not be able to pick up.

'Come back here tomorrow morning, around eleven. It's the day before the referendum, so the place will be in a frenzy and no one will notice you. Take her in the car she arrived in, drive it over towards my place, then head out into the marshes and do it there. There's plenty of shooting out there at this time of year. No one will take any notice. The tide will do the rest.'

Alois lit a Turkish cigarette and walked slowly out of the temple, past the remains of a grotto and into the rose garden. Olivia Kite, watching him from an upstairs window, thought he looked like an immaculately dressed young boy.

Aleksander urinated against a Doric column before rolling his motorbike down a cinder path, behind some cedars, away from the house.

In a locked bedroom Jen tasted blood in her mouth and squirmed vainly on the bed.

Olivia was still seething about Jen's treachery, as relayed to her by Alois. She'd like to thrash the living daylights out of her. But Alois was right; Jen had become a dangerous distraction, and the important thing was to keep her quiet. She would deal with Miss Lewis later, after the press conference was safely over.

Olivia took four sleeping pills downstairs to the kitchen, ground them into a powder and sprinkled it into a bowl of hot soup. She then went back upstairs, untied Jen, affecting to be horrified by the tape over her mouth, which she gently removed, and kissed her. Jen, woozy and scared, accepted her heartfelt apologies about the thugs who'd somehow wormed their way into Danskin, and gratefully swallowed the soup.

Olivia picked up her riding crop and left the room. She was beginning to feel rather curious about seeing that horrid little Alois Haydn without his clothes.

12

Wednesday, 20 September

Referendum Day Minus One

Phoebus Awakes: A Pageant

In the early hours of the following morning Rocks Point seemed not only a financial folly but a bleak joke. Rutted tracks led across dark-grey marshland to a small hillock on which a few scattered remnants of the old Victorian house were still standing. Once a place where Arthur Ransome had sought sanctuary with Trotsky's secretary, churning out 'nature note' columns for the *Guardian*, it was now reduced to a couple of walls of good red brick no more than a few feet high, and a tangled pile of ironwork.

An entire chimney, once constructed of fretted and artistic brickwork, lay on its side. Weather vanes in beaten metal poked through the nettles and the dead, grey remnants of the exotic plants which had once been lovingly reared in the Victorian greenhouse. Hundreds of smashed panes of glass reflected the moonlight, like broken ice on a still pond.

The monstrous growth of reinforced concrete and glass which now overshadowed the remains of the earlier house appeared to be a haphazard arrangement of geometrical shapes stolen from a child's mathematical primer; it was neither better nor worse than many other self-indulgent modern follies constructed by the new rich along the English coastline. North into East Anglia you could find green-glass palazzos, flying saucers, cast-iron spiders and rickety fantasies on timber legs. At the weekends hedge-fund managers, advertising men and Russians on the run would arrive by helicopter for a little shooting and swanking. Dorset was as bad, and Devon was on the turn.

Alois Haydn's Swiss architect had had reservations about his design being planted on the very edge of the shifting Essex coastline, where it had the general effect of a bijou nuclear power station — the addition of the mandatory helipad leading some of the bloggers to describe it as looking like a James Bond villain's lair. But wild-fowlers and birdwatchers alike could agree on this: Rocks Point was a blight. Inside the house giant windows, designed to flood Alois Haydn, Ajit Gupta and their weekend guests with radiant light, merely added to the sense of desolation.

There were no Rocks here, just ooze and scum and a huge raw sky. There was no Point either, just a radius of salty mud vanishing to the north and south into yellowish seawater. To the west lay the wreckage of the Victorian house, and to the east, whenever the rain lifted, the grey sea, regularly punctuated by ferries and container ships on their way to or from Harwich. Haydn had had to remort-gage the property, and had been too busy in London to furnish it to his taste, or even to finish the building work. Which was at least one saving grace.

Just a single room downstairs had been sufficiently completed to accommodate the shooters. Apart from that, only the concrete spiral staircase leading to the first-floor bedrooms had been painted. It was bright white, and was hung with lithographs of various tortures and executions, originally drawn by Goya but garishly redecorated by the Chapman brothers. Apart from the stairs and the shooting room the interior walls were bare concrete, still garlanded with electrical cables squirming out of ragged holes. There was some furniture downstairs, but it was mostly covered in polythene and dust. Upstairs, pacing from one of the almost empty bedrooms into Alois Haydn's 'library' (which contained no books) was a shrouded and moaning figure.

In silk pyjama bottoms, with a duvet wrapped around his head to keep out the chill, Ajit Gupta felt he must have woken up into a nightmare. This horrible house on this horrible piece of coastline seemed even more horrible since he had discovered yesterday, while picking through his partner's emails from the bank, that it was bankrupting the two of them. They must have been mad.

A seaside mansion, a piece of old England which had its dignity and history, had been smashed to pieces for this cold shed. What had they been thinking? And since, according to the most moderate estimate, this brand-new house required another two or three million spent on it just to make it weatherproof, let alone comfortable, Ajit was beginning to feel that nothing here in England was going to get any better for him.

Sleepless, he wandered to the back of the house and gazed down on the broken old brick walls. Still shivering with the cold, he realised he was thirsty. He had spent the evening waiting for Alois, drinking too much wine and wondering whether to confront him over their money troubles. What manner of man had he ended up with?

Ajit padded downstairs, the lithographs gurning at him, and into the temporary kitchen. This was dominated by a huge, brushed-steel fridge-freezer, standing in a corner of the room like an upright coffin. He reached in for a carton of orange juice. When he turned around he gave a start and dropped it with shock. A naked Alois Haydn was sitting on one of the kitchen chairs, staring at him.

'Ooops. Sorry. I came in late from Olivia Kite's place. I didn't want to wake you.'

Haydn stood and walked over to the window. In the moonlight Ajit could see livid red lines down his back.

The iron-grey nothingness that had hidden the sea and the ferries and the container ships was becoming tinged with the first whorls of pink. As Haydn spoke, little flecks of gold and tangerine began to decorate the hairs on his muscular legs and surprisingly powerful arms. He turned back to Ajit.

'When you look at me, what do you see?' He paused, and raised both arms in the air like a sporting hero.

I see a faun, thought Ajit. A baby god with a chest of brass, hair of beaten copper, and ankles and feet of clay.

But what he said was: 'I see a man who takes me for a whore, and a stupid whore at that. All these shady financial dealings, Alois. All the silences. Your sordid little mysteries. That terrible Pole. And now those marks on your back. What do you actually *do* all day? I know what I do. I sit on my arse and I write sentences. And when all the sentences are joined up I take them to my publisher and eventually I have a book. And even if not so many people read my books, enough of them do for me to make an honest living. And you? You live high on the hog, but what do you actually *do*? I'm sick to the teeth of all this flitting about in the shadows thinking you're so clever. Christ, I've even degraded myself by going through your accounts. So I know this folly is breaking us. I won't say it hasn't been fun, but I want out.'

Haydn stretched himself in the sun. Getting rid of Ajit would suit him quite well, but it would be a big risk. He knew too much, and these writers were always in search of material.

'Going to put me in a book are you, honey?'

'I'm not a blackmailer. But somebody should put you in a book one of these days. It would be a shame not to. . .'

Haydn felt he detected a threat. He began to pace back and forth, as if delivering a soliloquy on an empty stage.

'You write your sentences, Ajit. I take risks. We both use our brains as best we can. But yes, of course we're at a turning point. After this I can never go back to Westminster or Whitehall. All those contacts, those parties we gave, those favours still unredeemed, those little packets of golden information. . . all gone, all useless now.'

As the sun started to rise he became only a silhouette against the window. Ajit felt he was looking at a marionette, not the man he had once loved. Haydn talked on.

'I am an ambitious man. Yes, in this unambitious country I dare to say it. Here the politicians don't matter any more. Not the secretaries of state, not the ministers, not the lords. The British think they're democrats. But they're only shoppers. They don't vote very much, and they don't think very much either. Here the only people who count are the very rich, the people who can buy football teams and private jets and flash penthouses on the Thames. If you want power you have to become as rich as the robber Russians, the tyrannical Arabs, the Shanghai property developers and the Indian industrialists.

'So, Ajit, I am going to short the United Kingdom. It will make *me* as rich as those kinds of people. And to achieve that I will do anything, absolutely anything, that needs to be done. The world is divided between those who dream – or write – and men of action. So, Ajit Gupta, do you still want out?'

The sun was now fully up. Haydn placed one small foot in front of the other, raised his palms upright as if for applause, and bowed. Ajit found himself hypnotised by those little hands. They were so small and brown, so tapered. They looked more like the hands of a mole than a human being.

But he was having visions of his own. Haydn now appeared to him like one of Blake's engraved monsters, with speckled wings and leprous skin. He shuddered, and thought that as soon as he could he had to get away from here and back to London.

'Yes, Alois. I'm afraid I do.'

'Then I will give you some advice, as a parting gift. It should make you a few million pounds, which will make you financially secure for the rest of your life.' Haydn then went on to explain to Ajit exactly how to buy options on shorting British Airways, British Aerospace and a couple of the major banks. He gambled that Ajit would be unable to resist the temptation of such easy money, and that if Sir Solomon Dundas and Charmian Locke were right, he would certainly be caught, and would be safely locked away in one of His Majesty's prisons for several years. After that, no one would listen to anything a convicted fraudster said.

By now both of them were desperately hungry. There was a small camping stove in the kitchen, and the unsuspecting Ajit made bacon and eggs. They washed the frugal meal down with tumblers of Armagnac. Afterwards, Haydn, still naked and looking suddenly young and vulnerable, flopped back in his chair. Ajit ran a hand across his chest, tugged a nipple, and began to kiss him. An hour later they were lying sated, fast asleep, intertwined – and many miles apart.

Death in the Morning?

By 11 o'clock Danskin House was buzzing with activity in preparation for Olivia Kite's final press conference before the referendum. As Haydn had speculated, no one paid any attention to Aleksander. He marched boldly up the drive, opened the door of the Bristol with the key he had removed from Jen's handbag, and concealed his gun and some of the spare cartridges under the driver's seat. He then went into the house and, taking the stairs two at a time, up to the room where he had left Jen the previous evening. Thanks to Olivia's hot soup she was still fast asleep and snoring. He woke her gently. She recoiled in shock and loathing when she opened her eyes to see him standing over her.

'Shush, girl,' he said, and managed a smile. 'Mrs Kite says you are to go back with me to London. Things are getting too difficult here.'

Jennifer tried to protest, but Aleksander gently placed a large hand over her mouth. 'No, not yet, girl. I will speak to your questions in the car. You must dress. I wait outside, it's OK in this way. You must come down quietly with me and make no noise. Mrs Kite is angry for us both.'

It was only when the Bristol, which Aleksander drove very badly, turned off the main road to the village and began to bump and grind its way along a deeply rutted track into the marshes that Jen's mind began to turn over. The sky was colourless. A shimmering haze meant that it was hard to make out anything much beyond the clumps of sedge, the odd gatepost stump and the pools of brackish water in the road. The ghostly figures of stunted trees flickered in the near distance. Jen didn't like this at all.

Alois Haydn had been right. The isle was full of noises. Frequent pops and cracks betrayed the fact that the wildfowlers were out, and finding targets in the soupy brightness. When he was sure there was nobody within sight, Aleksander turned off the road and very gently asked Jen to get out for a moment. Feeling like an automaton, swallowing her fears, she dully unfastened her seatbelt, opened the door and stood by the side of the car. Her legs were shaking. Moving without haste or comment, Aleksander reached under his seat and pulled out the gun.

'Now you will walk, not run, to that ditch there. Do not worry, the water is quite shallow. You will kneel down please. This will be very quick.'

Jen, sobbing and gasping, found herself completely unable to speak. Crouching down in the ditch, she felt the cold water rising above her knees. She heard a metallic click. It must have been very loud, she thought, to penetrate the roar of the blood pounding in her head. She wondered about Ned Parminter.

Aleksander was standing behind her, his legs planted widely apart and his arms outstretched. The stubby barrels of the shotgun were no more than an inch or two from Jen's uncombed hair. This, he thought, was what he was good at. This was what he liked.

Turbulence

But far out above the North Sea a small area of low pres-
sure had created a bubble of turbulence over the water. Waves
ruffled the surface. The gust took a steward by surprise as he made
his way to the bar of a passing ferry. And as this lightest of breezes
reached the sopping, sucking edges of the marshland, the haze
suddenly lifted.

Trevor Kampusch had been a London taxi driver all his adult
life. There was nowhere, from Barnet to Croydon, that he didn't
know like the back of his mottled, liver-spotted hand. He hated it
out here in the sticks, fifty miles from the nearest falafel. He'd done
his best for the old lady and her gentleman admirer in the back,
and tried to find the bloody house they wanted, but he couldn't
for the life of him.

His passengers had been quiet to begin with. He'd thought the
old lady was asleep. But actually Myfanwy was thinking hard about
her ancient errors, the unprepossessing little baby boy she'd sold
for the price of a fortnight's holiday in Rome. Tiny pinpricks of
conscience reminded her of being a young girl herself. Well, maybe
she could still put things right. This would be a day for truth-telling.

Eventually the opportunity for a bit of gossip with Briskett had
proved irresistible, and she had embraced the opportunity of
retelling her life story to her eager listener. Briskett was suitably
impressed to find that so many of the men and women he had

written about in the course of his professional career had been friends or lovers of hers. They had talked of cabinet ministers and dashing former military officers, of self-serving memoirs and of diaries and collections of letters still to be published. They had talked about Jennifer and Ned Parminter too. It was proving a delightful adventure. Neither felt any sense of danger as they drew nearer to Danskin House.

But the taxi driver was now well and truly bloody lost. His AA road atlas lay on the seat beside him. These tangled lanes were almost enough to drive you to a bloody satnav. As the cabbie swore and tried to execute a seven-point turn without sinking into the malevolent-looking puddles on either side of the narrow track, Lord Briskett started, wound down the window and shouted, 'Ned?'

For there was no mistaking his protégé's beloved Bristol, badly parked, spattered with mud and leaning at an awkward angle.

Aleksander heard the shout, paused and turned around.

It was then that Lord Briskett noticed the girl huddled in the ditch and clearly in distress. He jumped out of the taxi and ran towards Aleksander, who straightened up and swivelled his gun in the direction of the elegantly dressed academic.

'Hey there! What do you think you're doing?' cried Briskett in his best, most commanding Oxford tones. They could have been his last words, but they were not. For his leather-soled brogues, perfect for city pavements, slipped on the mud and he was flung headlong to the ground just as the Pole fired, missing him by inches. The shot pinged against the taxi.

Immediately afterwards there was another loud report. Aleksander staggered backwards, looked down and was surprised to see a neat round hole in his left shoulder from which blood was not trickling but pumping. All sensation left his arm, the gun tumbled to his feet and he collapsed to the ground.

By the taxi, looking rather cavalier in a large blue felt fedora purchased at Liberty in 1960, Myfanwy Davies-Jones was experiencing an almost sexual satisfaction as she looked at the tiny ebony-handled object in her hand. 'I've always wanted to do that,' she said to the taxi driver. 'It felt divine.'

The Second Message

They left Aleksander lying by the side of the road. Jen, badly shaken but able to give the driver directions to Danskin House, sat with Myfanwy in the back of the taxi while Briskett followed them in the Bristol. Jen could give no coherent explanation as to why Aleksander had wanted to kill her, but she felt there might be safety in numbers. Myfanwy listened to her daughter's story with rare restraint, then asked exactly what Jen had taken to Olivia Kite.

'You see, Jennifer dear,' said Myfanwy, 'darling clever Lord Briskett found out that the prime minister was dead, and that there had been some terrible racket to cover it all up. It turns out that some friends of mine in London were actually helping to do it. Precious as you are, darling, it hardly seems worth killing you over an outlandish story that was about to leak out anyway. So we haven't yet reached the final chapter.'

Jen told her mother about the London Library and the message from Lucien McBryde. The information it contained had seemed such a bombshell, 'But the funny thing was, when I told Olivia she didn't seem surprised at all. How do you suppose she knew?'

Suddenly Jen remembered McBryde's second message, which she had only glanced at as she arrived at Olivia's the previous day. The one that – although she didn't know it – he had scribbled down in haste at Gordon's wine bar on the night he died. It was still there, tightly folded into the back pocket of her jeans. She fished it out, smoothed it over and carefully read it through twice, then handed it to Myfanwy, who had been loudly debating with the taxi driver about her right to smoke in the back of his cab. The note read:

Addendum

Jen, there's a bit of a twist, though I can't properly stand it up. We were always told in hack school to answer all the Ws — Who? What? When? Where?

But the greatest of the Ws is Why? And it was nagging away at me ever since that conversation last night with Alois Haydn. He was part of the plot. So why did he want to destroy it? And why did he tell me, of all people?

I couldn't let it alone. I've just asked an old school friend of mine, who used to work in the City, whether it was possible that Haydn could benefit in some way from knowing the result of the referendum in advance. He couldn't give me many details, but he said that Haydn could make an awful lot of money. I just had to ask the right questions of the right people and it would all become clear. I don't know what that means exactly, but I'll bet Olivia Kite's people do. Hope this helps. I think I still love you.

Lucien xxx

'It does help, it certainly does,' said Myfanwy. 'It's the final chapter. Now it all makes sense. If Alois is working some scam and he doesn't want Olivia Kite to know about it, well. . .' She inhaled deeply, then fell silent and stared at the low hedges lining the road towards Danskin House.

'It's obviously about money,' she said after a few minutes. 'Alois is up to something, and he thinks you might know what it is. I suppose he thinks McBryde must have told you. As to what he's planning exactly, I know just the man who will know how to find out. But it seems that Alois really was prepared to bump you off. I'd never have believed it of him, even though he's been a little shit all his life.'

She yawned. 'I'll have to have a word with him.'

A Dénouement

As they drew nearer to the house they found the narrow road almost blocked by vehicles parked on either side. Lumbering BBC outside-broadcast vans festooned with aerials and dishes, a Channel 4 minibus and a huge pantechnicon with 'Sky News' stencilled on its side were all wedged among numerous cars. Men employed to unwind black cabling were happily unwinding black cabling. Self-important adolescents were barking into mobile phones.

Lord Briskett paid off the still-grumbling taxi driver and plunged eagerly into the middle of all this. He was soon having a lovely time. He knew almost all the senior political correspondents by name, and found himself at the centre of a huddle of dark jackets, busily telling them the sensational news that Olivia Kite intended to reveal at her press conference. None of them believed him. Their sceptical expressions, which showed quite clearly that they thought he must be demented, made him even more pleased.

So he was almost jigging with pleasure when Myfanwy took him to one side and slipped him Lucien McBryde's second message. Ignoring her suggestion that he contact one of her many friends, Briskett immediately called Dame Cecily Morgan, convinced that she was one of the few people in London who would be able to find out within minutes exactly what Alois Haydn had done. After a brief telephone conversation with an embarrassed Sir Solomon

Dundas, who confessed everything, Dame Cecily called Briskett straight back.

'I'm not an easy woman to shock, but he's shorted the whole fucking country. He thinks sterling's going to tumble after the "No" campaign wins the referendum. In fact he wants it to. The damage to London will be immense. And we thought we were working with him all along. . .'

Just then, as if the media pack had a single brain (which, mostly, it does), the scrum of cameramen, sound engineers, research assistants and junior reporters commissioned to keep the best seats free for their superiors poured through the gates and across the front lawn of Danskin House. Behind them strolled the senior correspondents and television presenters, for it is a curious fact that as politics has diminished in stature and importance, those who merely report it have grown steadily grander. Bringing up the rear were four BBC work-experience trainees in their early twenties, straining under the weight of a palanquin, or sedan chair, on which reposed the corporation's political editor.

In front of several score gold-painted chairs and a raised enclosure for the cameras Olivia Kite's team had erected a four-foot-high platform festooned with Union flags. Behind it a banner hung from the top storey of Danskin House, reading 'BRITAIN'S SHAME! THE GREATEST LIE EVER TOLD?'

On the platform were a dozen well-known faces – actors, businesspeople, even a couple of politicians. Sitting centre-stage, Olivia herself had rejected her customary black trouser suit and was strikingly dressed in a cobalt-blue outfit with scarlet piping and a frilled white shirt. Always pale-faced, she was now chalk-white, her eyes dark and flashing, her mouth a wanton strip of carmine. The effect was of a collision between Elizabeth I and Lady Thatcher, but it was undeniably effective. Beside her, small, mouse-coloured and with a nervous smirk on his face, sat Alois Haydn.

As the hubbub of journalists arranged itself on the seats with much elbowing and jostling for position, Olivia spotted Jennifer Lewis standing at the back of the crowd between Myfanwy Davies-Jones and Lord Briskett. So did Alois Haydn, who was by now looking decidedly uneasy. But Olivia gestured imperiously at Jen, summoning her up beside her on the platform. It was a brilliant stroke. The presence of the dishevelled and mud-stained young woman confirmed that this would be a press conference like no other.

Olivia, her slim fingers holding, for no apparent reason, a riding crop, opened proceedings by bringing it slashing down on the long desk in front of her. A shiver ran through the press pack. Then she leaned into the microphone.

'For almost a year now, ladies and gentlemen, I have been telling you that we, the British people, have been *lied to*. (The crop slashed down again for emphasis.) We were *lied to* (Whack!) when we were first invited to join the Common Market by Edward Heath. We were *lied to at every turn* (Crash! Wallop! Bang!) by almost – but not quite – every subsequent prime minister as the market became a union and the union became a superstate. So my accusations of deceit levelled against this *wretched* (Crack!), *cowardly* (Ker-rack!), *dishonest* (a bigger crack, as the desk began to splinter), *contemptible* government will hardly surprise you. Today, however, the British people will finally discover – just in time – the depths to which that government has been prepared to sink in order to pull the wool over their eyes.

'Yesterday I learned, through unimpeachable sources, that the prime minister – to whom even now I pay tribute as an impeccable public servant and a man of honour – passed away nearly a week ago. His speeches, his interviews, his public appearances and his political broadcasts since then have been mere fakery, accomplished by means of a series of childish tricks. The country has yet again been lied to. Now, I say, that is not the fault of the late prime minister himself, and today I demand, on behalf of all of the people of Great Britain, a state funeral for a man who in death has been cynically misused by midgets. . .'

The rest of Olivia Kite's superb speech, which has passed into political history and is still taught in English grammar schools, is too well-known to repeat here. She was so overcome by her indignant eloquence that she completely forgot to put Alois Haydn on the spot about his involvement in the conspiracy, but her fiery words were broadcast in their entirety by every television and radio network. Every newspaper devoted pages to her speech the following day, along with pieces by their commentators explaining why they had suspected all along that something of this kind was going on. Reactions to the speech trended on Witter for an unheard-of eighty hours.

Back at the offices of PLS in London phones were ringing off the hook and inboxes were pinging frantically as clients scrambled for inside information. The company had been up to its neck in a national – indeed an international – scandal, and now found itself comprehensively outsmarted. If the referendum went against Europe, vast sums would be written off the balance sheets of half its clients – the very clients that paid PLS handsomely to be kept well-informed about such events.

General Sir Mike Patten was trying to reassure Baroness Tessie Fremantle. No one, he said confidently, would ever know about PLS's part in this wretched business – and in any case, he was by no means certain that the referendum *was* lost, despite all the furore.

'The whole Lazarus trick is just too bizarre, frankly. In this day and age, who would believe it?'

Dame Cecily Morgan had had enough. It had not been an easy week. She leaned across her desk, her lip curling and her formidable bosom aimed squarely at the retired general. 'Quite *right*, Mike. The whole thing is simply incredible. Oh no, it couldn't happen here. It's as bonkers as – what? – two brothers fighting each other for the leadership of the Labour Party, or a husband and wife jailing each other over a pretty minor traffic offence, or two eminent members of the Conservative Party being in a gay relationship even as they proclaim family values, or a prime minister having an affair with one of his own ministers. . . Loopy. Loony. It's as bonkers as manufacturing the case for an entire war and thinking no one would notice. Mad as cheese. No, no, none of that could ever happen here. The great British public simply wouldn't let them get away with it. Quite *right*, Mike.' With that Dame Cecily stomped off for a beer.

In Essex the journalists, who had been well-trained to believe anything they were told, were so excited by the sheer scale of the tale they had just been served up by Olivia Kite that they had all immediately fled Danskin House for their offices in London, or to feed pictures back from their vans. And so they missed the rest of the story, which began only once the cameras had been turned off and the miles of cable neatly rewound.

Female Wrestling

Sweet peas and tea roses. Lavender and freshly cut grass.
Olivia Kite, trembling, had made her way down from the platform
and was walking in a kind of post-coital daze back through the
garden towards her library when she was interrupted by a shout.

'You silly woman! You *utter* fool!'

Olivia swivelled. Myfanwy Davies-Jones stood with her legs apart,
her purple face crowned by her blue fedora. Her gaudy tartan wool
jacket, fine Welsh bones and emerald stare made her appear even
more exotically colourful than the garden around her.

Olivia looked just as garish, and just as formidable. Behind her,
in her shadow, stood Alois Haydn. Behind Myfanwy, with the gleeful
expression of a small boy about to break his first window, was Lord
Briskett. It was as if two female samurai, with their attendants,
were preparing for a fight to the death.

Olivia brandished her riding crop. 'I don't know who you are.
You look like Vivienne Westwood's drunken elder sister. And I don't
know what you're doing in my garden slinging insults at me either.
But since this is my house I insist we go indoors. Whatever it is
you want to say you can say to me there.'

Once they were inside Olivia, looking for any advantage she
could grab hold of, chose a chair by the fireplace and sat there,
stiff-backed.

Myfanwy strode across the room and stood over her. But her voice when she spoke was almost gentle. 'Mrs Kite, all you need to know is that I am a woman of the world. And you have been manipulated, like a helpless puppet, by that man there' – she indicated Alois Haydn with a contemptuous jerk of her thumb. 'He has been pulling your strings for days. Even if you win this referendum your victory will be a hollow one. It will be tainted by the stink of corruption – and what's more, Mrs Kite, of treason.'

Even the most devoted reader of her novels would have had to admit that Myfanwy Davies-Jones had a weakness for bombast.

'Now look here, you mad old bat,' retorted Olivia. 'The treason is all on the other side. Lies. Bribery. The abuse of office. The only crime Mr Haydn here is guilty of is coming to his senses in time and making sure the British people heard the truth.'

Lord Briskett stepped forward and folded his arms to appear more authoritative, Oxonian. 'Miss Davies-Jones here is one of the very finest novelists our islands have known, as well as having been a personal friend of mine for many years. And Mrs Kite, she is quite right. I have persuasive evidence that your friend Mr Haydn has bet a fabulous amount in the markets on a "No" vote tomorrow. He has done this by shorting the currency of Great Britain. But if that was intended to be a secret, it is already leaking out. Even now, other speculators are piling in. The combined effect of that and the referendum result on confidence in the City, and indeed on the entire British economy at this most sensitive and difficult time, will be catastrophic. And this man here is responsible. He is a corrupt, seedy little wrecker.'

Myfanwy took up the baton. 'Alois here needed you to win the vote, so he gave you the ammunition for victory – but only in order to enrich himself in the most discreditable way possible. I have no particular hostility to his wish to become filthy rich, but I must protest when he tries to have his own sister, who is no more than a harmless girl, murdered to keep her quiet about his schemes.'

'His sister?' said Olivia.

'My sister?' quavered Alois.

Myfanwy suddenly remembered her pistol, took it out of her purse and waggled it in Haydn's general direction. She drew herself up to her full five feet.

'I can see right through you, Alois. I've always been able to, ever since you first appeared – wet and pink and horrid then, but much worse now. Yes, I realise this must come as a shock to you. But I can assure you that being your mother is a serious embarrassment for me as well.'

But Where is Ned?

Lord Briskett, Myfanwy Davies-Jones and Jennifer Lewis
retired, reeling but victorious, to the Chelmsford Arms public
house, which trumpeted food all day. Three microwaved meals
explained the boast, accompanied by three large glasses of unspeak-
able wine. But the atmosphere around the battered wooden table
seemed snug, homely and reassuring.

Actually it wasn't, quite. Lord Briskett had not asked about Ned
Parminter yet. But he would surely do so soon. Jen felt that she
had some explaining to do.

Eyeing her mother with a new respect, she decided that she and
her boyfriend could cope with the truth.

'You must be wondering what's happened to Ned,' she began
uncertainly, dipping a finger in her wine and drawing spirals on the
tabletop. 'Well, he was hot for me, you see. I was rather keen on
him too. But I panicked, I'm afraid. I don't know him very well
really, and with everything feeling so weird, and me not knowing
who was on who's side, it seemed best just to give him a bit of a
bop on the head. I left him at the side of the road about forty miles
back, in a bit of woodland. I think he'll be all right, though he'll be
having a headache today.'

Briskett did not take the news well. This girl was clearly more
her mother's daughter than either of them realised. Ned Parminter,

for all his eccentricities, was a kindly and unworldly man, as well as a fine scholar. Apart from anything else, he had many of the notes Briskett would need when he came to write the full story of the referendum. Briskett's worry and irritation were shown by his determination to go straight off in search of his assistant. But Myfanwy strongly approved of the bopping of Ned, and suggested that he must surely have hitchhiked to Danskin House, or more probably back to London, long ago.

'I'm fagged out for the day,' she added. 'No wild geese for me.'

At the same time, in a bedroom on the third floor of the tower at the centre of Danskin House, with the shutters open and rich scents from the garden blowing in through the window, Olivia Kite and Alois Haydn were talking.

Alois had assumed that since they both wanted the referendum to go the same way their interests were in harmony. But Olivia was a keen student of all the media, from Witter to the Pirate website and the reviving *Independent*. She knew that the revelation of widespread betting against the pound by members of her inner circle would be something she could never shake off – like Gordon Brown selling the country's gold reserves, or Tony Blair and Bernie Ecclestone. She had been educating Alois in all the ways his gamble would be exaggerated, excoriated and pinned on her.

'You can't campaign to make things better and then put money on the assumption that you're going to make them a lot worse, you half-Welsh ninny. You can't promise to save the people and steal their future at the same time. It's an absolute political disaster. I should beat you into the dust.'

But the passion had gone out of her voice. Both of them realised it was too late. If the British people voted to leave Europe, Alois would become exceedingly rich – and exceedingly useful. And it was now too late for anyone to stop that happening. Clever Alois, she thought. No foreigner after all, but his mother's son.

Before their conversation, which took place in Olivia's bed, Alois Haydn had experienced a certain amount of mental anguish. All his life his sense of himself had been based on his solitary, free, independent state. He'd known from childhood that he wasn't a blood Haydn, that the exotic and talented family had taken him in under mysterious circumstances that his adoptive father Ludwig Mises-Berlin Haydn never discussed. As a boy he'd fantasised about his true origins. Camille and Liddell had slyly called him 'brother', but he'd come to think of himself as an orphan, the self-directed author of his own fate. To discover at his time of life that he was not only not an orphan, but that he was closely related to that ridiculous woman and that dreary girl, was not something he relished.

No family instinct surged through him. After Myfanwy, Jen and Briskett had taken their leave he had retreated for almost an hour to Olivia's bathroom, where he lathered himself with expensive unguents, lolling in warm water and scented oil. To massage his own body, to press his fingers into his own face and through his own hair – which was, yes, reddish, if not as red as Jennifer's, or as spun-gold-auburn as Myfanwy's – slowly helped him to calm down.

Eventually he began to think tactically again. Where was Aleksander, and could he rely on him to keep quiet? Would Jen press charges against her own brother, as he now was? Surely not – not now that she knew he had a witness to her mad moment with the wrench by the side of the road. That led back to Aleksander and his roll of tape. But nothing was irredeemable. By the time Alois had towelled himself dry, changed into clean clothes and was preparing to leave the bathroom, he was feeling almost optimistic.

His mood changed, however, the moment he opened the door and found Olivia standing before him dressed in nothing but a short black silk gown. 'I am going to grind you into the dust. I'm going to have you weeping. And after that I'm going to fuck you,' announced the next first minister of the United and Independent Kingdom of Great Britain. 'So follow me,' she added, turning on her heel and leading him up a spiral staircase to the rooftop.

Alois knew the story of Sir Rufus Panzer's walk, and was therefore half prepared for what was coming. And indeed, with her gown blowing open and her feet entirely bare, Olivia Kite walked the length of the wall. At the end, without a wobble, she turned and beckoned to him. He took a deep breath, locked his eyes on hers and, attended by the spirits of Danskin past, did not fall.

The nature of the deal that the two of them struck, first on the wall and then in the satin luxury of Olivia's bed, would be speculated upon by journalists, politicians and historians for many years to come. A dynasty was being born which would one day be spoken of, without irony, in the same breath as the Marlborough-Churchills or the Pitts. In its way it would change the course of British history just as much as any Westminster pact. The marriage of nationalist politics and City wealth began that day at Danskin House.

Marshmalice

Ajit Gupta had always disliked blood sports. So he was unfriendly when, as he was packing up his things at Rocks Point, two local wildfowlers hammered at the door. Both were dressed in a cheap mimicry of military fatigues and were carrying weapons under their arms. Bundles of bloody feathers protruded from bags strapped across their chests.

But the elder of the two, Bill Whiteford, who had taken the day off from his desk job in Chelmsford, wore a haunted expression as he grabbed Ajit by the hand.

'You have to help us,' he said urgently. 'There's something terrible out in the marshes, and it's coming this way.'

Sure enough, through the miasma a bulky and shambling silhouette could be seen tramping towards the house. It was smeared from head to toe in mud and blood. Its face was a mask. The thing slowly raised one hand, and pointed. The hunters shrank against the house's wall.

'Gupta,' said Aleksander. 'We have to talk.'

It Isn't Over

In the offices of the *National Courier* **Ken Cooper ground** his fingertips into his skull in an attempt to push the Lucien McBryde story from the front of his mind. It was distracting him too much. He was becoming too emotionally involved.

And things were changing terribly fast, by the minute. The cover-up of the prime minister's death was the biggest British political story of modern times – bigger than the fall of Thatcher, bigger than Blair and Iraq. The twenty-four-hour news media were running Olivia Kite almost on a loop – she appeared on-screen every few minutes. Meanwhile, with their customary plonking sense of theatre, the police had arrived at Number 10 just in time to catch the early editions of tomorrow's papers. According to the BBC's political editor, who was standing outside the famous front door, for the first time in history the police were treating Number 10, 'astonishingly, as a conventional crime scene'.

Indeed, there were far more police in Downing Street than usual, and they seemed less deferential too. The late PM's communications secretary Nelson Fraser, his face pale but his back upright, was ushered out through the front door. He had one protective hand around Amanda Andrews, who was nonetheless perky enough to blow a kiss at the watching huddle of cameras. A police van was waiting for them. Then Ken leaned forward in his chair and uttered an expletive so dark, so long-forgotten, that it shocked even him. For after Amanda and Fraser the police led out the chief whip, Ronnie Ashe, and the foreign secretary, Jason Latimer. Both were wearing handcuffs.

Only after the police vans had driven away with their eminent detainees was the Downing Street podium carried out and set up a yard or two in front of the metal barrier behind which the world's press and broadcasters were penned. After a long pause a new figure emerged from Number 10. The chancellor of the exchequer, Jo Johnson, had not been seen in London for a fortnight: he had been leading the pro-European campaign in Wales and the West Country. Now he stepped up to the microphone and gave the official confirmation of the prime minister's death, which had taken place, he said, 'some days ago' but had been 'illegally and improperly' covered up, including from himself.

Even his own office in Downing Street, said Johnson, had been appropriated by persons unknown, some of whom apparently had detailed inside knowledge of the workings of Whitehall. The police were investigating, but, mysteriously, these people seemed to have left little evidence behind them. The late prime minister would, as Olivia Kite had generously suggested, be given a state funeral; and there would be a full independent inquiry into the recent deplorable events, with all its sessions held in public. Lord Aaronovitch had agreed to chair it, and it would report within seven years.

Johnson added that on the advice of the justice secretary, Mr Alois Haydn, who had been involved in the cover-up from its very earliest stages, would not be prosecuted, as he had provided invaluable information to Mrs Kite which had brought about the exposure of the plot before even more damage could be done.

Ken Cooper's picture editor, who had also been watching events unfolding in Downing Street, banged on his boss's office door and entered. After so many years working together the two men thought more or less exactly alike.

'Ditch the front, boss?'

'Yep. I want four sharp fucking grabs, one of each of the bastards.'

The pictures would run across the front page, the subjects' expressions ranging from Jason Latimer's calm dignity to Amanda Andrews's flirtatious smirk, over the single-word headline, which Cooper sketched out himself – he still liked to work on paper with his first ideas: 'TRAITORS'.

As any newspaper editor knows, when the story is really big, front pages are easy to do; the agonising problem is the rejection of the alternative fronts which would have conveyed a radically different message. Cooper was gutted about his own decision to reject his original plan. He was also surprised and upset by the suggestion that Alois Haydn was going to get away with it. Still, the story of the 'nest of traitors' took things forward. And Cooper knew that if you have to choose between sorrow and anger, go for anger every time.

He compromised with a picture of the late prime minister on the bottom half of the front, and a full pullout about him, written at breakneck speed by Lucy Scadding and the comment team. It dwelt on the PM's long struggle to hammer out a workable deal for a leaner and more democratic Europe with the Germans, the Dutch and the other northern countries, his deeply disappointing summit in Paris, his passionate speeches. A separate article posed the question whether or not his apparently devastating final political broadcast had been no more than an elaborate fake. There were photos going back to his early years in the navy, his by-election success and his service as a junior minister in successive governments. The paper's untrustworthy diarist was allowed to write a spiky little article about his failed marriage, but the overall tone was of admiration, sorrow and reverence.

When, later that night, Ken scanned the early editions of the *Courier*'s rivals, he was relieved to see that none of them was entirely clear about which story to run with. Both the *Sun* and the *Mirror* refused to be deflected from the vote that still lay just ahead – 'Vote "No" for Britain' and 'Vote "Yes" for Britain', they chirruped. *The Times* had a picture of Olivia Kite, whom it portrayed as a latterday Gloriana, in full spate, and a wry column by Matthew Parris. The *Guardian* had a complex story which appeared to suggest that the Downing Street plot had been run by the CIA, and that the prime minister might have been killed because of his opposition to Guantánamo Bay. The *Daily Telegraph* had found a picture of a beautiful young woman who was unsure which way to vote – or, apparently, how to fasten her bra. The *Independent* ran with a story about a refugee camp in Thailand.

Only the *Daily Mail* had a front page that made Ken feel a little jealous. Under a photograph that caught Jason Latimer with a particularly agonised look on his face was the headline 'The Stab in the Back'. A piece by Simon Heffer said that Latimer had been prepared to betray his country and his prime minister for the possibility of seizing power. Only by voting 'No' to the EU could British citizens show their contempt for the man. Across the top of the paper Liz Jones was speculating about whether, at her age, Amanda Andrews should be wearing such a short skirt.

The age of newspapers was ending, Ken knew. But the blogosphere, Witter and the main political websites were equally divided in their reactions. Trolls gabbled about what they would like to do to Amanda Andrews or Olivia Kite. Conspiracy theorists were inflamed by the appearance of Alois Haydn sitting alongside Kite at the press conference – what did that mean? 'Fuzzy Blue Oatcake', the most influential right-wing blogger, went against the consensus, suggesting that millions of people might vote 'Yes' to Europe just to pay tribute to the deceased prime minister. Few agreed with that. Most commentators expressed their opinion that the plot was proof of the anti-democratic instincts of the pro-European camp, and made a 'No' vote even more urgent.

13

Thursday, 21 September

Referendum Day

The Rise of Lord Croaker

The early-morning rain had passed and the sun was already drying off the grass in the garden of Number 10 as Alois Haydn pulled out a deckchair and settled himself in a position where he would be shielded from prying eyes by a high wall. The children's slide and swing brought in by David Cameron were still there, a bit battered-looking by now. The police had been bumbling loudly around, but had now left. Peace at last.

He turned and gazed up at the windows of the flat in which the prime minister had been dismembered. Having been sent up to London by Olivia, who had phone calls to make, early the previous evening, Haydn had gone straight up there. Sidling through the private rooms he had found the foreign secretary, who had seemed unsurprised to see him, and had been perfectly friendly. He, the chief whip and most of the rest of them had known that the game was up as soon as they saw Olivia Kite's press conference. They weren't certain about Haydn's role, exactly, though they had all seen him on the platform next to Olivia, and had drawn their own conclusions. Insultingly perhaps, they had all assumed that he had simply switched camps when it became clear which side was likely to win the referendum. Was it he who had blown the secret?. . . Anyway, it didn't really matter now.

Only Amanda Andrews, the prime minister's personal warrior, had been visibly upset to see Haydn. Red-eyed and tear-smeared, she had grabbed him by the shoulders and shaken him with both hands. 'You bloody little traitor. You owe him a decent ending at the very least. Where is his head?'

It was a reasonable question.

'Amanda, the head was used for that final broadcast; it really looked as if the PM was there, and was speaking to us all. Some computer people were able to make good use of it, and it worked rather well. It's what he would have wanted, surely. But I'll make sure it's returned to you before the funeral.'

Haydn noted that, even here in the lions' den, he felt entirely calm and unaffected. After all those years of placating, reassuring and wheedling, he was safe at last. Olivia had had a word with the justice secretary. Jen was alive. Aleksander had disappeared. The McBryde business was an unsolvable conundrum. And he had broken no financial laws. He would be rich and, standing behind the caretaker prime minister, as great a power in the land as Sir Stuart Mountstewart of Danskin House had been at the court of James II.

He had had an unhappy telephone conversation with Myfanwy – 'Don't you dare call me "Mummy", toad-breath' – who had confirmed that he was the son, and presumably the heir, of Lord Croaker. So he had a decent shot at a seat in the upper house; the papers to prove it had been in her lawyers' hands for years. Rich, titled, and the close friendship of the prime minister. Not so bad.

Haydn stretched himself like a cat and luxuriated in the morning sun. He thought back to the confrontation on the wall at Danskin House, and how he'd kept his nerve. A military band was rehearsing in Horse Guards Parade. He hadn't yet been presented to the king, but that couldn't be far off. He would be dignified, would bow just a little, and would not be too impressed. He smiled to himself. He did like a happy ending.

The Nation Decides

Voting was heavy from the start, despite the light summer rain that had blown in from the continent before dawn. Up and down the country people had been arguing about Olivia Kite's speech and the arrests in London. Hard-core Europhiles thought Kite had seemed bonkers, and would turn people off. But the most common reaction was of disgust and disbelief at the concealment of the prime minister's death.

There was a strong sense that this was the way the political establishment always behaved, given half a chance, and that they must therefore be punished. A vote against Europe was a vote against the career politicians, against the kind of people who had been conspiring in Downing Street. There was also a lot of genuine sadness about the departed PM. He had been trusted, even loved, in a way that very few of his predecessors had been. Somehow, in his heft, his creased face and unfashionable suits, and the earthy though formal cadences of his speech, he reminded millions of Britons of their grandparents' generation – more substantial, more serious people than they were themselves. One way or another, many millions of voters found on this morning that the old, much-mocked duty of exercising their democratic right felt more urgent than usual.

At every polling station from the Shetland Islands to Cornwall rival groups of canvassers were surprised and elated by the sheer numbers of people who were turning up. This was a cause which had divided all the main parties, so socialists, Liberals and Conservatives stood side by side, marking down names, ticking off addresses and wearing the same rosettes – red, white and blue for independence, blue and gold for a European future.

Far from London, in his pebbledashed rented constituency house, Peter Collingwood had had a tricky few days. After his pep talk from the chief whip he had summoned up all his reserves of political courage, called his constituency chairman and told him that he would be voting with the prime minister, and in favour of Britain's continued membership of the EU. He understood the arguments for withdrawal, but this was a point of personal honour. He pinned a blue-and-gold badge to his cardigan.

An hour later, half a dozen of his most dedicated party workers – the sturdy souls who knocked on doors, photocopied leaflets and addressed envelopes, and who would reliably be waiting for him with a coffee or a brandy late at night when he had been out pounding the streets and was stiff with cold – had turned up on his doorstep. Not one of them was seriously angry with him, but all were disappointed, disgruntled and disillusioned. They would not, they said, be working with him again. In the damp, sad little wake that followed, Peter Collingwood contemplated the end of his political career. It was over.

When he phoned his wife in London to tell her the bad news she replied briskly, 'Good-oh. Why don't you pop back home and put in some human-being practice then?'

Instead Collingwood had remained in the constituency, in mourning, unable to sleep at night and spending the days poring over the newspapers.

But when he saw Olivia Kite's broadcast he instantly grasped that everything had changed – and so must he. Like many MPs throughout the country at that moment he allowed the grave, complicated questions of economics and national destiny to swim away and bob dimly at the back of his mind, while instead he asked himself the only thing that really mattered: 'Is it too late? Can I row back with enough dignity to hold on to them, and even to keep my seat?' The chief whip, he realised, had been lying to him, which meant that he was released from his word of honour. In an overexcited phone call he told his constituency chairman that he would be switching his vote, and that he hoped the unpleasantness of the last few days could be quickly forgotten. On went a red-white-and-blue rosette.

All his key party workers came back to him, barring one lady doctor who had previously stuck with him, but who now told him to his face that she found him spineless. Voting in his constituency went heavily against the EU, and the pressure on him eased off. He would be re-elected at the next general election, though with a reduced majority.

But somehow, even long after the event, he felt that his U-turn was never forgotten, and that some people laughed at him behind his back. Certainly he never got much credit from Olivia Kite for changing his vote. And some years later, when he was lamenting the stalling of his political career over the breakfast table, his daughter came up behind him and massaged his neck.

'Poor Daddy,' she said. 'Once a tosser, always a tosser.'

The sensational news from Westminster had not, of course, wiped away all other calculations. Voters had been struggling to translate what the European choice would mean to their own lives. Butchers dreamed of selling traditional sausages and cuts of meat without worrying about EU directives and inspectors. Burgled householders voted for tougher policing. And many people voted furtively to keep 'them' out. Others, thinking of their holidays in France or the German owners of their businesses, voted for a more predictable future. Others still worried about the heaving tectonic plates on the continent, asked themselves whether they or their children might one day have to go to war once more, and voted to stay inside the tent.

Everything that could be said had been said, endlessly, over every medium. In truth, nobody knew what the future held, but for once everybody, not only the spectral creatures at Westminster, had to choose. On both sides, people stood in line at the polling stations and shivered, noticing their goosebumps with a certain pride. After a very long time, the people of Britain were making history.

Mingling with the supporters of the two causes was a small army equipped with clipboards and electronic hand-counters, conferring together and making whispered telephone calls. The frontline troops of the polling companies were gathering hard information, ticking boxes and sending back enough news for a story, a narrative, to begin to take shape by the early afternoon. It was a story that would echo around the world.

14

Friday, 22 September

Referendum Day Plus One

The Birth of a Free Nation?

The pound crashed. In Munich, members of a far-right party burned Union Jacks. In Paris, English couples with reservations at the most expensive restaurants were refused their tables. British embassies everywhere closed their doors and raised limp flags of mourning.

In Coventry, the management of the Frankfurt-Italia Automobile Combine was pelted with rotten fruit and a BMW 7-Series was overturned by the workforce after a board announcement that the plant was being shut down because of 'the present intense political uncertainty'. Imams in Birmingham and rabbis in Manchester, priests in Liverpool and bishops in East Anglia called publicly for calm. In Edinburgh they sat it out with folded arms and calculated the odds. At Windsor the king tugged nervously at his shirtcuffs.

But on the outskirts – almost all the outskirts of everywhere – there was rejoicing. Pubs stayed open late, and people inside them lit up celebratory cigarettes. Faded Jubilee bunting had been retrieved from lofts and from cupboards under stairs and draped across pebbledash and brick. Neighbours spilled out onto the streets rather than sitting at home and watching events unfold on television. This seemed a day that required presence, propinquity, even conversation. Today the soft late-summer air smelt different. The light fell across windows in an unfamiliar way. Britain was 'free'.

Olivia Kite click-clacked across the empty Members' Lobby of the House of Commons. Stunned into silence, frozen, Winston and Lloyd George, Margaret and Clem watched her pass from the library corridor to the government whips' office. Olivia Kite would never be seen alone again. Not by the people of Britain. From now on she would be surrounded by PR advisers and spin doctors, communications directors, personal secretaries, Special Branch officers, political aides and all the other hangers-on to power, the flapping gulls following the ship of state, living on the stinking scraps that were tossed to them. Gliding high above, grey and ominous, would be the predatory figure of Alois Haydn.

Ronnie Ashe, released on bail, awaited her in the chief whip's office. He contemplated the rubble of his own hopes not in symbols or words, but scattered across the floor and over every available surface: a haze of plastic sandwich containers, pizza boxes, empty wine and beer bottles, discarded ties, scraps of paper covered in scrawled numbers and lists of underlined names, one forgotten Savile Row jacket and two abandoned iPads. They'd nearly done it, by God. They'd got so close. If it hadn't been for Alois Haydn. . .

All the others had gone home, stumbling into the now-quiet streets, feeling like the undead as they staggered towards West End apartments and riverside flats. For himself, Ronnie thought, it would surely be an open prison. For how long? He wasn't a young man any more. Hoping that Olivia would put in a quiet word, he tugged his already loosened tie further from his throat and moistened his lips as he heard her approach.

At Canary Wharf the lights had been burning all night at the offices of Barclays Wealth, Raworth & Reid and Peabody-Swiss. Marcus Dutieux, with his £35 million salary, his £100 million bonus and his name machine-incised over a new wing of the National Portrait Gallery, his Chelsea townhouse and his Long Island modern-gothic summer house, his nervous wife and his troubled daughters, was already out. Finished. Gone. His chairman, Sir Sandy Pitcairn, had called him at 3 a.m. The conversation had been polite but brief.

Over at Peabody there had been a hubbub, with raised voices and muttered threats, but in the end the entire corporate takeover team had quit. New men had been summoned from hitherto obscure departments and branches on the remoter edges of the city. From Berkhamsted to Richmond, Highgate to Notting Hill, limousines were waiting outside houses in which podgy middle-aged men were hurriedly dressing, quieting confused children and promising their spouses they would call when they could. John Peabody, 'Pug' to his friends, was back in. He'd lead the relocation team to Frankfurt. In the skies above London great gusts of money whooshed on electronic jetstreams and over the horizon in every direction.

In Washington, after an emergency meeting at the State Department, the Oval Office, more like a nineteenth-century drawing room than a modern executive suite, was crowded: the secretary of state, the director of the CIA, a team from the Pentagon, Alberto Fournier from the Federal Reserve, a former ambassador to the Court of St James's. . . and all the usual suspects who wanted to feel part of a historic moment. The president, still bemused by her inability to send a message of condolence to her old friend the prime minister of Great Britain, was reading some notes hurriedly drafted for her call to Olivia Kite.

That would be followed by more calls, very different in tone, to Brussels, Berlin, Paris and Rome. Her current London ambassador had been on the conference-call screens, but had made stumblingly little sense. You got more, thought the president, from Huff-Po and the Beast. At least they had called the vote right.

At the steel-faced Holborn offices of the *Courier*, only the night team was still at work, rewriting stories for the morning commuters' free paper and tweeting for obsessive political insomniacs. Without Ken Cooper's floods of invective the place seemed pallid and listless.

In Downing Street itself only a cat stirred. The prime minister's flat was deserted. Every trace of his tenure – the photographs, the clothes, the trophies, the favourite pictures – had already been removed, some by the police, most by a discreet storage company. Almost every trace, at least: his hands, which had shaken so many others, drafted so many speeches and signed so many treaties, lay forgotten in the freezer compartment. Downstairs in the private office a lone diary secretary wondered why Francis Fieldfare wasn't answering his messages. Computer screens softly glowed.

Epilogue

Monday, 9 October

Francis Fieldfare, wrapped tightly in a Union flag, was in fact lying in the prime ministerial coffin, a fitting end for such an exemplary public servant. Next to him nestled a circular plastic bundle, still encased in a Waitrose 'bag for life'. Alois Haydn had kept his promise to Amanda, and made sure it was returned. Fieldfare and his old boss's head would be laid to rest under a small memorial tablet set into the floor of Westminster Abbey. Disinterment would, of course, be unthinkable.

The funeral was a huge political event. Among the hundreds of mourners could be seen Alois Haydn, the aspirant Lord Croaker, grave and calm; and, arm in arm, Myfanwy Davies-Jones and a top-hatted Lord Briskett. Ken Cooper had a face of thunder. He was not looking forward to the service, surrounded by so many rats, badgers and other enemies. But his presence there had some small significance: it meant that when a diminutive Indian gentleman and a large, one-armed Pole arrived to see him at his office, they were politely turned away.

Meanwhile, standing among the quietly anonymous throng out in the streets was a stringy, bearded man who started when Olivia Kite passed by in the back of a government limousine. But Ned Parminter couldn't place her. His head still hurt. Overall, he had been lucky. Lord Briskett had taken him in after the writer Ajit Gupta had discovered him wandering around the village. He could talk and walk. But he remembered nothing, and in consequence knew nothing. In time this would assist him in a new career, in daytime television.

In England, autumn can be a season of renewal – October brings a rebirth of the intellect, a freshening of the mind, as the fug, glare and daze of the hot months are blown away.

Somewhere in Wiltshire, Jennifer Lewis was walking. Her shoes were soaked with dew. Below her, fallow fields in acid green and ploughed ones, brown and flecked with chalk, which would soon be brimming with winter corn, stretched down the southern escarpment of the Ridgeway. All around, neat explosions of beeches hid mysterious humps of earth. Forts. Settlements. Ritual sites. Old England. But she was thinking of more recent history.

All her life she had been searching for ways to be loved. Little Jenny Wren; pass the parcel; cold, bright, June. None of them was really her.

The previous evening she had taken the same walk with Lord Briskett, who had wanted to tell her about the Ridgeway and the England it represented. But eventually even his inexhaustible eloquence had been conquered by her inconsolable expression. They had trudged on in silence.

'Your choice of mother, darling. That was your first mistake,' he'd said eventually.

Jen had grunted.

'Don't get me wrong. I love her. She excites me, and she makes me laugh. Life's just more colourful whenever Myfanwy's around.

But dear heart, you must have chosen the least maternal woman in the entire country.'

'She's never really been my mother. I've never thought of her like that.'

Briskett rubbed his long chin. 'So you were on the hunt, old thing, were you not? But you hunted in the wrong direction. Whatever led you to offer yourself to Olivia Kite, of all people? You might as well have hoped to be suckled by Queen Elizabeth the First.'

'Or Boudicca,' Jen replied. 'But yes, you're right. I went haring off to Danskin House looking for a safe embrace. And I very nearly got myself killed.'

'You very nearly did, that's true. It's one of the oddest ironies of this whole business, isn't it, that it was your own mother who helped to save you? Very nearly a happy ending.'

Jen did not look happy. She looked cold and raw.

'But then I found out about Alois Haydn.'

'Yes. Your new half-brother turned out to be your false mother's lover,' snorted Briskett. 'It's ridiculous. It's like a really mad Shakespeare plot. Something out of *Cymbeline*.' He had laughed.

And so had she. At some point she'd have to start thinking about Lucien McBryde – more a broken-winged charity case than a proper lover – and, of course, about Ned Parminter. But this was not the moment. Briskett put an arm around her shoulders as the last light died around them.

'Soup,' he said. 'Brandy.'

The following morning Jen had been up with the lark, supposing there were any larks left here, and walking the hills.

The wind freshened. She shivered. Strips of Marian blue

327

appeared in the sky, torn by fast-moving clouds. She noticed a curl of smoke billowing from the grey huddle of buildings in the valley below. Briskett must have cleared the grate and lit a morning fire. She imagined she could smell the burning wood, and suddenly felt hungry for breakfast. Myfanwy would still be abed, working her way doggedly through the first cigarettes of the day, her coverlet hidden by crumpled pages of the *Financial Times*. But Briskett would be making everything shipshape, his skinny calves protruding from his fine velvet dressing gown, fresh eggs ready for scrambling. He would, she imagined, be rubbing a finger along the spines of his beloved books, on parade in almost every part of the house like an impatient, jostling crowd, as he readied himself for another day's work on his masterpiece. He liked to *work himself in*, as he put it, with a bit of Gibbon, or Jorrocks, or Winterson, or whatever came to hand.

The sun was now properly up, despite the drop in temperature. Copper and gold gleamed from the hedgerows leading back to the farm. It was going to be a glorious autumn. Jen began to walk downhill, enjoying the chill on her face, along the track Lord Briskett had shown her. There would be coffee, toast, and a day stretching ahead with the promise of good work. She had lost two mothers and two lovers – which was, at the very least, bad organisation. But she had found, she told herself, a father. A kind man, a clever man; and as he had proved in Essex, a brave man.

And they were all living, after all, in a new country. There would be less money about, it was true. But all that money sloshing around in the old days hadn't made the British happier, or more useful, had it? Now they had the chance of a new start. Yes, as she and Trevor had discussed while tramping uphill on a long, rainy walk the previous evening, there was a bunch of crooks in charge. But as Trevor had pointed out, there was no time in Britain's history when there hadn't been a considerable number of crooks in charge. The difference was that this time she and he could, perhaps, do something about it.

Jen stopped beside a glittering haze of blackcurrant bushes, tugged her hair back from her face, looked up into the sky and said loudly, 'Ned, Ned, Ned. If you can hear me, I am so, so, sorry.' The truth was that poor Ned Parminter was not going to be much help to Trevor as his giant manuscript grew. Jen felt especially guilty that it was now she who was assisting him, filling in the gaps in his first-hand knowledge of the successful 'No' campaign, although she couldn't help being delighted at the discovery that a little of her mother's literary talent seemed to have passed down to her after all.

She passed through the kitchen garden, knocked the mud off her shoes, unlaced them and padded with wet feet across the coir matting onto smooth, clean flagstones. Sure enough, there was a basket of toast on the little round breakfast table, and a pot of coffee on the Aga. Lord Briskett was preparing a tray to take upstairs. A tiny cup of coffee, a single boiled egg and an unopened packet of Camel cigarettes. 'She's not a big eater your old mum, is she? Not first thing in the morning.'

When he returned, they settled down in a companionable silence. She chose the *Daily Mail*, whose headline asked: 'The Most Evil Men in Britain?' (The answer was no.) He was reading the *Guardian*, which had discovered new evidence that the CIA, financed by hedge funds, had been behind the prime minister's murder as part of a plot to undermine the European Union.

After some time Briskett yawned, put down his paper and said, 'It's going jolly well by the way, my dear, all things considered.

I've seen your latest stuff, and you know, we do have a sensational story to tell, though it doesn't suit the agenda of the press. I talked to Ed Victor first thing.'

'Ed who?'

'Oh, come on. Literary agent. Big in the States, even bigger here. He's got, apparently, three Bentleys, one for each seaboard. He represents Nigella, Matthew Parris, Ben Macintyre. . .'

'All right, Trevor, that's enough. I'm impressed. And he wants you?'

'He says it will make our fortune, darling. With your help I'll be the Dan Brown of the history world, apparently.'

'Hmm. You don't seem as delighted as you should be.'

'Well, Jen, we have a few problems. How much do we actually reveal? If we spill every bean, we have the most sensational book. But then there are the libel lawyers. I suppose they can be dealt with, with care. And there's the larger question of credibility. When you think about it, the whole story's just too ridiculous for words. But I can live with that. We also have the matter of contacts. You may never want to see your old boss, or your half-brother and his friends, again, but I don't fancy being left out in the cold just at the time when we have the most interesting new regime in British post-war history.'

Briskett got up, walked over to the washing basket and plucked out a pair of scarlet woollen socks; despite the fire, there was a chill draught in the room.

'It's going to be such a fascinating time, and we're stuck with the journalist's age-old dilemma – do we keep in with the boss classes, keep talking to them, and keep getting the stories; or do we burn our bridges and retire from the fray?'

There was a creak from the stairs. Preceded by a cloud of smoke and a sickly waft of scent, Myfanwy was beginning her day at last.

'No problem at all, sweetie,' she said. 'Make it a novel. *Much more fun.*'

Bill Stevenson was an exemplary public servant. Whether or not you agreed with him, he presented his arguments fairly and with admirable passion. Fierce in debate, he was always personally generous to his opponents. Although the disgraceful events of the days preceding last month's referendum, and the crushing of his private hopes in the results of that referendum, currently cloud his memory, history will be generous to him in turn.

Yesterday, the Bishop of London paid tribute to the former prime minister at a service in Westminster Abbey. His Majesty the King, and the Duke and Duchess of Cambridge, led the mourners. The German chancellor, Herr David McAllister, and the president of the French Republic, Nicolas Sarkozy, were among the many foreign dignitaries present. The new prime minister, Mrs Olivia Kite, and most of the cabinet attended. Crowds lined the streets of Westminster for the cortège's short journey from Downing Street.

Mr Stevenson leaves a country, which has voted to reclaim its national sovereignty, in perilous circumstances. He would have been appalled by this. As he told this newspaper in his final interview for us, 'My nightmare is that they are stupid enough to do it. The biggest problem with democracy has always been the electorate.' But let us never forget that it was he who gave the British people the right to vote on this crucial issue. We cannot believe that he would have approved of the audacious plot to hoodwink them following his untimely death. He was, when all is said and done, a greater man than that.

National Courier, London, Tuesday, 10 October 2017